ROARINGS FROM
FURTHER OUT

ROARINGS FROM FURTHER OUT

Four Weird Novellas by
ALGERNON BLACKWOOD

edited by
XAVIER ALDANA REYES

This edition published 2019 by
The British Library
96 Euston Road
London NW1 2DB

Introduction © 2019 Xavier Aldana Reyes

'The Willows', 'Ancient Sorceries', 'The Wendigo' and 'The Man
Whom the Trees Loved' © The Estate of Algernon Blackwood

Dates attributed to each story relate to first publication.

Cataloguing in Publication Data

A catalogue record for this publication is
available from the British Library

ISBN 978 0 7123 5305 2
Limited edition ISBN 978 0 7123 5350 2
e-ISBN 978 0 7123 6710 3

Frontispiece illustration by W. Graham Robertson from the first
edition of the collection *Pan's Garden* by Algernon Blackwood.

Cover design by Mauricio Villamayor with
illustration by Enrique Bernardou

Text design and typesetting by Tetragon, London
Printed in England by CPI Group (UK) Ltd, Croydon, CR0 4YY

MIX
Paper | Supporting
responsible forestry
FSC
www.fsc.org
FSC® C171272

CONTENTS

INTRODUCTION

The reputation of early twentieth-century British writer Algernon Blackwood currently resides with his two novellas "The Willows" (1907) and "The Wendigo" (1910), and with good reason. They are perfectly crafted horror tales that convey feelings of mystical otherness; they hint at the possibility that there are forces which lie beyond the confines of our everyday understanding of the world and which may, given the right circumstances, manifest to humans. In "The Willows", "unearthly" creatures are responsible for arousing "some dim ancestral sense of terror more profoundly disturbing than anything" the protagonists have ever known. In "The Wendigo", fear of the titular monster from Native American folklore is used to create a discombobulating atmosphere of dread. In both novellas, as in many other of Blackwood's fictions, wild landscapes (a desolate island, a labyrinthine forest) act as more than mere enhancing backdrops to the action—they become essential elements to the generation of anxiety and metaphysical awe. Both stories have become staples of the weird literary tradition, of which Blackwood was undoubtedly a modern master. Blackwood's slow and measured prose, deeply psychological and descriptive, grants his fiction an intrinsic cumulative effect. It both builds up to potent climaxes and brilliantly chronicles the aftermath of horrific encounters. His poignant narrative pace, sparse use of action and marked interest in how the mind filters perceptions, rather than on objective physical descriptions, makes Blackwood truly unique. Only a handful of other stories in horror fiction manage to conjure up the type of uncanny ambiance found in

"The Willows" and "The Wendigo". This is why they are included in this collection.

Blackwood was no stranger to horror during his early career. His first two short story collections, *The Empty House and Other Ghost Stories* (1906), and *The Listener and Other Stories* (1907), were full of ghostly retributions and visionary hallucinations. One of Blackwood's distinctive traits, his emphasis on the physiological reactions that the presence of spirits cause on individuals (the contagion of moods, in particular), is in full display in these collections. Blackwood was also very interested in the occult, a passion which would lead him to join the Hermetic Order of the Golden Dawn and would influence his collection *John Silence: Physician Extraordinary* (1908), in which the eponymous doctor explores strange phenomena such as psychic invasions, the revival of memories from previous lives and astral body projections. From this key collection, so successful upon publication that it allowed Blackwood to become a full-time writer, I extract "Ancient Sorceries". A tale about a northern town in France where its inhabitants appear to turn into cats at night, it famously inspired Jacques Tourneur's classic 1942 horror film *Cat People*. Although the bulk of Blackwood's writing would only sparingly return to the ghost and horror story in collections like *Shocks* (1935) and *The Doll and One Other* (1946), his many appearances on radio and TV as teller of strange tales cemented an image of the man as horror auteur. And yet, the reader who turns to Blackwood's large bibliography in search of "weird" horror might well be disappointed. This is not because the quality of the rest of Blackwood's fictional output is not on a par with his earlier efforts. There are indeed several gems to discover, such as "The Glamour of the Snow" (1911), "Sand" (1912) and "The Regeneration of Lord Ernie" (1914), none of which could be included in this collection due to their length. Rather, the issue is that Blackwood was equally interested in the expansive aspects of fantasy, especially in the two collections that best showcase his spiritual-natural vision, *Pan's Garden: A Volume of Nature Stories* (1912) and *Incredible Adventures* (1914).

Blackwood's philosophy of the world stemmed from a very singular perception of the connection between human beings and the Earth. In his autobiography, *Episodes Before Thirty* (1923), he explained that, in his younger years, nature had "remained dominant, a truly magical spell" that always brought him "comfort, companionship, inspiration, joy". Blackwood's fascination with the natural world was not purely a consequence of the wanderlust that took him to continental Europe, Canada and Egypt, among other places, but of his conception of nature as somehow sacred and godly, as providing access to a deeper sense of self and matter. As he put it, "[t]he early feeling that everything was alive, a dim sense that some kind of consciousness struggled through every form, even that a sort of inarticulate communication with this 'other life' was possible, could I but discover the way" often coloured his mood. It is said of O'Malley, the protagonist of *The Centaur* (1914), that he appeared to have "sought [...] a development, if not a revival, of some faultless instinct, due to kinship with [Nature], which—to take extremes—shall direct alike the animal and the inspired man, guiding the wild bee and the homing pigeon and—the soul towards its God". The passage may as well have been written about Blackwood himself. Given the emphasis on wild landscapes, regeneration and inner connection to all organic life, it is not surprising that paganism, satyrs, elementals and the God Pan recur in his fiction as sources of hidden knowledge and revelation. These forces may be scary, but as in stories like "May Day Eve" (1907) and "The Touch of Pan" (1921), they also open up perceptual doors that can change a human's entire existence.

What distinguishes Blackwood from other weird writers is not just his interest in the occult and his intrinsic style, but his outlook on life and its spiritual links to nature. Where horror underpins his writing, it is usually rooted in the discovery of powers that belittle humans and which connect them directly to a superstitious past that modern technology has made difficult to access. In this sense, we may call some of his writing "weird". Like the best of the weird-ists, Blackwood's narrative effects are permeated by his worldview, and it would be limiting, and somewhat disingenuous, to examine Blackwood exclusively through a horrific lens. It is more accurate to conceive of him as a man obsessed with the "super-natural", as Mike Ashley puts it, and whose flights of imagination sometimes revelled in the horrors of awakening to a deeper knowledge of, and attachment to, the environment. Ancient magic, including human sacrifice, as well as returns to the wild and to primeval states of being, pepper his stories. In some cases, these extraordinary experi-ences lead to apparent transcendental changes, from resurrection to the death of the body as we know it. A clear message emerges from the bulk of Blackwood's writing: there is more to our rela-tionship with this Earth than meets the eye, and the desire to learn from it, to become one with it, emerges as an inevitable human disposition. In selecting the tales for this collection, I have thus tried to balance out Blackwood's weird horror novellas with "The Man Whom the Trees Loved", which, apart from being one of his most powerful pieces, best captures Blackwood's wonder of nature. This tale demonstrates there is at least one other side to this captivating writer and, more broadly, to weird literature.

XAVIER ALDANA REYES

Dr. Xavier Aldana Reyes is Reader in English Literature and Film at Manchester Metropolitan University and a member of the Manchester Centre for Gothic Studies. He is the editor of Horror: A Literary History *(2016),* The Gothic Tales of H. P. Lovecraft *(2018),* The Weird Tales of William Hope Hodgson *(2019) and* Promethean Horrors: Classic Tales of Mad Science *(2019), all published by the British Library.*

A NOTE FROM THE PUBLISHER

The original short stories reprinted in the British Library's Tales of the Weird series were written and published in a period ranging across the nineteenth and twentieth centuries. There are many elements of these stories which continue to entertain modern readers; however, in some cases there are also uses of language, instances of stereotyping and some attitudes expressed by narrators or characters which may not be endorsed by the publishing standards of today. We acknowledge therefore that some elements in the stories selected for reprinting may continue to make uncomfortable reading for some of our audience. With these new editions British Library Publishing aims to offer a new readership a chance to read some of the rare material of the British Library's collections in an affordable format, to enjoy their merits and to look back into the worlds of the past two centuries as portrayed by their writers. The following stories are presented as they were originally published with minor edits made for consistency of style and sense, and with pejorative terms of an extremely offensive nature partly obscured. We welcome feedback from our readers, which can be sent to the following address:

British Library Publishing, The British Library, 96 Euston Road

London, NW1 2DB, United Kingdom

I would like to dedicate this book to Linnie Blake and to thank her for her trust in me, her professional advice through the years and, most importantly, her friendship.

"The Wise are silent, the Foolish speak, and the children are thus led astray, for wisdom is not knowledge, it is a realization of the scheme and of one's own part in it."

ACKNOWLEDGEMENTS

I would like to thank Rob Davies and Jonny Davidson at the British Library for their enthusiasm and support. It is incredibly exciting to see the British Library supporting weird fiction and rescuing worthy writers from oblivion. I am grateful for their help with the acquisition and reproduction of the stories selected for this volume, too.

I would like to thank Mike Ashley and S. T. Joshi for the work they have carried out on Blackwood, and to Stark House books for keeping the vast majority of the author's bibliography in print.

Finally, I am very grateful to Imma Ferri and Emily Alder for the time they spent looking over the introduction.

The Willows

—1907—

I

A FTER LEAVING VIENNA, AND LONG BEFORE YOU COME TO Buda-Pesth, the Danube enters a region of singular loneliness and desolation, where its waters spread away on all sides regardless of a main channel, and the country becomes a swamp for miles upon miles, covered by a vast sea of low willow bushes. On the big maps this deserted area is painted in a fluffy blue, growing fainter in colour as it leaves the banks, and across it may be seen in large straggling letters the word *Sümpfe*, meaning marshes.

In high flood this great acreage of sand, shingle-beds, and willow-grown islands is almost topped by the water, but in normal seasons the bushes bend and rustle in the free winds, showing their silver leaves to the sunshine in an ever-moving plain of bewildering beauty. These willows never attain to the dignity of trees; they have no rigid trunks; they remain humble bushes, with rounded tops and soft outline, swaying on slender stems that answer to the least pressure of the wind; supple as grasses, and so continually shifting that they somehow give the impression that the entire plain is moving and *alive*. For the wind sends waves rising and falling over the whole surface, waves of leaves instead of waves of water, green swells like the sea, too, until the branches turn and lift, and then silvery white as their under-side turns to the sun.

Happy to slip beyond the control of stern banks, the Danube here wanders about at will among the intricate network of channels intersecting the islands everywhere with broad avenues down which the waters pour with a shouting sound; making whirlpools, eddies, and foaming rapids; tearing at the sandy banks; carrying away masses of shore and willow-clumps; and forming new islands innumerable which shift daily in size and shape and possess at best an impermanent life, since the flood-time obliterates their very existence.

Properly speaking, this fascinating part of the river's life begins soon after leaving Pressburg, and we, in our Canadian canoe, with gipsy tent and frying-pan on board, reached it on the crest of a rising flood about mid-July. That very same morning, when the sky was reddening before sunrise, we had slipped swiftly through still-sleeping Vienna, leaving it a couple of hours later a mere patch of smoke against the blue hills of the Wienerwald on the horizon; we had breakfasted below Fischeramend under a grove of birch trees roaring in the wind; and had then swept on the tearing current past Orth, Hainburg, Petronell (the old Roman Carnuntum of Marcus Aurelius), and so under the frowning heights of Theben on a spur of the Carpathians, where the March steals in quietly from the left and the frontier is crossed between Austria and Hungary.

Racing along at twelve kilometres an hour soon took us well into Hungary, and the muddy waters—sure sign of flood—sent us aground on many a shingle-bed, and twisted us like a cork in many a sudden belching whirlpool before the towers of Pressburg (Hungarian, Poszóny) showed against the sky; and then the canoe, leaping like a spirited horse, flew at top speed under the grey walls, negotiated safely the sunken chain of the Fliegende Brücke ferry, turned the corner sharply to the left, and plunged on yellow foam into the wilderness of islands, sand-banks, and swamp-land beyond— the land of the willows.

The change came suddenly, as when a series of bioscope pictures snaps down on the streets of a town and shifts without warning into the scenery of lake and forest. We entered the land of desolation on wings, and in less than half an hour there was neither boat nor fishing-hut nor red roof, nor any single sign of human habitation and civilisation within sight. The sense of remoteness from the world of human kind, the utter isolation, the fascination of this singular world of willows, winds, and waters, instantly laid its spell upon us both, so that we allowed laughingly to one another that we ought by rights to have held some special kind of passport to admit us, and that we had, somewhat audaciously, come without asking leave into a separate little kingdom of wonder and magic—a kingdom that was reserved for the use of others who had a right to it, with everywhere unwritten warnings to trespassers for those who had the imagination to discover them.

Though still early in the afternoon, the ceaseless buffetings of a most tempestuous wind made us feel weary, and we at once began casting about for a suitable camping-ground for the night. But the bewildering character of the islands made landing difficult; the swirling flood carried us in-shore and then swept us out again; the willow branches tore our hands as we seized them to stop the canoe, and we pulled many a yard of sandy bank into the water before at length we shot with a great sideways blow from the wind into a backwater and managed to beach the bows in a cloud of spray. Then we lay panting and laughing after our exertions on hot yellow sand, sheltered from the wind, and in the full blaze of a scorching sun, a cloudless blue sky above, and an immense army of dancing, shouting willow bushes, closing in from all sides, shining with spray and clapping their thousand little hands as though to applaud the success of our efforts.

"What a river!" I said to my companion, thinking of all the way we had travelled from the source in the Black Forest, and how we had often been obliged to wade and push in the upper shallows at the beginning of June.

"Won't stand much nonsense now, will it?" he said, pulling the canoe a little farther into safety up the sand, and then composing himself for a nap.

I lay by his side, happy and peaceful in the bath of the elements—water, wind, sand, and the great fire of the sun—thinking of the long journey that lay behind us, and of the great stretch before us to the Black Sea, and how lucky I was to have such a delightful and charming travelling companion as my friend, the Swede.

We had made many similar journeys together, but the Danube, more than any other river I knew, impressed us from the very beginning with its *aliveness*. From its tiny bubbling entry into the world among the pinewood gardens of Donaueschingen, until this moment when it began to play the great river-game of losing itself among the deserted swamps, unobserved, unrestrained, it had seemed to us like following the growth of some living creature. Sleepy at first, but later developing violent desires as it became conscious of its deep soul, it rolled, like some huge fluid being, through all the countries we had passed, holding our little craft on its mighty shoulders, playing roughly with us sometimes, yet always friendly and well-meaning, till at length we had come inevitably to regard it as a Great Personage.

How, indeed, could it be otherwise, since it told us so much of its secret life? At night we heard it singing to the moon as we lay in our tent, uttering that odd sibilant note peculiar to itself and said to be caused by the rapid tearing of the pebbles along its bed, so great is its hurrying speed. We knew, too, the voice of its gurgling whirlpools, suddenly bubbling up on a surface previously quite calm; the roar of its shallows and swift rapids; its constant steady thundering below all mere surface sounds; and that ceaseless tearing of its icy waters at the banks. How it stood up and shouted when the rains fell flat upon its face! And how its laughter roared out when the wind blew upstream and tried to stop its growing speed! We knew all its sounds and voices, its tumblings and foamings, its unnecessary splashing against the bridges; that self-conscious chatter when there were hills to look on; the affected dignity of its speech when it passed through the little towns, far too important to laugh; and all these faint, sweet whisperings when the sun caught it fairly in some slow curve and poured down upon it till the steam rose.

It was full of tricks, too, in its early life before the great world knew it. There were places in the upper reaches among the Swabian forests, when yet the first whispers of its destiny had not reached it, where it elected to disappear through holes in the ground, to appear again on the other side of the porous limestone hills and start a new river with another name; leaving, too, so little water in its own bed that we had to climb out and wade and push the canoe through miles of shallows!

And a chief pleasure, in those early days of its irresponsible youth, was to lie low, like Brer Fox, just before the little turbulent tributaries came to join it from the Alps, and to refuse to acknowledge them when in, but to run for miles side by side, the dividing line well marked, the very levels different, the Danube utterly declining to recognise the newcomer. Below Passau, however, it gave up this particular trick, for there the Inn comes in with a thundering power impossible to ignore, and so pushes and incommodes the parent river that there is hardly room for them in the long twisting gorge that follows, and the Danube is shoved this way and that against the cliffs, and forced to hurry itself with great waves and much dashing to and fro in order to get through in time. And during the fight our canoe slipped down from its shoulder to its breast, and had the time of its life among the struggling waves. But the Inn taught the old river a lesson, and after Passau it no longer pretended to ignore new arrivals.

This was many days back, of course, and since then we had come to know other aspects of the great creature, and across the Bavarian wheat plain of Straubing she wandered so slowly under the blazing June sun that we could well imagine only the surface inches were water, while below there moved, concealed as by a silken mantle, a whole army of Undines, passing silently and unseen down to the sea, and very leisurely too, lest they be discovered.

Much, too, we forgave her because of her friendliness to the birds and animals that haunted the shores. Cormorants lined the banks in lonely places in rows like short black palings; grey crows crowded the shingle beds; storks stood fishing in the vistas of shallower water that opened up between the islands, and hawks, swans, and marsh birds of all sorts filled the air with glinting wings and singing, petulant cries. It was impossible to feel annoyed with the river's vagaries after seeing a deer leap with a splash into the water at sunrise and swim past the bows of the canoe; and often we saw fawns peering at us from the underbrush, or looked straight into the brown eyes of a stag as we charged full tilt round a corner and entered another reach of the river. Foxes, too, everywhere haunted the banks, tripping daintily among the driftwood and disappearing so suddenly that it was impossible to see how they managed it.

But now, after leaving Pressburg, everything changed a little, and the Danube became more serious. It ceased trifling. It was half-way to the Black Sea, within scenting distance almost of other, stranger countries where no tricks would be permitted or understood. It became suddenly grown-up, and claimed our respect and even our awe. It broke out into three arms, for one thing, that only met again a hundred kilometres farther down, and for a canoe there were no indications which one was intended to be followed.

"If you take a side channel," said the Hungarian officer we met in the Pressburg shop while buying provisions, "you may find yourselves, when the flood subsides, forty miles from anywhere, high and dry, and you may easily starve. There are no people, no farms, no fishermen. I warn you not to continue. The river, too, is still rising, and this wind will increase."

The rising river did not alarm us in the least, but the matter of being left high and dry by a sudden subsidence of the waters might be serious, and we had consequently laid in an extra stock of provisions. For the rest, the officer's prophecy held true, and the wind, blowing down a perfectly clear sky, increased steadily till it reached the dignity of a westerly gale.

It was earlier than usual when we camped, for the sun was a good hour or two from the horizon, and leaving my friend still asleep on the hot sand, I wandered about in desultory examination of our hotel. The island, I found, was less than an acre in extent, a mere sandy bank standing some two or three feet above the level of the river. The far end, pointing into the sunset, was covered with flying spray which the tremendous wind drove off the crests of the broken waves. It was triangular in shape, with the apex up stream.

I stood there for several minutes, watching the impetuous crimson flood bearing down with a shouting roar, dashing in waves against the bank as though to sweep it bodily away, and then swirling by in two foaming streams on either side. The ground seemed to shake with the shock and rush, while the furious movement of the willow bushes as the wind poured over them increased the curious illusion that the island itself actually moved. Above, for a mile or two, I could see the great river descending upon me: it was like looking up the slope of a sliding hill, white with foam, and leaping up everywhere to show itself to the sun.

The rest of the island was too thickly grown with willows to make walking pleasant, but I made the tour, nevertheless. From the lower end the light, of course, changed, and the river looked dark and angry. Only the backs of the flying waves were visible, streaked with foam, and pushed forcibly by the great puffs of wind that fell upon them from behind. For a short mile it was visible, pouring in and out among the islands, and then disappearing with a huge sweep into the willows, which closed about it like a herd of monstrous antediluvian creatures crowding down to drink. They made me think of gigantic sponge-like growths that sucked the river up into themselves. They caused it to vanish from sight. They herded there together in such overpowering numbers.

Altogether it was an impressive scene, with its utter loneliness, its bizarre suggestion; and as I gazed, long and curiously, a singular emotion began to stir somewhere in the depths of me. Midway in my delight of the wild beauty, there crept, unbidden and unexplained, a curious feeling of disquietude, almost of alarm.

A rising river, perhaps, always suggests something of the ominous: many of the little islands I saw before me would probably have been swept away by the morning; this resistless, thundering flood of water touched the sense of awe. Yet I was aware that my uneasiness lay deeper far than the emotions of awe and wonder. It was not that I felt. Nor had it directly to do with the power of the driving wind—this shouting hurricane that might almost carry up a few acres of willows into the air and scatter them like so much chaff over the landscape. The wind was simply enjoying itself, for nothing rose out of the flat landscape to stop it, and I was conscious of sharing its great game with a kind of pleasurable excitement. Yet this novel emotion had nothing to do with the wind. Indeed, so vague was the sense of distress I experienced, that it was impossible to trace it to its source and deal with it accordingly, though I was aware somehow that it had to do with my realisation of our utter insignificance before this unrestrained power of the elements about me. The huge-grown river had something to do with it too—a vague, unpleasant idea that we had somehow trifled with these great elemental forces in whose power we lay helpless every hour of the day and night. For here, indeed, they were gigantically at play together, and the sight appealed to the imagination.

But my emotion, so far as I could understand it, seemed to attach itself more particularly to the willow bushes, to these acres and acres of willows, crowding, so thickly growing there, swarming everywhere the eye could reach, pressing upon the river as though to suffocate it, standing in dense array mile after mile beneath the sky, watching, waiting, listening. And, apart quite from the elements, the willows connected themselves subtly with my malaise, attacking the mind insidiously somehow by reason of their vast numbers, and contriving in some way or other to represent to the imagination a new and mighty power, a power, moreover, not altogether friendly to us.

Great revelations of nature, of course, never fail to impress in one way or another, and I was no stranger to moods of the kind. Mountains overawe and oceans terrify, while the mystery of great forests exercises a spell peculiarly its own. But all these, at one point or another, somewhere link on intimately with human life and human experience. They stir comprehensible, even if alarming, emotions. They tend on the whole to exalt.

With this multitude of willows, however, it was something far different, I felt. Some essence emanated from them that besieged the heart. A sense of awe awakened, true, but of awe touched somewhere by a vague terror. Their serried ranks, growing everywhere darker about me as the shadows deepened, moving furiously yet softly in the wind, woke in me the curious and unwelcome suggestion that we had trespassed here upon the borders of an alien world, a world where we were intruders, a world where we were not wanted or invited to remain—where we ran grave risks perhaps!

The feeling, however, though it refused to yield its meaning entirely to analysis, did not at the time trouble me by passing into menace. Yet it never left me quite, even during the very practical business of putting up the tent in a hurricane of wind and building a fire for the stew-pot. It remained, just enough to bother and perplex, and to rob a most delightful camping-ground of a good portion of its charm. To my companion, however, I said nothing, for he was a man I considered devoid of imagination. In the first place, I could never have explained to him what I meant, and in the second, he would have laughed stupidly at me if I had.

There was a slight depression in the centre of the island, and here we pitched the tent. The surrounding willows broke the wind a bit.

"A poor camp," observed the imperturbable Swede when at last the tent stood upright; "no stones and precious little firewood. I'm for moving on early to-morrow—eh? This sand won't hold anything."

But the experience of a collapsing tent at midnight had taught us many devices, and we made the cosy gipsy house as safe as possible, and then set about collecting a store of wood to last till bedtime. Willow bushes drop no branches, and driftwood was our only source of supply. We hunted the shores pretty thoroughly.

Everywhere the banks were crumbling as the rising flood tore at them and carried away great portions with a splash and a gurgle.

"The island's much smaller than when we landed," said the accurate Swede. "It won't last long at this rate. We'd better drag the canoe close to the tent, and be ready to start a moment's notice. *I* shall sleep in my clothes."

He was a little distance off, climbing along the bank, and I heard his rather jolly laugh as he spoke.

"By Jove!" I heard him call, a moment later, and turned to see what had caused his exclamation. But for the moment he was hidden by the willows, and I could not find him.

"What in the world's this?" I heard him cry again, and this time his voice had become serious.

I ran up quickly and joined him on the bank. He was looking over the river, pointing at something in the water.

"Good Heavens, it's a man's body!" he cried excitedly. "Look!"

A black thing, turning over and over in the foaming waves, swept rapidly past. It kept disappearing and coming up to the surface again. It was about twenty feet from the shore, and just as it was opposite to where we stood it lurched round and looked straight at us. We saw its eyes reflecting the sunset, and gleaming an odd yellow as the body turned over. Then it gave a swift, gulping plunge, and dived out of sight in a flash.

"An otter, by gad!" we exclaimed in the same breath, laughing.

It *was* an otter, alive, and out on the hunt; yet it had looked exactly like the body of a drowned man turning helplessly in the current. Far below it came to the surface once again, and we saw its black skin, wet and shining in the sunlight.

Then, too, just as we turned back, our arms full of driftwood, another thing happened to recall us to the river bank. This time it really was a man, and what was more, a man in a boat. Now a small boat on the Danube was an unusual sight at any time, but here in this deserted region, and at flood-time, it was so unexpected as to constitute a real event. We stood and stared.

Whether it was due to the slanting sunlight, or the refraction from the wonderfully illumined water, I cannot say, but, whatever the cause, I found it difficult to focus my sight properly upon the flying apparition. It seemed, however, to be a man standing upright in a sort of flat-bottomed boat, steering with a long oar, and being carried down the opposite shore at a tremendous pace. He apparently was looking across in our direction, but the distance was too great and the light too uncertain for us to make out very plainly what he was about. It seemed to me that he was gesticulating and making signs at us. His voice came across the water to us shouting something furiously, but the wind drowned it so that no single word was audible. There was something curious about the whole appearance—man, boat, signs, voice—that made an impression on me out of all proportion to its cause.

"He's crossing himself!" I cried. "Look, he's making the sign of the Cross!"

"I believe you're right," the Swede said, shading his eyes with his hand and watching the man out of sight. He seemed to be gone in a moment, melting away down there into the sea of willows where the sun caught them in the bend of the river and turned them into a great crimson wall of beauty. Mist, too, had begun to rise, so that the air was hazy.

"But what in the world is he doing at night-fall on this flooded river?" I said, half to myself. "Where is he going at such a time, and what did he mean by his signs and shouting? D'you think he wished to warn us about something?"

"He saw our smoke, and thought we were spirits probably," laughed my companion. "These Hungarians believe in all sorts of rubbish: you remember the shopwoman at Pressburg warning us that no one ever landed here because it belonged to some sort of beings outside man's world! I suppose they believe in fairies and elementals, possibly demons too. That peasant in the boat saw people on the islands for the first time in his life," he added, after a slight pause, "and it scared him, that's all."

The Swede's tone of voice was not convincing, and his manner lacked something that was usually there. I noted the change instantly while he talked, though without being able to label it precisely.

"If they had enough imagination," I laughed loudly—I remember trying to make as much *noise* as I could—"they might well people a place like this with the old gods of antiquity. The Romans must have haunted all this region more or less with their shrines and sacred groves and elemental deities."

The subject dropped and we returned to our stew-pot, for my friend was not given to imaginative conversation as a rule. Moreover, just then I remember feeling distinctly glad that he was not imaginative; his stolid, practical nature suddenly seemed to me welcome and comforting. It was an admirable temperament, I felt: he could steer down rapids like a red Indian, shoot dangerous bridges and whirlpools better than any white man I ever saw in a canoe. He was a grand fellow for an adventurous trip, a tower of strength when untoward things happened. I looked at his strong face and light curly hair as he staggered along under his pile of driftwood (twice the size of mine!), and I experienced a feeling of relief. Yes, I was distinctly glad just then that the Swede was—what he was, and that he never made remarks that suggested more than they said.

"The river's still rising, though," he added, as if following out some thoughts of his own, and dropping his load with a gasp. "This island will be under water in two days if it goes on."

"I wish the *wind* would go down," I said. "I don't care a fig for the river."

The flood, indeed, had no terrors for us; we could get off at ten minutes' notice, and the more water the better we liked it. It meant an increasing current and the obliteration of the treacherous shingle-beds that so often threatened to tear the bottom out of our canoe.

Contrary to our expectations, the wind did not go down with the sun. It seemed to increase with the darkness, howling overhead and shaking the willows round us like straws. Curious sounds accompanied it sometimes, like the explosion of heavy guns, and it fell upon the water and the island in great flat blows of immense power. It made me think of the sounds a planet must make, could we only hear it, driving along through space.

But the sky kept wholly clear of clouds, and soon after supper the full moon rose up in the east and covered the river and the plain of shouting willows with a light like the day.

We lay on the sandy patch beside the fire, smoking, listening to the noises of the night round us, and talking happily of the journey we had already made, and of our plans ahead. The map lay spread in the door of the tent, but the high wind made it hard to study, and presently we lowered the curtain and extinguished the lantern. The firelight was enough to smoke and see each other's faces by, and the sparks flew about overhead like fireworks. A few yards beyond, the river gurgled and hissed, and from time to time a heavy splash announced the falling away of further portions of the bank.

Our talk, I noticed, had to do with the far-away scenes and inci-dents of our first camps in the Black Forest, or of other subjects altogether remote from the present setting, for neither of us spoke of the actual moment more than was necessary—almost as though we had agreed tacitly to avoid discussion of the camp and its incidents. Neither the otter nor the boatman, for instance, received the honour of a single mention, though ordinarily these would have furnished discussion for the greater part of the evening. They were, of course, distinct events in such a place.

The scarcity of wood made it a business to keep the fire going, for the wind, that drove the smoke in our faces wherever we sat, helped at the same time to make a forced draught. We took it in turn to make foraging expeditions into the darkness, and the quantity the Swede brought back always made me feel that he took an absurdly long time finding it; for the fact was I did not care much about being left alone, and yet it always seemed to be my turn to grub about among the bushes or scramble along the slippery banks in the moonlight. The long day's battle with wind and water—such wind and such water!—had tired us both, and an early bed was the obvious programme. Yet neither of us made the move for the tent. We lay there, tending the fire, talking in desultory fashion, peering about us into the dense willow bushes, and listening to the thunder of wind and river. The loneliness of the place had entered our very bones, and silence seemed natural, for after a bit the sound of our voices became a trifle unreal and forced; whispering would have been the fitting mode of communication, I felt, and the human voice, always rather absurd amid the roar of the elements, now carried with it something almost illegitimate. It was like talking out loud in church, or in some place where it was not lawful, perhaps not quite *safe*, to be overheard.

The eeriness of this lonely island, set among a million willows, swept by a hurricane, and surrounded by hurrying deep waters, touched us both, I fancy. Untrodden by man, almost unknown to man, it lay there beneath the moon, remote from human influence, on the frontier of another world, an alien world, a world tenanted by willows only and the souls of willows. And we, in our rashness, had dared to invade it, even to make use of it! Something more than the power of its mystery stirred in me as I lay on the sand, feet to fire, and peered up through the leaves at the stars. For the last time I rose to get firewood.

"When this has burnt up," I said firmly, "I shall turn in," and my companion watched me lazily as I moved off into the surrounding shadows.

For an unimaginative man I thought he seemed unusually receptive that night, unusually open to suggestion of things other than sensory. He too was touched by the beauty and loneliness of the place. I was not altogether pleased, I remember, to recognise this slight change in him, and instead of immediately collecting sticks, I made my way to the far point of the island where the moonlight on plain and river could be seen to better advantage. The desire to be alone had come suddenly upon me; my former dread returned in force; there was a vague feeling in me I wished to face and probe to the bottom.

When I reached the point of sand jutting out among the waves, the spell of the place descended upon me with a positive shock. No mere "scenery" could have produced such an effect. There was something more here, something to alarm.

I gazed across the waste of wild waters; I watched the whispering willows; I heard the ceaseless beating of the tireless wind; and, one and all, each in its own way, stirred in me this sensation of a strange distress. But the *willows* especially: for ever they went on chattering and talking among themselves, laughing a little, shrilly crying out, sometimes sighing—but what it was they made so much to-do about belonged to the secret life of the great plain they inhabited. And it was utterly alien to the world I knew, or to that of the wild yet kindly elements. They made me think of a host of beings from another plane of life, another evolution altogether, perhaps, all discussing a mystery known only to themselves. I watched them moving busily together, oddly shaking their big bushy heads, twirling their myriad leaves even when there was no wind. They moved of their own will as though alive, and they touched, by some incalculable method, my own keen sense of the *horrible*.

There they stood in the moonlight, like a vast army surrounding our camp, shaking their innumerable silver spears defiantly, formed all ready for an attack.

The psychology of places, for some imaginations at least, is very vivid; for the wanderer, especially, camps have their "note" either of welcome or rejection. At first it may not always be apparent, because the busy preparations of tent and cooking prevent, but with the first pause—after supper usually—it comes and announces itself. And the note of this willow-camp now became unmistakably plain to me: we were interlopers, trespassers; we were not welcomed. The sense of unfamiliarity grew upon me as I stood there watching. We touched the frontier of a region where our presence was resented. For a night's lodging we might perhaps be tolerated; but for a prolonged and inquisitive stay—No! by all the gods of the trees and the wilderness, no! We were the first human influences upon this island, and we were not wanted. *The willows were against us.*

Strange thoughts like these, bizarre fancies, borne I know not whence, found lodgment in my mind as I stood listening. What, I thought, if, after all, these crouching willows proved to be alive; if suddenly they should rise up, like a swarm of living creatures, marshalled by the gods whose territory we had invaded, sweep towards us off the vast swamps, booming overhead in the night—and then *settle down!* As I looked it was so easy to imagine they actually moved, crept nearer, retreated a little, huddled together in masses, hostile, waiting for the great wind that should finally start them a-running. I could have sworn their aspect changed a little, and their ranks deepened and pressed more closely together.

The melancholy shrill cry of a night-bird sounded overhead, and suddenly I nearly lost my balance as the piece of bank I stood upon fell with a great splash into the river, undermined by the flood. I stepped back just in time, and went on hunting for firewood again, half laughing at the odd fancies that crowded so thickly into my mind and cast their spell upon me. I recalled the Swede's remark about moving on next day, and I was just thinking that I fully agreed with him, when I turned with a start and saw the subject of my thoughts standing immediately in front of me. He was quite close. The roar of the elements had covered his approach.

"You've been gone so long," he shouted above the wind, "I thought something must have happened to you."

But there was that in his tone, and a certain look in his face as well, that conveyed to me more than his actual words, and in a flash I understood the real reason for his coming. It was because the spell of the place had entered his soul too, and he did not like being alone.

"River still rising," he cried, pointing to the flood in the moon-light, "and the wind's simply awful."

He always said the same things, but it was the cry for companionship that gave the real importance to his words.

"Lucky," I cried back, "our tent's in the hollow. I think it'll hold all right." I added something about the difficulty of finding wood, in order to explain my absence, but the wind caught my words and flung them across the river, so that he did not hear, but just looked at me through the branches, nodding his head.

"Lucky if we get away without disaster!" he shouted, or words to that effect; and I remember feeling half angry with him for putting the thought into words, for it was exactly what I felt myself. There was disaster impending somewhere, and the sense of presentiment lay unpleasantly upon me.

We went back to the fire and made a final blaze, poking it up with our feet. We took a last look round. But for the wind the heat would have been unpleasant. I put this thought into words, and I remember my friend's reply struck me oddly: that he would rather have the heat, the ordinary July weather, than this "diabolical wind."

Everything was snug for the night; the canoe lying turned over beside the tent, with both yellow paddles beneath her; the provision sack hanging from a willow-stem, and the washed-up dishes removed to a safe distance from the fire, all ready for the morning meal.

We smothered the embers of the fire with sand, and then turned in. The flap of the tent door was up, and I saw the branches and the stars and the white moonlight. The shaking willows and the heavy buffetings of the wind against our taut little house were the last things I remembered as sleep came down and covered all with its soft and delicious forgetfulness.

II

Suddenly I found myself lying awake, peering from my sandy mattress through the door of the tent. I looked at my watch pinned against the canvas, and saw by the bright moonlight that it was past twelve o'clock—the threshold of a new day—and I had therefore slept a couple of hours. The Swede was asleep still beside me; the wind howled as before; something plucked at my heart and made me feel afraid. There was a sense of disturbance in my immediate neighbourhood.

I sat up quickly and looked out. The trees were swaying violently to and fro as the gusts smote them, but our little bit of green canvas lay snugly safe in the hollow, for the wind passed over it without meeting enough resistance to make it vicious. The feeling of disquietude did not pass, however, and I crawled quietly out of the tent to see if our belongings were safe. I moved carefully so as not to waken my companion. A curious excitement was on me.

I was half-way out, kneeling on all fours, when my eye first took in that the tops of the bushes opposite, with their moving tracery of leaves, made shapes against the sky. I sat back on my haunches and stared. It was incredible, surely, but there, opposite and slightly above me, were shapes of some indeterminate sort among the willows, and as the branches swayed in the wind they seemed to group themselves about these shapes, forming a series of monstrous outlines that shifted rapidly beneath the moon. Close, about fifty feet in front of me, I saw these things.

My first instinct was to waken my companion, that he too might see them, but something made me hesitate—the sudden realisation, probably, that I should not welcome corroboration; and meanwhile I crouched there staring in amazement with smarting eyes. I was wide awake. I remember saying to myself that I was *not* dreaming.

They first became properly visible, these huge figures, just within the tops of the bushes—immense, bronze-coloured, moving, and wholly independent of the swaying of the branches. I saw them plainly and noted, now I came to examine them more calmly, that they were very much larger than human, and indeed that something in their appearance proclaimed them to be *not human* at all. Certainly they were not merely the moving tracery of the branches against the moonlight. They shifted independently. They rose upwards in a continuous stream from earth to sky, vanishing utterly as soon as they reached the dark of the sky. They were interlaced one with another, making a great column, and I saw their limbs and huge bodies melting in and out of each other, forming this serpentine line that bent and swayed and twisted spirally with the contortions of the wind-tossed trees. They were nude, fluid shapes, passing up the bushes, *within* the leaves almost—rising up in a living column into the heavens. Their faces I never could see. Unceasingly they poured upwards, swaying in great bending curves, with a hue of dull bronze upon their skins.

I stared, trying to force every atom of vision from my eyes. For a long time I thought they *must* every moment disappear and resolve themselves into the movements of the branches and prove to be an optical illusion. I searched everywhere for a proof of reality, when all the while I understood quite well that the standard of reality had changed. For the longer I looked the more certain I became that these figures were real and living, though perhaps not according to the standards that the camera and the biologist would insist upon.

Far from feeling fear, I was possessed with a sense of awe and wonder such as I have never known. I seemed to be gazing at the personified elemental forces of this haunted and primeval region. Our intrusion had stirred the powers of the place into activity. It was we who were the cause of the disturbance, and my brain filled to bursting with stories and legends of the spirits and deities of places that have been acknowledged and worshipped by men in all ages of the world's history. But, before I could arrive at any possible explanation, something impelled me to go farther out, and I crept forward on to the sand and stood upright. I felt the ground still warm under my bare feet; the wind tore at my hair and face; and the sound of the river burst upon my ears with a sudden roar. These things, I knew, were real, and proved that my senses were acting normally. Yet the figures still rose from earth to heaven, silent, majestically, in a great spiral of grace and strength that overwhelmed me at length with a genuine deep emotion of worship. I felt that I must fall down and worship—absolutely worship.

Perhaps in another minute I might have done so, when a gust of wind swept against me with such force that it blew me sideways, and I nearly stumbled and fell. It seemed to shake the dream violently out of me. At least it gave me another point of view somehow. The figures still remained, still ascended into heaven from the heart of the night, but my reason at last began to assert itself. It must be a subjective experience, I argued—none the less real for that, but still subjective. The moonlight and the branches combined to work out these pictures upon the mirror of my imagination, and for some reason I projected them outwards and made them appear objective. I knew this must be the case, of course. I was the subject of a vivid and interesting hallucination. I took courage, and began to move forward across the open patches of sand. By Jove, though, was it all hallucination? Was it merely subjective? Did not my reason argue in the old futile way from the little standard of the known?

I only know that great column of figures ascended darkly into the sky for what seemed a very long period of time, and with a very complete measure of reality as most men are accustomed to gauge reality. Then suddenly they were gone!

And, once they were gone and the immediate wonder of their great presence had passed, fear came down upon me with a cold rush. The esoteric meaning of this lonely and haunted region suddenly flamed up within me, and I began to tremble dreadfully. I took a quick look round—a look of horror that came near to panic—calculating vainly ways of escape; and then, realising how helpless I was to achieve anything really effective, I crept back silently into the tent and lay down again upon my sandy mattress, first lowering the door-curtain to shut out the sight of the willows in the moonlight, and then burying my head as deeply as possibly beneath the blankets to deaden the sound of the terrifying wind.

III

As though further to convince me that I had not been dreaming, I remember that it was a long time before I fell again into a troubled and restless sleep; and even then only the upper crust of me slept, and underneath there was something that never quite lost consciousness, but lay alert and on the watch.

But this second time I jumped up with a genuine start of terror. It was neither the wind nor the river that woke me, but the slow approach of something that caused the sleeping portion of me to grow smaller and smaller till at last it vanished altogether, and I found myself sitting bolt upright—listening.

Outside there was a sound of multitudinous little patterings. They had been coming, I was aware, for a long time, and in my sleep they had first become audible. I sat there nervously wide awake as though I had not slept at all. It seemed to me that my breathing came with difficulty, and that there was a great weight upon the surface of my body. In spite of the hot night, I felt clammy with cold and shivered. Something surely was pressing steadily against the sides of the tent and weighing down upon it from above. Was it the body of the wind? Was this the pattering rain, the dripping of the leaves? The spray blown from the river by the wind and gathering in big drops? I thought quickly of a dozen things.

Then suddenly the explanation leaped into my mind: a bough from the poplar, the only large tree on the island, had fallen with the wind. Still half caught by the other branches, it would fall with the next gust and crush us, and meanwhile its leaves brushed and tapped upon the tight canvas surface of the tent. I raised the loose flap and rushed out, calling to the Swede to follow.

But when I got out and stood upright I saw that the tent was free. There was no hanging bough; there was no rain or spray; nothing approached.

A cold, grey light filtered down through the bushes and lay on the faintly gleaming sand. Stars still crowded the sky directly overhead, and the wind howled magnificently, but the fire no longer gave out any glow, and I saw the east reddening in streaks through the trees. Several hours must have passed since I stood there before watching the ascending figures, and the memory of it now came back to me horribly, like an evil dream. Oh, how tired it made me feel, that ceaseless raging wind! Yet, though the deep lassitude of a sleepless night was on me, my nerves were tingling with the activity of an equally tireless apprehension, and all idea of repose was out of the question. The river I saw had risen further. Its thunder filled the air, and a fine spray made itself felt through my thin sleeping shirt.

Yet nowhere did I discover the slightest evidences of anything to cause alarm. This deep, prolonged disturbance in my heart remained wholly unaccounted for.

My companion had not stirred when I called him, and there was no need to waken him now. I looked about me carefully, noting everything: the turned-over canoe; the yellow paddles—two of them, I'm certain; the provision sack and the extra lantern hanging together from the tree; and, crowding everywhere about me, enveloping all, the willows, those endless, shaking willows. A bird uttered its morning cry, and a string of duck passed with whirring flight overhead in the twilight. The sand whirled, dry and stinging, about my bare feet in the wind.

I walked round the tent and then went out a little way into the bush, so that I could see across the river to the farther landscape, and the same profound yet indefinable emotion of distress seized upon me again as I saw the interminable sea of bushes stretching to the horizon, looking ghostly and unreal in the wan light of dawn. I walked softly here and there, still puzzling over that odd sound of infinite pattering, and of that pressure upon the tent that had wakened me. It *must* have been the wind, I reflected—the wind beating upon the loose, hot sand, driving the dry particles smartly against the taut canvas—the wind dropping heavily upon our fragile roof.

Yet all the time my nervousness and malaise increased appreciably.

I crossed over to the farther shore and noted how the coast-line had altered in the night, and what masses of sand the river had torn away. I dipped my hands and feet into the cool current, and bathed my forehead. Already there was a glow of sunrise in the sky and the exquisite freshness of coming day. On my way back I passed purposely beneath the very bushes where I had seen the column of figures rising into the air, and midway among the clumps I suddenly found myself overtaken by a sense of vast terror. From the shadows a large figure went swiftly by. Some one passed me, as sure as ever man did...

It was a great staggering blow from the wind that helped me forward again, and once out in the more open space, the sense of terror diminished strangely. The winds were about and walking, I remember saying to myself; for the winds often move like great presences under the trees. And altogether the fear that hovered about me was such an unknown and immense kind of fear, so unlike anything I had ever felt before, that it woke a sense of awe and wonder in me that did much to counteract its worst effects; and when I reached a high point in the middle of the island from which I could see the wide stretch of river, crimson in the sunrise, the whole magical beauty of it all was so overpowering that a sort of wild yearning woke in me and almost brought a cry up into the throat.

But this cry found no expression, for as my eyes wandered from the plain beyond to the island round me and noted our little tent half hidden among the willows, a dreadful discovery leaped out at me, compared to which my terror of the walking winds seemed as nothing at all.

For a change, I thought, had somehow come about in the arrangement of the landscape. It was not that my point of vantage gave me a different view, but that an alteration had apparently been effected in the relation of the tent to the willows, and of the willows to the tent. Surely the bushes now crowded much closer—unnecessarily, unpleasantly close. *They had moved nearer.*

Creeping with silent feet over the shifting sands, drawing imperceptibly nearer by soft, unhurried movements, the willows had come closer during the night. But had the wind moved them, or had they moved of themselves? I recalled the sound of infinite small patterings and the pressure upon the tent and upon my own heart that caused me to wake in terror. I swayed for a moment in the wind like a tree, finding it hard to keep my upright position on the sandy hillock. There was a suggestion here of personal agency, of deliberate intention, of aggressive hostility, and it terrified me into a sort of rigidity.

Then the reaction followed quickly. The idea was so bizarre, so absurd, that I felt inclined to laugh. But the laughter came no more readily than the cry, for the knowledge that my mind was so respective to such dangerous imaginings brought the additional terror that it was through our minds and not through our physical bodies that the attack would come, and was coming.

The wind buffeted me about, and, very quickly it seemed, the sun came up over the horizon, for it was after four o'clock, and I must have stood on that little pinnacle of sand longer than I knew, afraid to come down at close quarters with the willows. I returned quietly, creepily, to the tent, first taking another exhaustive look round and—yes, I confess it—making a few measurements. I paced out on the warm sand the distances between the willows and the tent, making a note of the shortest distance particularly.

I crawled stealthily into my blankets. My companion, to all appearances, still slept soundly, and I was glad that this was so. Provided my experiences were not corroborated, I could find strength somehow to deny them, perhaps. With the daylight I could persuade myself that it was all a subjective hallucination, a fantasy of the night, a projection of the excited imagination.

Nothing further came to disturb me, and I fell asleep almost at once, utterly exhausted, yet still in dread of hearing again that weird sound of multitudinous pattering, or of feeling the pressure upon my heart that had made it difficult to breathe.

IV

The sun was high in the heavens when my companion woke me from a heavy sleep and announced that the porridge was cooked and there was just time to bathe. The grateful smell of frizzling bacon entered the tent door.

"River still rising," he said, "and several islands out in mid-stream have disappeared altogether. Our own island's much smaller."

"Any wood left?" I asked sleepily.

"The wood and the island will finish to-morrow in a dead heat," he laughed, "but there's enough to last us till then."

I plunged in from the point of the island, which had indeed altered a lot in size and shape during the night, and was swept down in a moment to the landing place opposite the tent. The water was icy, and the banks flew by like the country from an express train. Bathing under such conditions was an exhilarating operation, and the terror of the night seemed cleansed out of me by a process of evaporation in the brain. The sun was blazing hot; not a cloud showed itself anywhere; the wind, however, had not abated one little jot.

Quite suddenly then the implied meaning of the Swede's words flashed across me, showing that he no longer wished to leave post-haste, and had changed his mind. "Enough to last till to-morrow"— he assumed we should stay on the island another night. It struck me as odd. The night before he was so positive the other way. How had the change come about?

Great crumblings of the banks occurred at breakfast, with heavy splashings and clouds of spray which the wind brought into our frying-pan, and my fellow-traveller talked incessantly about the difficulty the Vienna-Pesth steamers must have to find the channel in flood. But the state of his mind interested and impressed me far more than the state of the river or the difficulties of the steamers. He had changed somehow since the evening before. His manner was different—a trifle excited, a trifle shy, with a sort of suspicion about his voice and gestures. I hardly know how to describe it now in cold blood, but at the time I remember being quite certain of one thing, viz., that he had become frightened!

He ate very little breakfast, and for once omitted to smoke his pipe. He had the map spread open beside him, and kept studying its markings.

"We'd better get off sharp in an hour," I said presently, feeling for an opening that must bring him indirectly to a partial confession at any rate. And his answer puzzled me uncomfortably: "Rather! If they'll let us."

"Who'll let us? The elements?" I asked quickly, with affected indifference.

"The powers of this awful place, whoever they are," he replied, keeping his eyes on the map. "The gods are here, if they are any-where at all in the world."

"The elements are always the true immortals," I replied, laugh-ing as naturally as I could manage, yet knowing quite well that my face reflected my true feelings when he looked up gravely at me and spoke across the smoke:

"We shall be fortunate if we get away without further disaster."

This was exactly what I had dreaded, and I screwed myself up to the point of the direct question. It was like agreeing to allow the dentist to extract the tooth; it *had* to come anyhow in the long run, and the rest was all pretence.

"Further disaster! Why, what's happened?"

"For one thing—the steering paddle's gone," he said quietly.

"The steering paddle gone!" I repeated, greatly excited, for this was our rudder, and the Danube in flood without a rudder was suicide. "But what—"

"And there's a tear in the bottom of the canoe," he added, with a genuine little tremor in his voice.

I continued staring at him, able only to repeat the words in his face somewhat foolishly. There, in the heat of the sun, and on this burning sand, I was aware of a freezing atmosphere descending round us. I got up to follow him, for he merely nodded his head gravely and led the way towards the tent a few yards on the other side of the fireplace. The canoe still lay there as I had last seen her in the night, ribs uppermost, the paddles, or rather, *the* paddle, on the sand beside her.

"There's only one," he said, stooping to pick it up. "And here's the rent in the base-board."

It was on the tip of my tongue to tell him that I had clearly noticed *two* paddles a few hours before, but a second impulse made me think better of it, and I said nothing. I approached to see.

There was a long, finely-made tear in the bottom of the canoe where a little slither of wood had been neatly taken clean out; it looked as if the tooth of a sharp rock or snag had eaten down her length, and investigation showed that the hole went through. Had we launched out in her without observing it we must inevitably have foundered. At first the water would have made the wood swell so as to close the hole, but once out in mid-stream the water must have poured in, and the canoe, never more than two inches above the surface, would have filled and sunk very rapidly.

"There, you see, an attempt to prepare a victim for the sacrifice," I heard him saying, more to himself than to me, "two victims rather," he added as he bent over and ran his fingers along the slit.

I began to whistle—a thing I always do unconsciously when utterly nonplussed—and purposely paid no attention to his words. I was determined to consider them foolish.

"It wasn't there last night," he said presently, straightening up from his examination and looking anywhere but at me.

"We must have scratched her in landing, of course," I stopped whistling to say. "The stones are very sharp—"

I stopped abruptly, for at that moment he turned round and met my eye squarely. I knew just as well as he did how impossible my explanation was. There were no stones, to begin with.

"And then there's this to explain too," he added quietly, handing me the paddle and pointing to the blade.

A new and curious emotion spread freezingly over me as I took and examined it. The blade was scraped down all over, beautifully scraped, as though some one had sand-papered it with care, making it so thin that the first vigorous stroke must have snapped it off at the elbow.

"One of us walked in his sleep and did this thing," I said feebly, "or—or it has been filed by the constant stream of sand particles blown against it by the wind, perhaps."

"Ah," said the Swede, turning away, laughing a little, "you can explain everything!"

"The same wind that caught the steering paddle and flung it so near the bank that it fell in with the next lump that crumbled," I called out after him, absolutely determined to find an explanation for everything he showed me.

"I see," he shouted back, turning his head to look at me before disappearing among the willow bushes.

Once alone with these perplexing evidences of personal agency, I think my first thought took the form of "One of us must have done this thing, and it certainly was not I." But my second thought decided how impossible it was to suppose, under all the circumstances, that either of us had done it. That my companion, the trusted friend of a dozen similar expeditions, could have knowingly had a hand in it, was a suggestion not to be entertained for a moment. Equally absurd seemed the explanation that this imperturbable and densely practical nature had suddenly become insane and was busied with insane purposes.

Yet the fact remained that what disturbed me most, and kept my fear actively alive even in this blaze of sunshine and wild beauty, was the clear certainty that some curious alteration had come about in his *mind*—that he was nervous, timid, suspicious, aware of goings on he did not speak about, watching a series of secret and hitherto unmentionable events—waiting, in a word, for a climax that he expected, and, I thought, expected very soon. This grew up in my mind intuitively—I hardly knew how.

I made a hurried examination of the tent and its surroundings, but the measurements of the night remained the same. There were deep hollows formed in the sand, I now noticed for the first time, basin-shaped and of various depths and sizes, varying from that of a tea-cup to a large bowl. The wind, no doubt, was responsible for these miniature craters, just as it was for lifting the paddle and tossing it towards the water. The rent in the canoe was the only thing that seemed quite inexplicable; and, after all, it *was* conceivable that a sharp point had caught it when we landed. The examination I made of the shore did not assist this theory, but all the same I clung to it with that diminishing portion of my intelligence which I called my "reason." An explanation of some kind was an absolute necessity, just as some working explanation of the universe is necessary—however absurd—to the happiness of every individual who seeks to do his duty in the world and face the problems of life. The simile seemed to me at the time an exact parallel.

I at once set the pitch melting, and presently the Swede joined me at the work, though under the best conditions in the world the canoe could not be safe for travelling till the following day. I drew his attention casually to the hollows in the sand.

"Yes," he said, "I know. They're all over the island. But *you* can explain them, no doubt!"

"Wind, of course," I answered without hesitation. "Have you never watched those little whirlwinds in the street that twist and twirl everything into a circle? This sand's loose enough to yield, that's all."

He made no reply, and we worked on in silence for a bit. I watched him surreptitiously all the time, and I had an idea he was watching me. He seemed, too, to be always listening attentively to something I could not hear, or perhaps for something that he expected to hear, for he kept turning about and staring into the bushes, and up into the sky, and out across the water where it was visible through the openings among the willows. Sometimes he even put his hand to his ear and held it there for several minutes. He said nothing to me, however, about it, and I asked no questions. And meanwhile, as he mended that torn canoe with the skill and address of a red Indian, I was glad to notice his absorption in the work, for there was a vague dread in my heart that he would speak of the changed aspect of the willows. And, if he had noticed *that*, my imagination could no longer be held a sufficient explanation of it.

At length, after a long pause, he began to talk.

"Queer thing," he added in a hurried sort of voice, as though he wanted to say something and get it over. "Queer thing, I mean, about that otter last night."

I had expected something so totally different that he caught me with surprise, and I looked up sharply.

"Shows how lonely this place is. Otters are awfully shy things—"

"I don't mean that, of course," he interrupted. "I mean—do you think—did you think it really *was* an otter?"

"What else, in the name of Heaven, what else?"

"You know, I saw it before you did, and at first it seemed—so *much* bigger than an otter."

"The sunset as you looked up-stream magnified it, or something," I replied.

He looked at me absently a moment, as though his mind were busy with other thoughts.

"It had such extraordinary yellow eyes," he went on half to himself.

"That was the sun too," I laughed, a trifle boisterously. "I suppose you'll wonder next if that fellow in the boat—"

I suddenly decided not to finish the sentence. He was in the act again of listening, turning his head to the wind, and something in the expression of his face made me halt. The subject dropped, and we went on with our caulking. Apparently he had not noticed my unfinished sentence. Five minutes later, however, he looked at me across the canoe, the smoking pitch in his hand, his face exceedingly grave.

"I *did* rather wonder, if you want to know," he said slowly, "what that thing in the boat was. I remember thinking at the time it was not a man. The whole business seemed to rise quite suddenly out of the water."

I laughed again boisterously in his face, but this time there was impatience, and a strain of anger too, in my feeling.

"Look here now," I cried, "this place is quite queer enough without going out of our way to imagine things! That boat was an ordinary boat, and the man in it was an ordinary man, and they were both going down stream as fast as they could lick. And that otter *was* an otter, so don't let's play the fool about it!"

He looked steadily at me with the same grave expression. He was not in the least annoyed. I took courage from his silence.

"And, for Heaven's sake," I went on, "don't keep pretending you hear things, because it only gives me the jumps, and there's nothing to hear but the river and this cursed old thundering wind."

"You *fool!*" he answered in a low, shocked voice, "you utter fool. That's just the way all victims talk. As if you didn't understand just as well as I do!" he sneered with scorn in his voice, and a sort of resignation. "The best thing you can do is to keep quiet and try to hold your mind as firm as possible. This feeble attempt at self-deception only makes the truth harder when you're forced to meet it."

My little effort was over, and I found nothing more to say, for I knew quite well his words were true, and that *I* was the fool, not *he*. Up to a certain stage in the adventure he kept ahead of me easily, and I think I felt annoyed to be out of it, to be thus proved less psychic, less sensitive than himself to these extraordinary happenings, and half ignorant all the time of what was going on under my very nose. *He knew* from the very beginning, apparently. But at the moment I wholly missed the point of his words about the necessity of there being a victim, and that we ourselves were destined to satisfy the want. I dropped all pretence thenceforward, but thenceforward likewise my fear increased steadily to the climax.

"But you're quite right about one thing," he added, before the subject passed, "and that is that we're wiser not to talk about it, or even to think about it, because what one *thinks* finds expression in words, and what one *says*, happens."

That afternoon, while the canoe dried and hardened, we spent
trying to fish, testing the leak, collecting wood, and watching the
enormous flood of rising water. Masses of driftwood swept near
our shores sometimes, and we fished for them with long willow
branches. The island grew perceptibly smaller as the banks were
torn away with great gulps and splashes. The weather kept brilliantly
fine till about four o'clock, and then for the first time for three days
the wind showed signs of abating. Clouds began to gather in the
south-west, spreading thence slowly over the sky.

This lessening of the wind came as a great relief, for the incessant roaring, banging, and thundering had irritated our nerves.
Yet the silence that came about five o'clock with its sudden cessation was in a manner quite as oppressive. The booming of the
river had everything its own way then: it filled the air with deep
murmurs, more musical than the wind noises, but infinitely more
monotonous. The wind held many notes, rising, falling, always
beating out some sort of great elemental tune; whereas the river's
song lay between three notes at most—dull pedal notes, that held
a lugubrious quality foreign to the wind, and somehow seemed
to me, in my then nervous state, to sound wonderfully well the
music of doom.

It was extraordinary, too, how the withdrawal suddenly of bright
sunlight took everything out of the landscape that made for cheer-
fulness; and since this particular landscape had already managed to
convey the suggestion of something sinister, the change of course
was all the more unwelcome and noticeable. For me, I know, the
darkening outlook became distinctly more alarming, and I found
myself more than once calculating how soon after sunset the full
moon would get up in the east, and whether the gathering clouds
would greatly interfere with her lighting of the little island.

With this general hush of the wind—though it still indulged in occasional brief gusts—the river seemed to me to grow blacker, the willows to stand more densely together. The latter, too, kept up a sort of independent movement of their own, rustling among themselves when no wind stirred, and shaking oddly from the roots upwards. When common objects in this way become charged with the suggestion of horror, they stimulate the imagination far more than things of unusual appearance; and these bushes, crowding huddled about us, assumed for me in the darkness a bizarre *grotesquerie* of appearance that lent to them somehow the aspect of purposeful and living creatures. Their very ordinariness, I felt, masked what was malignant and hostile to us. The forces of the region drew nearer with the coming of night. They were focussing upon our island, and more particularly upon ourselves. For thus, somehow, in the terms of the imagination, did my really indescribable sensations in this extraordinary place present themselves.

I had slept a good deal in the early afternoon, and had thus recovered somewhat from the exhaustion of a disturbed night, but this only served apparently to render me more susceptible than before to the obsessing spell of the haunting. I fought against it, laughing at my feelings as absurd and childish, with very obvious physiological explanations, yet, in spite of every effort, they gained in strength upon me so that I dreaded the night as a child lost in a forest must dread the approach of darkness.

The canoe we had carefully covered with a waterproof sheet during the day, and the one remaining paddle had been securely tied by the Swede to the base of a tree, lest the wind should rob us of that too. From five o'clock onwards I busied myself with the stew-pot and preparations for dinner, it being my turn to cook that night. We had potatoes, onions, bits of bacon fat to add flavour, and a general thick residue from former stews at the bottom of the pot; with black bread broken up into it the result was most excellent, and it was followed by a stew of plums with sugar and a brew of strong tea with dried milk. A good pile of wood lay close at hand, and the absence of wind made my duties easy. My companion sat lazily watching me, dividing his attentions between cleaning his pipe and giving useless advice—an admitted privilege of the off-duty man. He had been very quiet all the afternoon, engaged in re-caulking the canoe, strengthening the tent ropes, and fishing for driftwood while I slept. No more talk about undesirable things had passed between us, and I think his only remarks had to do with the gradual destruction of the island, which he declared was now fully a third smaller than when we first landed.

The pot had just begun to bubble when I heard his voice calling to me from the bank, where he had wandered away without my noticing. I ran up.

"Come and listen," he said, "and see what you make of it." He held his hand cupwise to his ear, as so often before.

"*Now* do you hear anything?" he asked, watching me curiously.

We stood there, listening attentively together. At first I heard only the deep note of the water and the hissings rising from its turbulent surface. The willows, for once, were motionless and silent. Then a sound began to reach my ears faintly, a peculiar sound—something like the humming of a distant gong. It seemed to come across to us in the darkness from the waste of swamps and willows opposite. It was repeated at regular intervals, but it was certainly neither the sound of a bell nor the hooting of a distant steamer. I can liken it to nothing so much as to the sound of an immense gong, suspended far up in the sky, repeating incessantly its muffled metallic note, soft and musical, as it was repeatedly struck. My heart quickened as I listened.

"I've heard it all day," said my companion. "While you slept this afternoon it came all round the island. I hunted it down, but could never get near enough to see—to localise it correctly. Sometimes it was overhead, and sometimes it seemed under the water. Once or twice, too, I could have sworn it was not outside at all, but *within myself*—you know—the way a sound in the fourth dimension is supposed to come."

I was too much puzzled to pay much attention to his words. I listened carefully, striving to associate it with any known familiar sound I could think of, but without success. It changed in direction, too, coming nearer, and then sinking utterly away into remote distance. I cannot say that it was ominous in quality, because to me it seemed distinctly musical, yet I must admit it set going a distressing feeling that made me wish I had never heard it.

"The wind blowing in those sand-funnels," I said, determined to find an explanation, "or the bushes rubbing together after the storm perhaps."

"It comes off the whole swamp," my friend answered. "It comes from everywhere at once." He ignored my explanations. "It comes from the willow bushes somehow—"

"But now the wind has dropped," I objected. "The willows can hardly make a noise by themselves, can they?"

His answer frightened me, first because I had dreaded it, and secondly, because I knew intuitively it was true.

"It is *because* the wind has dropped we now hear it. It was drowned before. It is the cry, I believe, of the—"

I dashed back to my fire, warned by a sound of bubbling that the stew was in danger, but determined at the same time to escape from further conversation. I was resolute, if possible, to avoid the exchanging of views. I dreaded, too, that he would begin again about the gods, or the elemental forces, or something else disquieting, and I wanted to keep myself well in hand for what might happen later. There was another night to be faced before we escaped from this distressing place, and there was no knowing yet what it might bring forth.

"Come and cut up bread for the pot," I called to him, vigorously stirring the appetising mixture. That stew-pot held sanity for us both, and the thought made me laugh.

He came over slowly and took the provision sack from the tree, fumbling in its mysterious depths, and then emptying the entire contents upon the ground-sheet at his feet.

"Hurry up!" I cried; "it's boiling."

The Swede burst out into a roar of laughter that startled me. It was forced laughter, not artificial exactly, but mirthless.

"There's nothing here!" he shouted, holding his sides.

"Bread, I mean."

"It's gone. There is no bread. They've taken it!"

I dropped the long spoon and ran up. Everything the sack had contained lay upon the ground-sheet, but there was no loaf.

The whole dead weight of my growing fear fell upon me and shook me. Then I burst out laughing too. It was the only thing to do: and the sound of my own laughter also made me understand his. The strain of psychical pressure caused it—this explosion of unnatural laughter in both of us; it was an effort of repressed forces to seek relief; it was a temporary safety valve. And with both of us it ceased quite suddenly.

"How criminally stupid of me!" I cried, still determined to be consistent and find an explanation. "I clean forgot to buy a loaf at Pressburg. That chattering woman put everything out of my head, and I must have left it lying on the counter or—"

"The oatmeal, too, is much less than it was this morning," the Swede interrupted.

Why in the world need he draw attention to it? I thought angrily.

"There's enough for to-morrow," I said, stirring vigorously, "and we can get lots more at Komorn or Gran. In twenty-four hours we shall be miles from here."

"I hope so—to God," he muttered, putting the things back into the sack, "unless we're claimed first as victims for the sacrifice," he added with a foolish laugh. He dragged the sack into the tent, for safety's sake, I suppose, and I heard him mumbling on to himself, but so indistinctly that it seemed quite natural for me to ignore his words.

Our meal was beyond question a gloomy one, and we ate it almost in silence, avoiding one another's eyes, and keeping the fire bright. Then we washed up and prepared for the night, and, once smoking, our minds unoccupied with any definite duties, the apprehension I had felt all day long became more and more acute. It was not then active fear, I think, but the very vagueness of its origin distressed me far more than if I had been able to ticket and face it squarely. The curious sound I have likened to the note of a gong became now almost incessant, and filled the stillness of the night with a faint, continuous ringing rather than a series of distinct notes. At one time it was behind and at another time in front of us. Sometimes I fancied it came from the bushes on our left, and then again from the clumps on our right. More often it hovered directly overhead like the whirring of wings. It was really everywhere at once, behind, in front, at our sides and over our heads, completely surrounding us. The sound really defies description. But nothing within my knowledge is like that ceaseless muffled humming rising off the deserted world of swamps and willows.

We sat smoking in comparative silence, the strain growing every minute greater. The worst feature of the situation seemed to me that we did not know what to expect, and could therefore make no sort of preparation by way of defence. We could anticipate nothing. My explanations made in the sunshine, moreover, now came to haunt me with their foolish and wholly unsatisfactory nature, and it was more and more clear to us that some kind of plain talk with my companion was inevitable, whether I liked it or not. After all, we had to spend the night together, and to sleep in the same tent side by side. I saw that I could not get along much longer without the support of his mind, and for that, of course, plain talk was imperative. As long as possible, however, I postponed this little climax, and tried to ignore or laugh at the occasional sentences he flung into the emptiness.

Some of these sentences, moreover, were confoundedly disquieting to me, coming as they did to corroborate much that I felt myself: corroboration, too—which made it so much more convincing—from a totally different point of view. He composed such curious sentences, and hurled them at me in such an inconsequential sort of way, as though his main line of thought was secret to himself, and these fragments were the bits he found it impossible to digest. He got rid of them by uttering them. Speech relieved him. It was like being sick.

"There are things about us, I'm sure, that make for disorder, disintegration, destruction, *our* destruction," he said once, while the fire blazed between us. "We've strayed out of a safe line somewhere."

And another time, when the gong sounds had come nearer, ringing much louder than before, and directly over our heads, he said, as though talking to himself:

"I don't think a phonograph would show any record of that. The sound doesn't come to me by the ears at all. The vibrations reach me in another manner altogether, and seem to be within me, which is precisely how a fourth dimensional sound might be supposed to make itself heard."

I purposely made no reply to this, but I sat up a little closer to the fire and peered about me into the darkness. The clouds were massed all over the sky, and no trace of moonlight came through. Very still, too, everything was, so that the river and the frogs had things all their own way.

"It has that about it," he went on, "which is utterly out of common experience. It is *unknown*. Only one thing describes it really: it is a nonhuman sound; I mean a sound outside humanity."

Having rid himself of this indigestible morsel, he lay quiet for a time; but he had so admirably expressed my own feeling that it was a relief to have the thought out, and to have confined it by the limitation of words from dangerous wandering to and fro in the mind.

The solitude of that Danube camping-place, can I ever forget it? The feeling of being utterly alone on an empty planet! My thoughts ran incessantly upon cities and the haunts of men. I would have given my soul, as the saying is, for the "feel" of those Bavarian villages we had passed through by the score; for the normal, human commonplaces: peasants drinking beer, tables beneath the trees, hot sunshine, and a ruined castle on the rocks behind the red-roofed church. Even the tourists would have been welcome.

Yet what I felt of dread was no ordinary ghostly fear. It was infinitely greater, stranger, and seemed to arise from some dim ancestral sense of terror more profoundly disturbing than anything I had known or dreamed of. We had "strayed," as the Swede put it, into some region or some set of conditions where the risks were great, yet unintelligible to us; where the frontiers of some unknown world lay close about us. It was a spot held by the dwellers in some outer space, a sort of peep-hole whence they could spy upon the earth, themselves unseen, a point where the veil between had worn a little thin. As the final result of too long a sojourn here, we should be carried over the border and deprived of what we called "our lives," yet by mental, not physical, processes. In that sense, as he said, we should be the victims of our adventure—a sacrifice.

It took us in different fashion, each according to the measure of his sensitiveness and powers of resistance. I translated it vaguely into a personification of the mightily disturbed elements, investing them with the horror of a deliberate and malefic purpose, resentful of our audacious intrusion into their breeding-place; whereas my friend threw it into the unoriginal form at first of a trespass on some ancient shrine, some place where the old gods still held sway, where the emotional forces of former worshippers still clung, and the ancestral portion of him yielded to the old pagan spell.

At any rate, here was a place unpolluted by men, kept clean by the winds from coarsening human influences, a place where spiritual agencies were within reach and aggressive. Never, before or since, have I been so attacked by indescribable suggestions of a "beyond region," of another scheme of life, another evolution not parallel to the human. And in the end our minds would succumb under the weight of the awful spell, and we should be drawn across the frontier into *their* world.

Small things testified to this amazing influence of the place, and now in the silence round the fire they allowed themselves to be noted by the mind. The very atmosphere had proved itself a magnifying medium to distort every indication: the otter rolling in the current, the hurrying boatman making signs, the shifting willows, one and all had been robbed of its natural character, and revealed in something of its other aspect—as it existed across the border in that other region. And this changed aspect I felt was new not merely to me, but to the race. The whole experience whose verge we touched was unknown to humanity at all. It was a new order of experience, and in the true sense of the word *unearthly*.

"It's the deliberate, calculating purpose that reduces one's courage to zero," the Swede said suddenly, as if he had been actually following my thoughts. "Otherwise imagination might count for much. But the paddle, the canoe, the lessening food—"

"Haven't I explained all that once?" I interrupted viciously.

"You have," he answered dryly; "you have indeed."

He made other remarks too, as usual, about what he called the "plain determination to provide a victim"; but, having now arranged my thoughts better, I recognised that this was simply the cry of his frightened soul against the knowledge that he was being attacked in a vital part, and that he would be somehow taken or destroyed. The situation called for a courage and calmness of reasoning that neither of us could compass, and I have never before been so clearly conscious of two persons in me—the one that explained everything, and the other that laughed at such foolish explanations, yet was horribly afraid.

Meanwhile, in the pitchy night the fire died down and the wood pile grew small. Neither of us moved to replenish the stock, and the darkness consequently came up very close to our faces. A few feet beyond the circle of firelight it was inky black. Occasionally a stray puff of wind set the willows shivering about us, but apart from this not very welcome sound a deep and depressing silence reigned, broken only by the gurgling of the river and the humming in the air overhead.

We both missed, I think, the shouting company of the winds.

At length, at a moment when a stray puff prolonged itself as though the wind were about to rise again, I reached the point for me of saturation, the point where it was absolutely necessary to find relief in plain speech, or else to betray myself by some hysterical extravagance that must have been far worse in its effect upon both of us. I kicked the fire into a blaze, and turned to my companion abruptly. He looked up with a start.

"I can't disguise it any longer," I said; "I don't like this place, and the darkness, and the noises, and the awful feelings I get. There's something here that beats me utterly. I'm in a blue funk, and that's the plain truth. If the other shore was—different, I swear I'd be inclined to swim for it!"

The Swede's face turned very white beneath the deep tan of sun and wind. He stared straight at me and answered quietly, but his voice betrayed his huge excitement by its unnatural calmness. For the moment, at any rate, he was the strong man of the two. He was more phlegmatic, for one thing.

"It's not a physical condition we can escape from by running away," he replied, in the tone of a doctor diagnosing some grave disease; "we must sit tight and wait. There are forces close here that could kill a herd of elephants in a second as easily as you or I could squash a fly. Our only chance is to keep perfectly still. Our insignificance perhaps may save us."

I put a dozen questions into my expression of face, but found no words. It was precisely like listening to an accurate description of a disease whose symptoms had puzzled me.

"I mean that so far, although aware of our disturbing presence, they have not *found* us—not 'located' us, as the Americans say," he went on. "They're blundering about like men hunting for a leak of gas. The paddle and canoe and provisions prove that. I think they *feel* us, but cannot actually see us. We must keep our minds quiet—it's our minds they feel. We must control our thoughts, or it's all up with us."

"Death you mean?" I stammered, icy with the horror of his suggestion.

"Worse—by far," he said. "Death, according to one's belief, means either annihilation or release from the limitations of the senses, but it involves no change of character. *You* don't suddenly alter just because the body's gone. But this means a radical alteration, a complete change, a horrible loss of oneself by substitution—far worse than death, and not even annihilation. We happen to have camped in a spot where their region touches ours, where the veil between has worn thin"—horrors! he was using my very own phrase, my actual words—"so that they are aware of our being in their neighbourhood."

"But *who* are aware?" I asked.

I forgot the shaking of the willows in the windless calm, the humming overhead, everything except that I was waiting for an answer that I dreaded more than I can possibly explain.

He lowered his voice at once to reply, leaning forward a little over the fire, an indefinable change in his face that made me avoid his eyes and look down upon the ground.

"All my life," he said, "I have been strangely, vividly conscious of another region—not far removed from our own world in one sense, yet wholly different in kind—where great things go on unceasingly, where immense and terrible personalities hurry by, intent on vast purposes compared to which earthly affairs, the rise and fall of nations, the destinies of empires, the fate of armies and continents, are all as dust in the balance; vast purposes, I mean, that deal directly with the soul, and not indirectly with mere expressions of the soul—"

"I suggest just now—" I began, seeking to stop him, feeling as though I was face to face with a madman. But he instantly overbore me with his torrent that *had* to come.

"You think," he said, "it is the spirits of the elements, and I thought perhaps it was the old gods. But I tell you now it is—*neither*. These would be comprehensible entities, for they have relations with men, depending upon them for worship or sacrifice, whereas these beings who are now about us have absolutely nothing to do with mankind, and it is mere chance that their space happens just at this spot to touch our own."

The mere conception, which his words somehow made so convincing, as I listened to them there in the dark stillness of that lonely island, set me shaking a little all over. I found it impossible to control my movements.

"And what do you propose?" I began again.

"A sacrifice, a victim, might save us by distracting them until we could get away," he went on, "just as the wolves stop to devour the dogs and give the sleigh another start. But—I see no chance of any other victim now."

I stared blankly at him. The gleam in his eyes was dreadful. Presently he continued.

"It's the willows, of course. The willows *mask* the others, but the others are feeling about for us. If we let our minds betray our fear, we're lost, lost utterly." He looked at me with an expression so calm, so determined, so sincere, that I no longer had any doubts as to his sanity. He was as sane as any man ever was. "If we can hold out through the night," he added, "we may get off in the daylight unnoticed, or rather, *undiscovered*."

"But you really think a sacrifice would—"

That gong-like humming came down very close over our heads as I spoke, but it was my friend's scared face that really stopped my mouth.

"Hush!" he whispered, holding up his hand. "Do not mention them more than you can help. Do not refer to them *by name*. To name is to reveal: it is the inevitable clue, and our only hope lies in ignoring them, in order that they may ignore us."

"Even in thought?" He was extraordinarily agitated.

"Especially in thought. Our thoughts make spirals in their world. We must keep them *out of our minds* at all costs if possible."

I raked the fire together to prevent the darkness having everything its own way. I never longed for the sun as I longed for it then in the awful blackness of that summer night.

"Were you awake all last night?" he went on suddenly.

"I slept badly a little after dawn," I replied evasively, trying to follow his instructions, which I knew instinctively were true, "but the wind, of course—"

"I know. But the wind won't account for all the noises."

"Then you heard it too?"

"The multiplying countless little footsteps I heard," he said, adding, after a moment's hesitation, "and that other sound—"

"You mean above the tent, and the pressing down upon us of something tremendous, gigantic?"

He nodded significantly.

"It was like the beginning of a sort of inner suffocation?" I said.

"Partly, yes. It seemed to me that the weight of the atmosphere had been altered—had increased enormously, so that we should be crushed."

"And *that*," I went on, determined to have it all out, pointing upwards where the gong-like note hummed ceaselessly, rising and falling like wind. "What do you make of that?"

"It's *their* sound," he whispered gravely. "It's the sound of their world, the humming in their region. The division here is so thin that it leaks through somehow. But, if you listen carefully, you'll find it's not above so much as around us. It's in the willows. It's the willows themselves humming, because here the willows have been made symbols of the forces that are against us."

I could not follow exactly what he meant by this, yet the thought and idea in my mind were beyond question the thought and idea in his. I realised what he realised, only with less power of analysis than his. It was on the tip of my tongue to tell him at last about my hallucination of the ascending figures and the moving bushes, when he suddenly thrust his face again close into mine across the firelight and began to speak in a very earnest whisper. He amazed me by his calmness and pluck, his apparent control of the situation. This man I had for years deemed unimaginative, stolid!

"Now listen," he said. "The only thing for us to do is to go on as though nothing had happened, follow our usual habits, go to bed, and so forth; pretend we feel nothing and notice nothing. It is a question wholly of the mind, and the less we think about them the better our chance of escape. Above all, don't *think*, for what you think happens!"

"All right," I managed to reply, simply breathless with his words and the strangeness of it all; "all right, I'll try, but tell me one thing more first. Tell me what you make of those hollows in the ground all about us, those sand-funnels?"

"No!" he cried, forgetting to whisper in his excitement. "I dare not, simply dare not, put the thought into words. If you have not guessed I am glad. Don't try to. *They* have put it into my mind; try your hardest to prevent their putting it into yours."

He sank his voice again to a whisper before he finished, and I did not press him to explain. There was already just about as much horror in me as I could hold. The conversation came to an end, and we smoked our pipes busily in silence.

Then something happened, something unimportant apparently, as the way is when the nerves are in a very great state of tension, and this small thing for a brief space gave me an entirely different point of view. I chanced to look down at my sandshoe—the sort we used for the canoe—and something to do with the hole at the toe suddenly recalled to me the London shop where I had bought them, the difficulty the man had in fitting me, and other details of the uninteresting but practical operation. At once, in its train, followed a wholesome view of the modern sceptical world I was accustomed to move in at home. I thought of roast beef and ale, motor-cars, policemen, brass bands, and a dozen other things that proclaimed the soul of ordinariness or utility. The effect was immediate and astonishing even to myself. Psychologically, I suppose, it was simply a sudden and violent reaction after the strain of living in an atmosphere of things that to the normal consciousness must seem impossible and incredible. But, whatever the cause, it momentarily lifted the spell from my heart, and left me for the short space of a minute feeling free and utterly unafraid. I looked up at my friend opposite.

"You damned old pagan!" I cried, laughing aloud in his face. "You imaginative idiot! You superstitious idolator! You—"

I stopped in the middle, seized anew by the old horror. I tried to smother the sound of my voice as something sacrilegious. The Swede, of course, heard it too—that strange cry overhead in the darkness—and that sudden drop in the air as though something had come nearer.

He had turned ashen white under the tan. He stood bolt upright in front of the fire, stiff as a rod, staring at me.

"After that," he said in a sort of helpless, frantic way, "we must go! We can't stay now; we must strike camp this very instant and go on—down the river."

He was talking, I saw, quite wildly, his words dictated by abject terror—the terror he had resisted so long, but which had caught him at last.

"In the dark?" I exclaimed, shaking with fear after my hysterical outburst, but still realising our position better than he did. "Sheer madness! The river's in flood, and we've only got a single paddle. Besides, we only go deeper into their country! There's nothing ahead for fifty miles but willows, willows, willows!"

He sat down again in a state of semi-collapse. The positions, by one of those kaleidoscopic changes nature loves, were suddenly reversed, and the control of our forces passed over into my hands. His mind at last had reached the point where it was beginning to weaken.

"What on earth possessed you to do such a thing?" he whispered, with the awe of genuine terror in his voice and face.

I crossed round to his side of the fire. I took both his hands in mine, kneeling down beside him and looking straight into his frightened eyes.

"We'll make one more blaze," I said firmly, "and then turn in for the night. At sunrise we'll be off full speed for Komorn. Now, pull yourself together a bit, and remember your own advice about *not thinking fear!*"

He said no more, and I saw that he would agree and obey. In

some measure, too, it was a sort of relief to get up and make an excursion into the darkness for more wood. We kept close together, almost touching, groping among the bushes and along the bank. The humming overhead never ceased, but seemed to me to grow louder as we increased our distance from the fire. It was shivery work!

We were grubbing away in the middle of a thickish clump of willows where some driftwood from a former flood had caught high among the branches, when my body was seized in a grip that made me half drop upon the sand. It was the Swede. He had fallen against me, and was clutching me for support. I heard his breath coming and going in short gasps.

"Look! By my soul!" he whispered, and for the first time in my experience I knew what it was to hear tears of terror in a human voice. He was pointing to the fire, some fifty feet away. I followed the direction of his finger, and I swear my heart missed a beat.

There, in front of the dim glow, *something was moving*.

I saw it through a veil that hung before my eyes like the gauze drop-curtain used at the back of a theatre—hazily a little. It was neither a human figure nor an animal. To me it gave the strange impression of being as large as several animals grouped together, like horses, two or three, moving slowly. The Swede, too, got a similar result, though expressing it differently, for he thought it was shaped and sized like a clump of willow bushes, rounded at the top, and moving all over upon its surface—"coiling upon itself like smoke," he said afterwards.

"I watched it settle downwards through the bushes," he sobbed at me. "Look, by God! It's coming this way! Oh, oh!"—he gave a kind of whistling cry. *"They've found us."*

I gave one terrified glance, which just enabled me to see that the shadowy form was swinging towards us through the bushes, and then I collapsed backwards with a crash into the branches. These failed, of course, to support my weight, so that with the Swede on the top of me we fell in a struggling heap upon the sand. I really hardly knew what was happening. I was conscious only of a sort of enveloping sensation of icy fear that plucked the nerves out of their fleshly covering, twisted them this way and that, and replaced them quivering. My eyes were tightly shut; something in my throat choked me; a feeling that my consciousness was expanding, extending out into space, swiftly gave way to another feeling that I was losing it altogether, and about to die.

An acute spasm of pain passed through me, and I was aware that the Swede had hold of me in such a way that he hurt me abominably. It was the way he caught at me in falling.

But it was this pain, he declared afterwards, that saved me: it caused me to *forget them* and think of something else at the very instant when they were about to find me. It concealed my mind from them at the moment of discovery, yet just in time to evade their terrible seizing of me. He himself, he says actually swooned at the same moment, and that was what saved him.

I only know that at a later time, how long or short is impossible to say, I found myself scrambling up out of the slippery network of willow branches, and saw my companion standing in front of me holding out a hand to assist me. I stared at him in a dazed way, rubbing the arm he had twisted for me. Nothing came to me to say, somehow.

"I lost consciousness for a moment or two," I heard him say. "That's what saved me. It made me stop thinking about them."

"You nearly broke my arm in two," I said, uttering my only connected thought at the moment. A numbness came over me.

"That's what saved *you!*" he replied. "Between us, we've managed to set them off on a false tack somewhere. The humming has ceased. It's gone—for the moment at any rate!"

A wave of hysterical laughter seized me again, and this time spread to my friend too—great healing gusts of shaking laughter that brought a tremendous sense of relief in their train. We made our way back to the fire and put the wood on so that it blazed at once. Then we saw that the tent had fallen over and lay in a tangled heap upon the ground.

We picked it up, and during the process tripped more than once and caught our feet in sand.

"It's those sand-funnels," exclaimed the Swede, when the tent was up again and the firelight lit up the ground for several yards about us. "And look at the size of them!"

All round the tent and about the fireplace where we had seen the moving shadows there were deep funnel-shaped hollows in the sand, exactly similar to the ones we had already found over the island, only far bigger and deeper, beautifully formed, and wide enough in some instances to admit the whole of my foot and leg.

Neither of us said a word. We both knew that sleep was the safest thing we could do, and to bed we went accordingly without further delay, having first thrown sand on the fire and taken the provision sack and the paddle inside the tent with us. The canoe, too, we propped in such a way at the end of the tent that our feet touched it, and the least motion would disturb and wake us.

In case of emergency, too, we again went to bed in our clothes, ready for a sudden start.

V

It was my firm intention to lie awake all night and watch, but the exhaustion of nerves and body decreed otherwise, and sleep after a while came over me with a welcome blanket of oblivion. The fact that my companion also slept quickened its approach. At first he fidgeted and constantly sat up, asking me if I "heard this" or "heard that." He tossed about on his cork mattress, and said the tent was moving and the river had risen over the point of the island; but each time I went out to look I returned with the report that all was well, and finally he grew calmer and lay still. Then at length his breathing became regular and I heard unmistakable sounds of snoring—the first and only time in my life when snoring has been a welcome and calming influence.

This, I remember, was the last thought in my mind before dozing off.

A difficulty in breathing woke me, and I found the blanket over my face. But something else besides the blanket was pressing upon me, and my first thought was that my companion had rolled off his mattress on to my own in his sleep. I called to him and sat up, and at the same moment it came to me that the tent was *surrounded*. That sound of multitudinous soft pattering was again audible outside, filling the night with horror.

I called again to him, louder than before. He did not answer, but I missed the sound of his snoring, and also noticed that the flap of the tent door was down. This was the unpardonable sin. I crawled out in the darkness to hook it back securely, and it was then for the first time I realised positively that the Swede was not there. He had gone.

I dashed out in a mad run, seized by a dreadful agitation, and the moment I was out I plunged into a sort of torrent of humming that surrounded me completely and came out of every quarter of the heavens at once. It was that same familiar humming—gone mad! A swarm of great invisible bees might have been about me in the air. The sound seemed to thicken the very atmosphere, and I felt that my lungs worked with difficulty.

But my friend was in danger, and I could not hesitate.

The dawn was just about to break, and a faint whitish light spread upwards over the clouds from a thin strip of clear horizon. No wind stirred. I could just make out the bushes and river beyond, and the pale sandy patches. In my excitement I ran frantically to and fro about the island, calling him by name, shouting at the top of my voice the first words that came into my head. But the willows smothered my voice, and the humming muffled it, so that the sound only travelled a few feet round me. I plunged among the bushes, tripping headlong, tumbling over roots, and scraping my face as I tore this way and that among the preventing branches.

Then, quite unexpectedly, I came out upon the island's point and saw a dark figure outlined between the water and the sky. It was the Swede. And already he had one foot in the river! A moment more and he would have taken the plunge.

I threw myself upon him, flinging my arms about his waist and dragging him shorewards with all my strength. Of course he struggled furiously, making a noise all the time just like that cursed humming, and using the most outlandish phrases in his anger about "going *inside* to Them," and "taking the way of the water and the wind," and God only knows what more besides, that I tried in vain to recall afterwards, but which turned me sick with horror and amazement as I listened. But in the end I managed to get him into the comparative safety of the tent, and flung him breathless and cursing upon the mattress, where I held him until the fit had passed.

I think the suddenness with which it all went and he grew calm, coinciding as it did with the equally abrupt cessation of the humming and pattering outside—I think this was almost the strangest part of the whole business perhaps. For he just opened his eyes and turned his tired face up to me so that the dawn threw a pale light upon it through the doorway, and said, for all the world just like a frightened child:

"My life, old man—it's my life I owe you. But it's all over now anyhow. They've found a victim in our place!"

Then he dropped back upon his blankets and went to sleep literally under my eyes. He simply collapsed, and began to snore again as healthily as though nothing had happened and he had never tried to offer his own life as a sacrifice by drowning. And when the sunlight woke him three hours later—hours of ceaseless vigil for me—it became so clear to me that he remembered absolutely nothing of what he had attempted to do, that I deemed it wise to hold my peace and ask no dangerous questions.

He woke naturally and easily, as I have said, when the sun was already high in a windless hot sky, and he at once got up and set about the preparation of the fire for breakfast. I followed him anxiously at bathing, but he did not attempt to plunge in, merely dipping his head and making some remark about the extra coldness of the water.

"River's falling at last," he said, "and I'm glad of it."

"The humming has stopped too," I said.

He looked up at me quietly with his normal expression. Evidently he remembered everything except his own attempt at suicide.

"Everything has stopped," he said, "because—"

He hesitated. But I knew some reference to that remark he had made just before he fainted was in his mind, and I was determined to know it.

"Because 'They've found another victim'?" I said, forcing a little laugh.

"Exactly," he answered, "exactly! I feel as positive of it as though—as though—I feel quite safe again, I mean," he finished.

He began to look curiously about him. The sunlight lay in hot patches on the sand. There was no wind. The willows were motionless. He slowly rose to feet.

"Come," he said; "I think if we look, we shall find it."

He started off on a run, and I followed him. He kept to the banks, poking with a stick among the sandy bays and caves and little back-waters, myself always close on his heels.

"Ah!" he exclaimed presently, "ah!"

The tone of his voice somehow brought back to me a vivid sense of the horror of the last twenty-four hours, and I hurried up to join him. He was pointing with his stick at a large black object that lay half in the water and half on the sand. It appeared to be caught by some twisted willow roots so that the river could not sweep it away. A few hours before the spot must have been under water.

"See," he said quietly, "the victim that made our escape possible!"

And when I peered across his shoulder I saw that his stick rested on the body of a man. He turned it over. It was the corpse of a peasant, and the face was hidden in the sand. Clearly the man had been drowned but a few hours before, and his body must have been swept down upon our island somewhere about the hour of the dawn—*at the very time the fit had passed*.

"We must give it a decent burial, you know."

"I suppose so," I replied. I shuddered a little in spite of myself, for there was something about the appearance of that poor drowned man that turned me cold.

The Swede glanced up sharply at me, an undecipherable expression on his face, and began clambering down the bank. I followed him more leisurely. The current, I noticed, had torn away much of the clothing from the body, so that the neck and part of the chest lay bare.

Half-way down the bank my companion suddenly stopped and held up his hand in warning; but either my foot slipped, or I had gained too much momentum to bring myself quickly to a halt, for I bumped into him and sent him forward with a sort of leap to save himself. We tumbled together on to the hard sand so that our feet splashed into the water. And, before anything could be done, we had collided a little heavily against the corpse.

The Swede uttered a sharp cry. And I sprang back as if I had been shot.

At the moment we touched the body there rose from its surface the loud sound of humming—the sound of several hummings—which passed with a vast commotion as of winged things in the air about us and disappeared upwards into the sky, growing fainter and fainter till they finally ceased in the distance. It was exactly as though we had disturbed some living yet invisible creatures at work.

My companion clutched me, and I think I clutched him, but before either of us had time properly to recover from the unexpected shock, we saw that a movement of the current was turning the corpse round so that it became released from the grip of the willow roots. A moment later it had turned completely over, the dead face uppermost, staring at the sky. It lay on the edge of the main stream. In another moment it would be swept away.

The Swede started to save it, shouting again something I did not catch about a "proper burial"—and then abruptly dropped upon his knees on the sand and covered his eyes with his hands. I was beside him in an instant.

I saw what he had seen.

For just as the body swung round to the current the face and the exposed chest turned full towards us, and showed plainly how the skin and flesh were indented with small hollows, beautifully formed, and exactly similar in shape and kind to the sand-funnels that we had found all over the island.

"Their mark!" I heard my companion mutter under his breath. "Their awful mark!"

And when I turned my eyes again from his ghastly face to the river, the current had done its work, and the body had been swept away into midstream and was already beyond our reach and almost out of sight, turning over and over on the waves like an otter.

Ancient Sorceries

—*1908*—

I

THERE ARE, IT WOULD APPEAR, CERTAIN WHOLLY UNREMARK-able persons, with none of the characteristics that invite adventure, who yet once or twice in the course of their smooth lives undergo an experience so strange that the world catches its breath—and looks the other way! And it was cases of this kind, perhaps, more than any other, that fell into the widespread net of John Silence, the psychic doctor, and, appealing to his deep human-ity, to his patience, and to his great qualities of spiritual sympathy, led often to the revelation of problems of the strangest complexity, and of the profoundest possible human interest.

Matters that seemed almost too curious and fantastic for belief he loved to trace to their hidden sources. To unravel a tangle in the very soul of things—and to release a suffering human soul in the process—was with him a veritable passion. And the knots he untied were, indeed, often passing strange. The world, of course, asks for some plausible basis to which it can attach credence—something it can, at least, pretend to explain. The adventurous type it can under-stand: such people carry about with them an adequate explanation of their exciting lives, and their characters obviously drive them into the circumstances which produce the adventures. It expects nothing else from them, and is satisfied. But dull, ordinary folk have no right to out-of-the-way experiences, and the world, having been led to expect otherwise, is disappointed with them, not to say shocked. Its complacent judgment has been rudely disturbed.

"Such a thing happen to *that* man!" it cries—"a commonplace person like that! It is too absurd! There must be something wrong!"

Yet there could be no question that something did actually happen to little Arthur Vezin, something of the curious nature he described to Dr. Silence. Outwardly, or inwardly, it happened beyond a doubt, and in spite of the jeers of his few friends who heard the tale, and observed wisely that "such a thing might perhaps have come to Iszard, that crack-brained Iszard, or to that odd fish Minski, but it could never have happened to commonplace little Vezin, who was fore-ordained to live and die according to scale."

But, whatever his method of death was, Vezin certainly did not "live according to scale" so far as this particular event in his otherwise uneventful life was concerned; and to hear him recount it, and watch his pale delicate features change, and hear his voice grow softer and more hushed as he proceeded, was to know the conviction that his halting words perhaps failed sometimes to convey. He lived the thing over again each time he told it. His whole personality became muffled in the recital. It subdued him more than ever, so that the tale became a lengthy apology for an experience that he deprecated. He appeared to excuse himself and ask your pardon for having dared to take part in so fantastic an episode. For little Vezin was a timid, gentle, sensitive soul, rarely able to assert himself, tender to man and beast, and almost constitutionally unable to say No, or to claim many things that should rightly have been his. His whole scheme of life seemed utterly remote from anything more exciting than missing a train or losing an umbrella on an omnibus. And when this curious event came upon him he was already more years beyond forty than his friends suspected or he cared to admit.

John Silence, who heard him speak of his experience more than once, said that he sometimes left out certain details and put in others; yet they were all obviously true. The whole scene was unforgettably cinematographed on to his mind. None of the details were imagined or invented. And when he told the story with them all complete, the effect was undeniable. His appealing brown eyes shone, and much of the charming personality, usually so carefully repressed, came forward and revealed itself. His modesty was always there, of course, but in the telling he forgot the present and allowed himself to appear almost vividly as he lived again in the past of his adventure.

He was on the way home when it happened, crossing northern France from some mountain trip or other where he buried himself solitary-wise every summer. He had nothing but an unregistered bag in the rack, and the train was jammed to suffocation, most of the passengers being unredeemed holiday English. He disliked them, not because they were his fellow-countrymen, but because they were noisy and obtrusive, obliterating with their big limbs and tweed clothing all the quieter tints of the day that brought him satisfaction and enabled him to melt into insignificance and forget that he was anybody. These English clashed about him like a brass band, making him feel vaguely that he ought to be more self-assertive and obstreperous, and that he did not claim insistently enough all kinds of things that he didn't want and that were really valueless, such as corner seats, windows up or down, and so forth.

So that he felt uncomfortable in the train, and wished the journey were over and he was back again living with his unmarried sister in Surbiton.

And when the train stopped for ten panting minutes at the little station in northern France, and he got out to stretch his legs on the platform, and saw to his dismay a further batch of the British Isles debouching from another train, it suddenly seemed impossible to him to continue the journey. Even *his* flabby soul revolted, and the idea of staying a night in the little town and going on next day by a slower, emptier train, flashed into his mind. The guard was already shouting "en voiture" and the corridor of his compartment was already packed when the thought came to him. And, for once, he acted with decision and rushed to snatch his bag.

Finding the corridor and steps impassable, he tapped at the window (for he had a corner seat) and begged the Frenchman who sat opposite to hand his luggage out to him, explaining in his wretched French that he intended to break the journey there. And this elderly Frenchman, he declared, gave him a look, half of warning, half of reproach, that to his dying day he could never forget; handed the bag through the window of the moving train; and at the same time poured into his ears a long sentence, spoken rapidly and low, of which he was able to comprehend only the last few words: "*à cause du sommeil et à cause des chats.*"

In reply to Dr. Silence, whose singular psychic acuteness at once seized upon this Frenchman as a vital point in the adventure, Vezin admitted that the man had impressed him favourably from the beginning, though without being able to explain why. They had sat facing one another during the four hours of the journey, and though no conversation had passed between them—Vezin was timid about his stuttering French—he confessed that his eyes were being continually drawn to his face, almost, he felt, to rudeness, and that each, by a dozen nameless little politenesses and attentions, had evinced the desire to be kind. The men liked each other and their personalities did not clash, or would not have clashed had they chanced to come to terms of acquaintance. The Frenchman, indeed, seemed to have exercised a silent protective influence over the insignificant little Englishman, and without words or gestures betrayed that he wished him well and would gladly have been of service to him.

"And this sentence that he hurled at you after the bag?" asked John Silence, smiling that peculiarly sympathetic smile that always melted the prejudices of his patient, "were you unable to follow it exactly?"

"It was so quick and low and vehement," explained Vezin, in his small voice, "that I missed practically the whole of it. I only caught the few words at the very end, because he spoke them so clearly, and his face was bent down out of the carriage window so near to mine."

"'À cause du sommeil et à cause des chats'?" repeated Dr. Silence, as though half speaking to himself.

"That's it exactly," said Vezin; "which, I take it, means something like 'because of sleep and because of the cats,' doesn't it?"

"Certainly, that's how I should translate it," the doctor observed shortly, evidently not wishing to interrupt more than necessary.

"And the rest of the sentence—all the first part I couldn't understand, I mean—was a warning not to do something—not to stop in the town, or at some particular place in the town, perhaps. That was the impression it made on me."

Then, of course, the train rushed off, and left Vezin standing on the platform alone and rather forlorn.

The little town climbed in straggling fashion up a sharp hill rising out of the plain at the back of the station, and was crowned by the twin towers of the ruined cathedral peeping over the summit. From the station itself it looked uninteresting and modern, but the fact was that the mediæval position lay out of sight just beyond the crest. And once he reached the top and entered the old streets, he stepped clean out of modern life into a bygone century. The noise and bustle of the crowded train seemed days away. The spirit of this silent hill-town, remote from tourists and motor-cars, dreaming its own quiet life under the autumn sun, rose up and cast its spell upon him. Long before he recognised this spell he acted under it. He walked softly, almost on tiptoe, down the winding narrow streets where the gables all but met over his head, and he entered the doorway of the solitary inn with a deprecating and modest demeanour that was in itself an apology for intruding upon the place and disturbing its dream.

At first, however, Vezin said, he noticed very little of all this. The attempt at analysis came much later. What struck him then was only the delightful contrast of the silence and peace after the dust and noisy rattle of the train. He felt soothed and stroked like a cat.

"Like a cat, you said?" interrupted John Silence, quickly catching him up.

"Yes. At the very start I felt that." He laughed apologetically. "I felt as though the warmth and the stillness and the comfort made me purr. It seemed to be the general mood of the whole place—then."

The inn, a rambling ancient house, the atmosphere of the old coaching days still about it, apparently did not welcome him too warmly. He felt he was only tolerated, he said. But it was cheap and comfortable, and the delicious cup of afternoon tea he ordered at once made him feel really very pleased with himself for leaving the train in this bold, original way. For to him it had seemed bold and original. He felt something of a dog. His room, too, soothed him with its dark panelling and low irregular ceiling, and the long sloping passage that led to it seemed the natural pathway to a real Chamber of Sleep—a little dim cubby hole out of the world where noise could not enter. It looked upon the courtyard at the back. It was all very charming, and made him think of himself as dressed in very soft velvet somehow, and the floors seemed padded, the walls provided with cushions. The sounds of the streets could not penetrate there. It was an atmosphere of absolute rest that surrounded him.

On engaging the two-franc room he had interviewed the only person who seemed to be about that sleepy afternoon, an elderly waiter with Dundreary whiskers and a drowsy courtesy, who had ambled lazily towards him across the stone yard; but on coming downstairs again for a little promenade in the town before dinner he encountered the proprietress herself. She was a large woman whose hands, feet, and features seemed to swim towards him out of a sea of person. They emerged, so to speak. But she had great dark, vivacious eyes that counteracted the bulk of her body, and betrayed the fact that in reality she was both vigorous and alert. When he first caught sight of her she was knitting in a low chair against the sunlight of the wall, and something at once made him see her as a great tabby cat, dozing, yet awake, heavily sleepy, and yet at the same time prepared for instantaneous action. A great mouser on the watch occurred to him.

She took him in with a single comprehensive glance that was polite without being cordial. Her neck, he noticed, was extraordinarily supple in spite of its proportions, for it turned so easily to follow him, and the head it carried bowed so very flexibly.

"But when she looked at me, you know," said Vezin, with that little apologetic smile in his brown eyes, and that faintly deprecating gesture of the shoulders that was characteristic of him, "the odd notion came to me that really she had intended to make quite a different movement, and that with a single bound she could have leaped at me across the width of that stone yard and pounced upon me like some huge cat upon a mouse."

He laughed a little soft laugh, and Dr. Silence made a note in his book without interrupting, while Vezin proceeded in a tone as though he feared he had already told too much and more than we could believe.

"Very soft, yet very active she was, for all her size and mass, and I felt she knew what I was doing even after I had passed and was behind her back. She spoke to me, and her voice was smooth and running. She asked if I had my luggage, and was comfortable in my room, and then added that dinner was at seven o'clock, and that they were very early people in this little country town. Clearly, she intended to convey that late hours were not encouraged."

Evidently, she contrived by voice and manner to give him the impression that here he would be "managed," that everything would be arranged and planned for him, and that he had nothing to do but fall into the groove and obey. No decided action or sharp personal effort would be looked for from him. It was the very reverse of the train. He walked quietly out into the street feeling soothed and peaceful. He realised that he was in a *milieu* that suited him and stroked him the right way. It was so much easier to be obedient. He began to purr again, and to feel that all the town purred with him.

About the streets of that little town he meandered gently, falling deeper and deeper into the spirit of repose that characterised it. With no special aim he wandered up and down, and to and fro. The September sunshine fell slantingly over the roofs. Down winding alleyways, fringed with tumbling gables and open casements, he caught fairylike glimpses of the great plain below, and of the meadows and yellow copses lying like a dream-map in the haze. The spell of the past held very potently here, he felt.

The streets were full of picturesquely garbed men and women, all busy enough, going their respective ways; but no one took any notice of him or turned to stare at his obviously English appearance. He was even able to forget that with his tourist appearance he was a false note in a charming picture, and he melted more and more into the scene, feeling delightfully insignificant and unimportant and unself-conscious. It was like becoming part of a softly-coloured dream which he did not even realise to be a dream.

On the eastern side the hill fell away more sharply, and the plain below ran off rather suddenly into a sea of gathering shadows in which the little patches of woodland looked like islands and the stubble fields like deep water. Here he strolled along the old ramparts of ancient fortifications that once had been formidable, but now were only vision-like with their charming mingling of broken grey walls and wayward vine and ivy. From the broad coping on which he sat for a moment, level with the rounded tops of clipped plane trees, he saw the esplanade far below lying in shadow. Here and there a yellow sunbeam crept in and lay upon the fallen yellow leaves, and from the height he looked down and saw that the townsfolk were walking to and fro in the cool of the evening. He could just hear the sound of their slow footfalls, and the murmur of their voices floated up to him through the gaps between the trees. The figures looked like shadows as he caught glimpses of their quiet movements far below.

He sat there for some time pondering, bathed in the waves of murmurs and half-lost echoes that rose to his ears, muffled by the leaves of the plane trees. The whole town, and the little hill out of which it grew as naturally as an ancient wood, seemed to him like a being lying there half asleep on the plain and crooning to itself as it dozed.

And, presently, as he sat lazily melting into its dream, a sound of horns and strings and wood instruments rose to his ears, and the town band began to play at the far end of the crowded terrace

below to the accompaniment of a very soft, deep-throated drum.
Vezin was very sensitive to music, knew about it intelligently, and
had even ventured, unknown to his friends, upon the composi-
tion of quiet melodies with low-running chords which he played
to himself with the soft pedal when no one was about. And this
music floating up through the trees from an invisible and doubtless
very picturesque band of the townspeople wholly charmed him.
He recognised nothing that they played, and it sounded as though
they were simply improvising without a conductor. No definitely
marked time ran through the pieces, which ended and began oddly
after the fashion of wind through an Æolian harp. It was part of
the place and scene, just as the dying sunlight and faintly-breathing
wind were part of the scene and hour, and the mellow notes of
old-fashioned plaintive horns, pierced here and there by the sharper
strings, all half smothered by the continuous booming of the deep
drum, touched his soul with a curiously potent spell that was almost
too engrossing to be quite pleasant.

There was a certain queer sense of bewitchment in it all. The
music seemed to him oddly unartificial. It made him think of
trees swept by the wind, of night breezes singing among wires
and chimney-stacks, or in the rigging of invisible ships; or—and
the simile leaped up in his thoughts with a sudden sharpness of
suggestion—a chorus of animals, of wild creatures, somewhere in
desolate places of the world, crying and singing as animals will, to
the moon. He could fancy he heard the wailing, half-human cries
of cats upon the tiles at night, rising and falling with weird intervals
of sound, and this music, muffled by distance and the trees, made
him think of a queer company of these creatures on some roof far
away in the sky, uttering their solemn music to one another and
the moon in chorus.

It was, he felt at the time, a singular image to occur to him, yet it expressed his sensation pictorially better than anything else. The instruments played such impossibly odd intervals, and the crescendos and diminuendos were so very suggestive of cat-land on the tiles at night, rising swiftly, dropping without warning to deep notes again, and all in such strange confusion of discords and accords. But, at the same time a plaintive sweetness resulted on the whole, and the discords of these half-broken instruments were so singular that they did not distress his musical soul like fiddles out of tune.

He listened a long time, wholly surrendering himself as his character was, and then strolled homewards in the dusk as the air grew chilly.

"There was nothing to alarm?" put in Dr. Silence briefly.

"Absolutely nothing," said Vezin; "but you know it was all so fantastical and charming that my imagination was profoundly impressed. Perhaps, too," he continued, gently explanatory, "it was this stirring of my imagination that caused other impressions; for, as I walked back, the spell of the place began to steal over me in a dozen ways, though all intelligible ways. But there were other things I could not account for in the least, even then."

"Incidents, you mean?"

"Hardly incidents, I think. A lot of vivid sensations crowded themselves upon my mind and I could trace them to no causes. It was just after sunset and the tumbled old buildings traced magical outlines against an opalescent sky of gold and red. The dusk was running down the twisted streets. All round the hill the plain pressed in like a dim sea, its level rising with the darkness. The spell of this kind of scene, you know, can be very moving, and it was so that night. Yet I felt that what came to me had nothing directly to do with the mystery and wonder of the scene."

"Not merely the subtle transformations of the spirit that come with beauty," put in the doctor, noticing his hesitation.

"Exactly," Vezin went on, duly encouraged and no longer so fearful of our smiles at his expense. "The impressions came from somewhere else. For instance, down the busy main street where men and women were bustling home from work, shopping at stalls and barrows, idly gossiping in groups, and all the rest of it, I saw that I aroused no interest and that no one turned to stare at me as a foreigner and stranger. I was utterly ignored, and my presence among them excited no special interest or attention.

"And then, quite suddenly, it dawned upon me with conviction that all the time this indifference and inattention were merely feigned. Everybody as a matter of fact was watching me closely. Every movement I made was known and observed. Ignoring me was all a pretence—an elaborate pretence."

He paused a moment and looked at us to see if we were smiling, and then continued, reassured—

"It is useless to ask me how I noticed this, because I simply cannot explain it. But the discovery gave me something of a shock. Before I got back to the inn, however, another curious thing rose up strongly in my mind and forced my recognition of it as true. And this, too, I may as well say at once, was equally inexplicable to me. I mean I can only give you the fact, as fact it was to me."

The little man left his chair and stood on the mat before the fire. His diffidence lessened from now onwards, as he lost himself again in the magic of the old adventure. His eyes shone a little already as he talked.

"Well," he went on, his soft voice rising somewhat with his excitement, "I was in a shop when it came to me first—though the idea must have been at work for a long time subconsciously to appear in so complete a form all at once. I was buying socks, I think," he laughed, "and struggling with my dreadful French, when it struck me that the woman in the shop did not care two pins whether I bought anything or not. She was indifferent whether she made a sale or did not make a sale. She was only pretending to sell.

"This sounds a very small and fanciful incident to build upon what follows. But really it was not small. I mean it was the spark that lit the line of powder and ran along to the big blaze in my mind.

"For the whole town, I suddenly realised, was something other than I so far saw it. The real activities and interests of the people were elsewhere and otherwise than appeared. Their true lives lay somewhere out of sight behind the scenes. Their busy-ness was but the outward semblance that masked their actual purposes. They bought and sold, and ate and drank, and walked about the streets, yet all the while the main stream of their existence lay somewhere beyond my ken, underground, in secret places. In the shops and at the stalls they did not care whether I purchased their articles or not; at the inn, they were indifferent to my staying or going; their life lay remote from my own, springing from hidden, mysterious sources, coursing out of sight, unknown. It was all a great elaborate pretence, assumed possibly for my benefit, or possibly for purposes of their own. But the main current of their energies ran elsewhere. I almost felt as an unwelcome foreign substance might be expected to feel when it has found its way into the human system and the whole body organises itself to eject it or to absorb it. The town was doing this very thing to me.

"This bizarre notion presented itself forcibly to my mind as I walked home to the inn, and I began busily to wonder wherein the true life of this town could lie and what were the actual interests and activities of its hidden life.

"And, now that my eyes were partly opened, I noticed other things too that puzzled me, first of which, I think, was the extraordinary silence of the whole place. Positively, the town was muffled. Although the streets were paved with cobbles the people moved about silently, softly, with padded feet, like cats. Nothing made noise. All was hushed, subdued, muted. The very voices were quiet, low-pitched like purring. Nothing clamorous, vehement or emphatic seemed able to live in the drowsy atmosphere of soft dreaming that soothed this little hill-town into its sleep. It was like the woman at the inn—an outward repose screening intense inner activity and purpose.

"Yet there was no sign of lethargy or sluggishness anywhere about it. The people were active and alert. Only a magical and uncanny softness lay over them all like a spell."

Vezin passed his hand across his eyes for a moment as though the memory had become very vivid. His voice had run off into a whisper so that we heard the last part with difficulty. He was telling a true thing obviously, yet something that he both liked and hated telling.

"I went back to the inn," he continued presently in a louder voice, "and dined. I felt a new strange world about me. My old world of reality receded. Here, whether I liked it or no, was something new and incomprehensible. I regretted having left the train so impulsively. An adventure was upon me, and I loathed adventures as foreign to my nature. Moreover, this was the beginning apparently of an adventure somewhere deep within me, in a region I could not check or measure, and a feeling of alarm mingled itself with my wonder—alarm for the stability of what I had for forty years recognised as my 'personality.'

"I went upstairs to bed, my mind teeming with thoughts that were unusual to me, and of rather a haunting description. By way of relief I kept thinking of that nice, prosaic noisy train and all those wholesome, blustering passengers. I almost wished I were with them again. But my dreams took me elsewhere. I dreamed of cats, and soft-moving creatures, and the silence of life in a dim muffled world beyond the senses."

II

Vezin stayed on from day to day, indefinitely, much longer than he had intended. He felt in a kind of dazed, somnolent condition. He did nothing in particular, but the place fascinated him and he could not decide to leave. Decisions were always very difficult for him, and he sometimes wondered how he had ever brought himself to the point of leaving the train. It seemed as though some one else must have arranged it for him, and once or twice his thoughts ran to the swarthy Frenchman who had sat opposite. If only he could have understood that long sentence ending so strangely with "*à cause du sommeil et à cause des chats.*" He wondered what it all meant.

Meanwhile the hushed softness of the town held him prisoner, and he sought in his muddling, gentle way to find out where the mystery lay, and what it was all about. But his limited French and his constitutional hatred of active investigation made it hard for him to buttonhole anybody and ask questions. He was content to observe, and watch, and remain negative.

The weather held on calm and hazy, and this just suited him. He wandered about the town till he knew every street and alley. The people suffered him to come and go without let or hindrance, though it became clearer to him every day that he was never free himself from observation. The town watched him as a cat watches a mouse. And he got no nearer to finding out what they were all so busy with or where the main stream of their activities lay. This remained hidden. The people were as soft and mysterious as cats.

But that he was continually under observation became more evident from day to day.

For instance, when he strolled to the end of the town and entered a little green public garden beneath the ramparts and seated himself upon one of the empty benches in the sun, he was quite alone—at first. Not another seat was occupied; the little park was empty, the paths deserted. Yet, within ten minutes of his coming, there must have been fully twenty persons scattered about him, some strolling aimlessly along the gravel walks, staring at the flowers, and others seated on the wooden benches enjoying the sun like himself. None of them appeared to take any notice of him; yet he understood quite well they had all come there to watch. They kept him under close observation. In the street they had seemed busy enough, hurrying upon various errands; yet these were suddenly all forgotten and they had nothing to do but loll and laze in the sun, their duties unremembered. Five minutes after he left, the garden was again deserted, the seats vacant. But in the crowded street it was the same thing again; he was never alone. He was ever in their thoughts.

By degrees, too, he began to see how it was he was so cleverly watched, yet without the appearance of it. The people did nothing *directly*. They behaved *obliquely*. He laughed in his mind as the thought thus clothed itself in words, but the phrase exactly described it. They looked at him from angles which naturally should have led their sight in another direction altogether. Their movements were oblique, too, so far as these concerned himself. The straight, direct thing was not their way evidently. They did nothing obviously. If he entered a shop to buy, the woman walked instantly away and busied herself with something at the farther end of the counter, though answering at once when he spoke, showing that she knew he was there and that this was only her way of attending to him. It was the fashion of the cat she followed. Even in the dining-room of the inn, the be-whiskered and courteous waiter, lithe and silent in all his movements, never seemed able to come straight to his table for an order or a dish. He came by zigzags, indirectly, vaguely, so that he appeared to be going to another table altogether, and only turned suddenly at the last moment, and was there beside him.

Vezin smiled curiously to himself as he described how he began to realise these things. Other tourists there were none in the hostel, but he recalled the figures of one or two old men, inhabitants, who took their *déjeuner* and dinner there, and remembered how fantastically they entered the room in similar fashion. First, they paused in the doorway, peering about the room, and then, after a temporary inspection, they came in, as it were, sideways, keeping close to the walls so that he wondered which table they were making for, and at the last minute making almost a little quick run to their particular seats. And again he thought of the ways and methods of cats.

Other small incidents, too, impressed him as all part of this queer, soft town with its muffled, indirect life, for the way some of the people appeared and disappeared with extraordinary swiftness puzzled him exceedingly. It may have been all perfectly natural, he knew, yet he could not make it out how the alleys swallowed them up and shot them forth in a second of time when there were no visible doorways or openings near enough to explain the phenomenon. Once he followed two elderly women who, he felt, had been particularly examining him from across the street—quite near the inn this was—and saw them turn the corner a few feet only in front

of him. Yet when he sharply followed on their heels he saw nothing but an utterly deserted alley stretching in front of him with no
sign of a living thing. And the only opening through which they
could have escaped was a porch some fifty yards away, which not
the swiftest human runner could have reached in time.

And in just such sudden fashion people appeared when he never
expected them. Once when he heard a great noise of fighting going
on behind a low wall, and hurried up to see what was going on, what
should he see but a group of girls and women engaged in vociferous
conversation which instantly hushed itself to the normal whispering
note of the town when his head appeared over the wall. And even
then none of them turned to look at him directly, but slunk off with
the most unaccountable rapidity into doors and sheds across the
yard. And their voices, he thought, had sounded so like, so strangely
like, the angry snarling of fighting animals, almost of cats.

The whole spirit of the town, however, continued to evade
him as something elusive, protean, screened from the outer world,
and at the same time intensely, genuinely, vital; and, since he now
formed part of its life, this concealment puzzled and irritated him;
more—it began rather to frighten him.

Out of the mists that slowly gathered about his ordinary surface
thoughts, there rose again the idea that the inhabitants were waiting for him to declare himself, to take an attitude, to do this, or to
do that; and that when he had done so they in their turn would at
length make some direct response, accepting or rejecting him. Yet
the vital matter concerning which his decision was awaited came
no nearer to him.

Once or twice he purposely followed little processions or groups
of the citizens in order to find out, if possible, on what purpose they
were bent; but they always discovered him in time and dwindled

away, each individual going his or her own way. It was always the same: he never could learn what their main interest was. The cathedral was ever empty, the old church of St. Martin, at the other end of the town, deserted. They shopped because they had to, and not because they wished to. The booths stood neglected, the stalls unvisited, the little cafés desolate. Yet the streets were always full, the townsfolk ever on the bustle.

"Can it be," he thought to himself, yet with a deprecating laugh that he should have dared to think anything so odd, "can it be that these people are people of the twilight, that they live only at night their real life, and come out honestly only with the dusk? That during the day they make a sham though brave pretence, and after the sun is down their true life begins? Have they the souls of night-things, and is the whole blessed town in the hands of the cats?"

The fancy somehow electrified him with little shocks of shrinking and dismay. Yet, though he affected to laugh, he knew that he was beginning to feel more than uneasy, and that strange forces were tugging with a thousand invisible cords at the very centre of his being. Something utterly remote from his ordinary life, something that had not waked for years, began faintly to stir in his soul, sending feelers abroad into his brain and heart, shaping queer thoughts and penetrating even into certain of his minor actions. Something exceedingly vital to himself, to his soul, hung in the balance.

And, always when he returned to the inn about the hour of sunset, he saw the figures of the townsfolk stealing through the dusk from their shop doors, moving sentry-wise to and fro at the corners of the streets, yet always vanishing silently like shadows at his near approach. And as the inn invariably closed its doors at ten o'clock he had never yet found the opportunity he rather half-heartedly sought to see for himself what account the town could give of itself at night.

"—*à cause du sommeil et à cause des chats*"—the words now rang in his ears more and more often, though still as yet without any definite meaning.

Moreover, something made him sleep like the dead.

III

It was, I think, on the fifth day—though in this detail his story sometimes varied—that he made a definite discovery which increased his alarm and brought him up to a rather sharp climax. Before that he had already noticed that a change was going forward and certain subtle transformations being brought about in his character which modified several of his minor habits. And he had affected to ignore them. Here, however, was something he could no longer ignore; and it startled him.

At the best of times he was never very positive, always negative rather, compliant and acquiescent; yet, when necessity arose he was capable of reasonably vigorous action and could take a strongish decision. The discovery he now made that brought him up with such a sharp turn was that this power had positively dwindled to nothing. He found it impossible to make up his mind. For, on this fifth day, he realised that he had stayed long enough in the town and that for reasons he could only vaguely define to himself it was wiser *and safer* that he should leave.

And he found that he could not leave!

This is difficult to describe in words, and it was more by gesture and the expression of his face that he conveyed to Dr. Silence the state of impotence he had reached. All this spying and watching, he said, had as it were spun a net about his feet so that he was trapped and powerless to escape; he felt like a fly that had blundered into the intricacies of a great web; he was caught, imprisoned, and could not get away. It was a distressing sensation. A numbness had crept over his will till it had become almost incapable of decision. The mere thought of vigorous action—action towards escape—began to terrify him. All the currents of his life had turned inwards upon himself, striving to bring to the surface something that lay buried almost beyond reach, determined to force his recognition of something he had long forgotten—forgotten years upon years, centuries almost ago. It seemed as though a window deep within his being would presently open and reveal an entirely new world, yet somehow a world that was not unfamiliar. Beyond that, again, he fancied a great curtain hung; and when that too rolled up he would see still farther into this region and at last understand something of the secret life of these extraordinary people.

"Is this why they wait and watch?" he asked himself with rather a shaking heart, "for the time when I shall join them—or refuse to join them? Does the decision rest with me after all, and not with them?"

And it was at this point that the sinister character of the adventure first really declared itself, and he became genuinely alarmed. The stability of his rather fluid little personality was at stake, he felt, and something in his heart turned coward.

Why otherwise should he have suddenly taken to walking stealthily, silently, making as little sound as possible, for ever looking behind him? Why else should he have moved almost on tiptoe about the passages of the practically deserted inn, and when he was abroad have found himself deliberately taking advantage of what cover presented itself? And why, if he was not afraid, should the

wisdom of staying indoors after sundown have suddenly occurred
to him as eminently desirable? Why, indeed?

And, when John Silence gently pressed him for an explanation
of these things, he admitted apologetically that he had none to give.

"It was simply that I feared something might happen to me
unless I kept a sharp look-out. I felt afraid. It was instinctive," was
all he could say. "I got the impression that the whole town was
after me—wanted me for something; and that if it got me I should
lose myself, or at least the Self I knew, in some unfamiliar state of
consciousness. But I am not a psychologist, you know," he added
meekly, "and I cannot define it better than that."

It was while lounging in the courtyard half an hour before the
evening meal that Vezin made this discovery, and he at once went
upstairs to his quiet room at the end of the winding passage to
think it over alone. In the yard it was empty enough, true, but there
was always the possibility that the big woman whom he dreaded
would come out of some door, with her pretence of knitting, to
sit and watch him. This had happened several times, and he could
not endure the sight of her. He still remembered his original fancy,
bizarre though it was, that she would spring upon him the moment
his back was turned and land with one single crushing leap upon
his neck. Of course it was nonsense, but then it haunted him, and
once an idea begins to do that it ceases to be nonsense. It has clothed
itself in reality.

He went upstairs accordingly. It was dusk, and the oil lamps
had not yet been lit in the passages. He stumbled over the uneven
surface of the ancient flooring, passing the dim outlines of doors
along the corridors—doors that he had never once seen opened—
rooms that seemed never occupied. He moved, as his habit now
was, stealthily and on tiptoe.

Half-way down the last passage to his own chamber there was a sharp turn, and it was just here, while groping round the walls with outstretched hands, that his fingers touched something that was not wall—something that moved. It was soft and warm in texture, indescribably fragrant, and about the height of his shoulder; and he immediately thought of a furry, sweet-smelling kitten. The next minute he knew it was something quite different.

Instead of investigating, however,—his nerves must have been too overwrought for that, he said,—he shrank back as closely as possible against the wall on the other side. The thing, whatever it was, slipped past him with a sound of rustling, and retreating with light footsteps down the passage behind him, was gone. A breath of warm, scented air was wafted to his nostrils.

Vezin caught his breath for an instant and paused, stock-still, half leaning against the wall—and then almost ran down the remaining distance and entered his room with a rush, locking the door hurriedly behind him. Yet it was not fear that made him run: it was excitement, pleasurable excitement. His nerves were tingling, and a delicious glow made itself felt all over his body. In a flash it came to him that this was just what he had felt twenty-five years ago as a boy when he was in love for the first time. Warm currents of life ran all over him and mounted to his brain in a whirl of soft delight. His mood was suddenly become tender, melting, loving.

The room was quite dark, and he collapsed upon the sofa by the window, wondering what had happened to him and what it all meant. But the only thing he understood clearly in that instant was that something in him had swiftly, magically changed: he no longer wished to leave, or to argue with himself about leaving. The encounter in the passage-way had changed all that. The strange perfume of it still hung about him, bemusing his heart and mind.

For he knew that it was a girl who had passed him, a girl's face that his fingers had brushed in the darkness, and he felt in some extraordinary way as though he had been actually kissed by her, kissed full upon the lips.

Trembling, he sat upon the sofa by the window and struggled to collect his thoughts. He was utterly unable to understand how the mere passing of a girl in the darkness of a narrow passage-way could communicate so electric a thrill to his whole being that he still shook with the sweetness of it. Yet, there it was! And he found it as useless to deny as to attempt analysis. Some ancient fire had entered his veins, and now ran coursing through his blood; and that he was forty-five instead of twenty did not matter one little jot. Out of all the inner turmoil and confusion emerged the one salient fact that the mere atmosphere, the merest casual touch, of this girl, unseen, unknown in the darkness, had been sufficient to stir dormant fires in the centre of his heart, and rouse his whole being from a state of feeble sluggishness to one of tearing and tumultuous excitement.

After a time, however, the number of Vezin's years began to assert their cumulative power; he grew calmer; and when a knock came at length upon his door and he heard the waiter's voice suggesting that dinner was nearly over, he pulled himself together and slowly made his way downstairs into the dining-room.

Every one looked up as he entered, for he was very late, but he took his customary seat in the far corner and began to eat. The trepidation was still in his nerves, but the fact that he had passed through the courtyard and hall without catching sight of a petticoat served to calm him a little. He ate so fast that he had almost caught up with the current stage of the table d'hôte, when a slight commotion in the room drew his attention.

His chair was so placed that the door and the greater portion of the long *salle à manger* were behind him, yet it was not necessary to turn round to know that the same person he had passed in the dark passage had now come into the room. He felt the presence long before he heard or saw any one. Then he became aware that the old men, the only other guests, were rising one by one in their places, and exchanging greetings with some one who passed among them from table to table. And when at length he turned with his heart beating furiously to ascertain for himself, he saw the form of a young girl, lithe and slim, moving down the centre of the room and making straight for his own table in the corner. She moved wonderfully, with sinuous grace, like a young panther, and her approach filled him with such delicious bewilderment that he was utterly unable to tell at first what her face was like, or discover what it was about the whole presentment of the creature that filled him anew with trepidation and delight.

"Ah, Ma'mselle est de retour!" he heard the old waiter murmur at his side, and he was just able to take in that she was the daughter of the proprietress, when she was upon him, and he heard her voice. She was addressing him. Something of red lips he saw and laughing white teeth, and stray wisps of fine dark hair about the temples; but all the rest was a dream in which his own emotion rose like a thick cloud before his eyes and prevented his seeing accurately, or knowing exactly what he did. He was aware that she greeted him with a charming little bow; that her beautiful large eyes looked searchingly into his own; that the perfume he had noticed in the dark passage again assailed his nostrils, and that she was bending a little towards him and leaning with one hand on the table at his side. She was quite close to him—that was the chief thing he knew—explaining that she had been asking after the comfort of her mother's guests, and was now introducing herself to the latest arrival—himself.

"M'sieur has already been here a few days," he heard the waiter say; and then her own voice, sweet as singing replied—

"Ah, but M'sieur is not going to leave us just yet, I hope. My mother is too old to look after the comfort of our guests properly, but now I am here I will remedy all that." She laughed deliciously. "M'sieur shall be well looked after."

Vezin, struggling with his emotion and desire to be polite, half rose to acknowledge the pretty speech, and to stammer some sort of reply, but as he did so his hand by chance touched her own that was resting upon the table, and a shock that was for all the world like a shock of electricity, passed from her skin into his body. His soul wavered and shook deep within him. He caught her eyes fixed upon his own with a look of most curious intentness, and the next moment he knew that he had sat down wordless again on his chair, that the girl was already half-way across the room, and that he was trying to eat his salad with a dessert-spoon and a knife.

Longing for her return, and yet dreading it, he gulped down the remainder of his dinner, and then went at once to his bedroom to be alone with his thoughts. This time the passages were lighted, and he suffered no exciting contretemps; yet the winding corridor was dim with shadows, and the last portion, from the bend of the walls onwards, seemed longer than he had ever known it. It ran downhill like the pathway on a mountain side, and as he tiptoed softly down it he felt that by rights it ought to have led him clean out of the house into the heart of a great forest. The world was singing with him. Strange fancies filled his brain, and once in the room, with the door securely locked, he did not light the candles, but sat by the open window thinking long, long thoughts that came unbidden in troops to his mind.

IV

This part of the story he told to Dr. Silence, without special coaxing, it is true, yet with much stammering embarrassment. He could not in the least understand, he said, how the girl had managed to affect him so profoundly, and even before he had set eyes upon her. For her mere proximity in the darkness had been sufficient to set him on fire. He knew nothing of enchantments, and for years had been a stranger to anything approaching tender relations with any member of the opposite sex, for he was encased in shyness, and realised his overwhelming defects only too well. Yet this bewitching young creature came to him deliberately. Her manner was unmistakable, and she sought him out on every possible occasion. Chaste and sweet she was undoubtedly, yet frankly inviting; and she won him utterly with the first glance of her shining eyes, even if she had not already done so in the dark merely by the magic of her invisible presence.

"You felt she was altogether wholesome and good?" queried the doctor. "You had no reaction of any sort—for instance, of alarm?"

Vezin looked up sharply with one of his inimitable little apologetic smiles. It was some time before he replied. The mere memory of the adventure had suffused his shy face with blushes, and his brown eyes sought the floor again before he answered.

"I don't think I can quite say that," he explained presently. "I acknowledged certain qualms, sitting up in my room afterwards. A conviction grew upon me that there was something about her—how shall I express it?—well, something unholy. It is not impurity in any sense, physical or mental, that I mean, but something quite indefinable that gave me a vague sensation of the creeps. She drew me, and at the same time repelled me, more than—than—"

He hesitated, blushing furiously, and unable to finish the sentence.

"Nothing like it has ever come to me before or since," he concluded, with lame confusion. "I suppose it was, as you suggested just now, something of an enchantment. At any rate, it was strong enough to make me feel that I would stay in that awful little haunted town for years if only I could see her every day, hear her voice, watch her wonderful movements, and sometimes, perhaps, touch her hand."

"Can you explain to me what you felt was the source of her power?" John Silence asked, looking purposely anywhere but at the narrator.

"I am surprised that *you* should ask me such a question," answered Vezin, with the nearest approach to dignity he could manage. "I think no man can describe to another convincingly wherein lies the magic of the woman who ensnares him. I certainly cannot. I can only say this slip of a girl bewitched me, and the mere knowledge that she was living and sleeping in the same house filled me with an extraordinary sense of delight.

"But there's one thing I can tell you," he went on earnestly, his eyes aglow, "namely, that she seemed to sum up and synthesise in herself all the strange hidden forces that operated so mysteriously in the town and its inhabitants. She had the silken movements of the panther, going smoothly, silently to and fro, and the same indirect, oblique methods as the townsfolk, screening, like them, secret purposes of her own—purposes that I was sure had *me* for their objective. She kept me, to my terror and delight, ceaselessly under observation, yet so carelessly, so consummately, that another man less sensitive, if I may say so"—he made a deprecating gesture—"or less prepared by what had gone before, would never have noticed it at all. She was always still, always reposeful, yet she seemed to be everywhere at once, so that I never could escape from her. I was continually meeting the stare and laughter of her great eyes, in the corners of the rooms, in the passages, calmly looking at me through the windows, or in the busiest parts of the public streets."

Their intimacy, it seems, grew very rapidly after this first encounter which had so violently disturbed the little man's equilibrium. He was naturally very prim, and prim folk live mostly in so small a world that anything violently unusual may shake them clean out of it, and they therefore instinctively distrust originality. But Vezin began to forget his primness after awhile. The girl was always modestly behaved, and as her mother's representative she naturally had to do with the guests in the hotel. It was not out of the way that a spirit of camaraderie should spring up. Besides, she was young, she was charmingly pretty, she was French, and—she obviously liked him.

At the same time, there was something indescribable—a certain indefinable atmosphere of other places, other times—that made him try hard to remain on his guard, and sometimes made him catch his breath with a sudden start. It was all rather like a delirious dream, half delight, half dread, he confided in a whisper to Dr. Silence; and more than once he hardly knew quite what he was doing or saying, as though he were driven forward by impulses he scarcely recognised as his own.

And though the thought of leaving presented itself again and again to his mind, it was each time with less insistence, so that he stayed on from day to day, becoming more and more a part of the sleepy life of this dreamy mediæval town, losing more and more of his recognisable personality. Soon, he felt, the Curtain within would roll up with an awful rush, and he would find himself suddenly admitted into the secret purposes of the hidden life that lay behind it all. Only, by that time, he would have become transformed into an entirely different being.

And, meanwhile, he noticed various little signs of the intention to make his stay attractive to him: flowers in his bedroom, a more comfortable arm-chair in the corner, and even special little extra dishes on his private table in the dining-room. Conversations, too, with "Mademoiselle Ilsé" became more and more frequent and pleasant, and although they seldom travelled beyond the weather, or the details of the town, the girl, he noticed, was never in a hurry to bring them to an end, and often contrived to interject little odd sentences that he never properly understood, yet felt to be significant.

And it was these stray remarks, full of a meaning that evaded him, that pointed to some hidden purpose of her own and made him feel uneasy. They all had to do, he felt sure, with reasons for his staying on in the town indefinitely.

"And has M'sieur not even yet come to a decision?" she said softly in his ear, sitting beside him in the sunny yard before *déjeuner*, the acquaintance having progressed with significant rapidity. "Because, if it's so difficult, we must all try together to help him!"

The question startled him, following upon his own thoughts. It was spoken with a pretty laugh, and a stray bit of hair across one eye, as she turned and peered at him half roguishly. Possibly he did not quite understand the French of it, for her near presence always confused his small knowledge of the language distressingly. Yet the words, and her manner, and something else that lay behind it all in her mind, frightened him. It gave such point to his feeling that the town was waiting for him to make his mind up on some important matter.

At the same time, her voice, and the fact that she was there so close beside him in her soft dark dress, thrilled him inexpressibly.

"It is true I find it difficult to leave," he stammered, losing his way deliciously in the depths of her eyes, "and especially now that Mademoiselle Ilsé has come."

He was surprised at the success of his sentence, and quite delighted with the little gallantry of it. But at the same time he could have bitten his tongue off for having said it.

"Then after all you like our little town, or you would not be pleased to stay on," she said, ignoring the compliment.

"I am enchanted with it, and enchanted with you," he cried, feeling that his tongue was somehow slipping beyond the control of his brain. And he was on the verge of saying all manner of other things of the wildest description, when the girl sprang lightly up from her chair beside him, and made to go.

"It is *soupe à l'oignon* to-day!" she cried, laughing back at him through the sunlight, "and I must go and see about it. Otherwise, you know, M'sieur will not enjoy his dinner, and then, perhaps, he will leave us!"

He watched her cross the courtyard, moving with all the grace and lightness of the feline race, and her simple black dress clothed her, he thought, exactly like the fur of the same supple species. She turned once to laugh at him from the porch with the glass door, and then stopped a moment to speak to her mother, who sat knitting as usual in her corner seat just inside the hall-way.

But how was it, then, that the moment his eye fell upon this ungainly woman, the pair of them appeared suddenly as other than they were? Whence came that transforming dignity and sense of power that enveloped them both as by magic? What was it about that massive woman that made her appear instantly regal, and set her on a throne in some dark and dreadful scenery, wielding a sceptre over the red glare of some tempestuous orgy? And why did this slender stripling of a girl, graceful as a willow, lithe as a young leopard, assume suddenly an air of sinister majesty, and move with flame and smoke about her head, and the darkness of night beneath her feet?

Vezin caught his breath and sat there transfixed. Then, almost simultaneously with its appearance, the queer notion vanished again, and the sunlight of day caught them both, and he heard her laughing to her mother about the *soupe à l'oignon*, and saw her glancing back at him over her dear little shoulder with a smile that made him think of a dew-kissed rose bending lightly before summer airs.

And, indeed, the onion soup was particularly excellent that day, because he saw another cover laid at his small table and, with fluttering heart, heard the waiter murmur by way of explanation that "Ma'mselle Ilsé would honour M'sieur to-day at *déjeuner*, as her custom sometimes is with her mother's guests."

So actually she sat by him all through that delirious meal, talking quietly to him in easy French, seeing that he was well looked after, mixing the salad-dressing, and even helping him with her own hand. And, later in the afternoon, while he was smoking in the courtyard, longing for a sight of her as soon as her duties were done, she came again to his side, and when he rose to meet her, she stood facing him a moment, full of a perplexing sweet shyness before she spoke—

"My mother thinks you ought to know more of the beauties of our little town, and I think so too! Would M'sieur like me to be his guide, perhaps? I can show him everything, for our family has lived here for many generations."

She had him by the hand, indeed, before he could find a single word to express his pleasure, and led him, all unresisting, out into the street, yet in such a way that it seemed perfectly natural she should do so, and without the faintest suggestion of boldness or immodesty. Her face glowed with the pleasure and interest of it, and with her short dress and tumbled hair she looked every bit the charming child of seventeen that she was, innocent and playful, proud of her native town, and alive beyond her years to the sense of its ancient beauty.

So they went over the town together, and she showed him what she considered its chief interest: the tumble-down old house where her forebears had lived; the sombre, aristocratic-looking mansion where her mother's family dwelt for centuries, and the ancient market-place where several hundred years before the witches had been burnt by the score. She kept up a lively running stream of talk about it all, of which he understood not a fiftieth part as he trudged along by her side, cursing his forty-five years and feeling all the yearnings of his early manhood revive and jeer at him. And, as she talked, England and Surbiton seemed very far away indeed, almost in another age of the world's history. Her voice touched something immeasurably old in him, something that slept deep. It lulled the surface parts of his consciousness to sleep, allowing what was far more ancient to awaken. Like the town, with its elaborate pretence of modern active life, the upper layers of his being became dulled, soothed, muffled, and what lay underneath began to stir in its sleep. That big Curtain swayed a little to and fro. Presently it might lift altogether...

He began to understand a little better at last. The mood of the town was reproducing itself in him. In proportion as his ordinary external self became muffled, that inner secret life, that was far more real and vital, asserted itself. And this girl was surely the high-priestess of it all, the chief instrument of its accomplishment. New thoughts, with new interpretations, flooded his mind as she walked beside him through the winding streets, while the picturesque old gabled town, softly coloured in the sunset, had never appeared to him so wholly wonderful and seductive.

And only one curious incident came to disturb and puzzle him, slight in itself, but utterly inexplicable, bringing white terror into the child's face and a scream to her laughing lips. He had merely pointed to a column of blue smoke that rose from the burning autumn leaves and made a picture against the red roofs, and had then run to the wall and called her to his side to watch the flames shooting here and there through the heap of rubbish. Yet, at the sight of it, as though taken by surprise, her face had altered dreadfully, and she had turned and run like the wind, calling out wild sentences to him as she ran, of which he had not understood a single word, except that the fire apparently frightened her, and she wanted to get quickly away from it, and to get him away too.

Yet five minutes later she was as calm and happy again as though nothing had happened to alarm or waken troubled thoughts in her, and they had both forgotten the incident.

They were leaning over the ruined ramparts together listening to the weird music of the band as he had heard it the first day of his arrival. It moved him again profoundly as it had done before, and somehow he managed to find his tongue and his best French. The girl leaned across the stones close beside him. No one was about. Driven by some remorseless engine within he began to stammer something—he hardly knew what—of his strange admiration for her. Almost at the first word she sprang lightly off the wall and came up smiling in front of him, just touching his knees as he sat there. She was hatless as usual, and the sun caught her hair and one side of her cheek and throat.

"Oh, I'm *so* glad!" she cried, clapping her little hands softly in his face, "so very glad, because that means that if you like me you must also like what I do, and what I belong to."

Already he regretted bitterly having lost control of himself. Something in the phrasing of her sentence chilled him. He knew the fear of embarking upon an unknown and dangerous sea.

"You will take part in our real life, I mean," she added softly, with an indescribable coaxing of manner, as though she noticed his shrinking. "You will come back to us."

Already this slip of a child seemed to dominate him; he felt her power coming over him more and more; something emanated from her that stole over his senses and made him aware that her personality, for all its simple grace, held forces that were stately, imposing, august. He saw her again moving through smoke and flame amid broken and tempestuous scenery, alarmingly strong, her terrible mother by her side. Dimly this shone through her smile and appearance of charming innocence.

"You will, I know," she repeated, holding him with her eyes.

They were quite alone up there on the ramparts, and the sensation that she was overmastering him stirred a wild sensuousness in his blood. The mingled abandon and reserve in her attracted him furiously, and all of him that was man rose up and resisted the creeping influence, at the same time acclaiming it with the full delight of his forgotten youth. An irresistible desire came to him to question her, to summon what still remained to him of his own little personality in an effort to retain the right to his normal self.

The girl had grown quiet again, and was now leaning on the broad wall close beside him, gazing out across the darkening plain, her elbows on the coping, motionless as a figure carved in stone. He took his courage in both hands.

"Tell me, Ilsé," he said, unconsciously imitating her own purring softness of voice, yet aware that he was utterly in earnest, "what is the meaning of this town, and what is this real life you speak of? And why is it that the people watch me from morning to night? Tell me what it all means? And, tell me," he added more quickly with passion in his voice, "what you really are—yourself?"

She turned her head and looked at him through half-closed eyelids, her growing inner excitement betraying itself by the faint colour that ran like a shadow across her face.

"It seems to me,"—he faltered oddly under her gaze—"that I have some right to know—"

Suddenly she opened her eyes to the full. "You love me, then?" she asked softly.

"I swear," he cried impetuously, moved as by the force of a rising tide, "I never felt before—I have never known any other girl who—"

"Then you *have* the right to know," she calmly interrupted his confused confession; "for love shares all secrets."

She paused, and a thrill like fire ran swiftly through him. Her words lifted him off the earth, and he felt a radiant happiness, followed almost the same instant in horrible contrast by the thought of death. He became aware that she had turned her eyes upon his own and was speaking again.

"The real life I speak of," she whispered, "is the old, old life within, the life of long ago, the life to which you, too, once belonged, and to which you still belong."

A faint wave of memory troubled the deeps of his soul as her low voice sank into him. What she was saying he knew instinctively to be true, even though he could not as yet understand its full purport. His present life seemed slipping from him as he listened, merging his personality in one that was far older and greater. It was this loss of his present self that brought to him the thought of death.

"You came here," she went on, "with the purpose of seeking it, and the people felt your presence and are waiting to know what you decide, whether you will leave them without having found it, or whether—"

Her eyes remained fixed upon his own, but her face began to change, growing larger and darker with an expression of age.

"It is their thoughts constantly playing about your soul that makes you feel they watch you. They do not watch you with their eyes. The purposes of their inner life are calling to you, seeking to claim you. You were all part of the same life long, long ago, and now they want you back again among them."

Vezin's timid heart sank with dread as he listened; but the girl's eyes held him with a net of joy so that he had no wish to escape. She fascinated him, as it were, clean out of his normal self.

"Alone, however, the people could never have caught and held you," she resumed. "The motive force was not strong enough; it has faded through all these years. But I"—she paused a moment and looked at him with complete confidence in her splendid eyes—"I possess the spell to conquer you and hold you: the spell of old love. I can win you back again and make you live the old life with me, for the force of the ancient tie between us, if I choose to use it, is irresistible. And I do choose to use it. I still want you. And you, dear soul of my dim past"—she pressed closer to him so that her breath passed across his eyes, and her voice positively sang—"I mean to have you, for you love me and are utterly at my mercy."

Vezin heard, and yet did not hear; understood, yet did not understand. He had passed into a condition of exaltation. The world was beneath his feet, made of music and flowers, and he was flying somewhere far above it through the sunshine of pure delight. He was breathless and giddy with the wonder of her words. They intoxicated him. And, still, the terror of it all, the dreadful thought of death, pressed ever behind her sentences. For flames shot through her voice out of black smoke and licked at his soul.

And they communicated with one another, it seemed to him, by a process of swift telepathy, for his French could never have compassed all he said to her. Yet she understood perfectly, and what she said to him was like the recital of verses long since known. And the mingled pain and sweetness of it as he listened were almost more than his little soul could hold.

"Yet I came here wholly by chance—" he heard himself saying.

"No," she cried with passion, "you came here because I called to you. I have called to you for years, and you came with the whole force of the past behind you. You had to come, for I own you, and I claim you."

She rose again and moved closer, looking at him with a certain insolence in the face—the insolence of power.

The sun had set behind the towers of the old cathedral and the darkness rose up from the plain and enveloped them. The music of the band had ceased. The leaves of the plane trees hung motionless, but the chill of the autumn evening rose about them and made Vezin shiver. There was no sound but the sound of their voices and the occasional soft rustle of the girl's dress. He could hear the blood rushing in his ears. He scarcely realised where he was or what he was doing. Some terrible magic of the imagination drew him deeply down into the tombs of his own being, telling him in no unfaltering voice that her words shadowed forth the truth. And this simple little French maid, speaking beside him with so strange authority, he saw curiously alter into quite another being. As he stared into her eyes, the picture in his mind grew and lived, dressing itself vividly to his inner vision with a degree of reality he was compelled to acknowledge. As once before, he saw her tall and stately, moving through wild and broken scenery of forests and mountain caverns, the glare of flames behind her head and clouds of shifting smoke about her feet. Dark leaves encircled her hair, flying loosely in the wind, and her limbs shone through the merest rags of clothing. Others were about her too, and ardent eyes on all sides cast delirious glances upon her, but her own eyes were always for One only, one whom she held by the hand. For she was leading the dance in some tempestuous orgy to the music of chanting voices, and the dance she led circled about a great and awful Figure on a throne, brooding over the scene through lurid vapours, while innumerable other wild faces and forms crowded furiously about her in the dance. But the one she held by the hand he knew to be himself, and the monstrous shape upon the throne he knew to be her mother.

The vision rose within him, rushing to him down the long years of buried time, crying aloud to him with the voice of memory reawakened… And then the scene faded away and he saw the clear circle of the girl's eyes gazing steadfastly into his own, and she became once more the pretty little daughter of the innkeeper, and he found his voice again.

"And you," he whispered tremblingly—"you child of visions and enchantment, how is it that you so bewitch me that I loved you even before I saw?"

She drew herself up beside him with an air of rare dignity.

"The call of the Past," she said; "and besides," she added proudly, "in the real life I am a princess—"

"A princess!" he cried.

"—and my mother is a queen!"

At this, little Vezin utterly lost his head. Delight tore at his heart and swept him into sheer ecstasy. To hear that sweet singing voice, and to see those adorable little lips utter such things, upset his balance beyond all hope of control. He took her in his arms and covered her unresisting face with kisses.

But even while he did so, and while the hot passion swept him, he felt that she was soft and loathsome, and that her answering kisses stained his very soul... And when, presently, she had freed herself and vanished into the darkness, he stood there, leaning against the wall in a state of collapse, creeping with horror from the touch of her yielding body, and inwardly raging at the weakness that he already dimly realised must prove his undoing.

And from the shadows of the old buildings into which she disappeared there rose in the stillness of the night a singular, long-drawn cry, which at first he took for laughter, but which later he was sure he recognised as the almost human wailing of a cat.

V

For a long time Vezin leant there against the wall, alone with his surging thoughts and emotions. He understood at length that he had done the one thing necessary to call down upon him the whole force of this ancient Past. For in those passionate kisses he had acknowledged the tie of olden days, and had revived it. And the memory of that soft impalpable caress in the darkness of the inn corridor came back to him with a shudder. The girl had first mastered him, and then led him to the one act that was necessary for her purpose. He had been waylaid, after the lapse of centuries— caught, and conquered.

Dimly he realised this, and sought to make plans for his escape. But, for the moment at any rate, he was powerless to manage his thoughts or will, for the sweet, fantastic madness of the whole adventure mounted to his brain like a spell, and he gloried in the feeling that he was utterly enchanted and moving in a world so much larger and wilder than the one he had ever been accustomed to.

The moon, pale and enormous, was just rising over the sea-like plain, when at last he rose to go. Her slanting rays drew all the houses into new perspective, so that their roofs, already glistening with dew, seemed to stretch much higher into the sky than usual, and their gables and quaint old towers lay far away in its purple reaches.

The cathedral appeared unreal in a silver mist. He moved softly, keeping to the shadows; but the streets were all deserted and very silent; the doors were closed, the shutters fastened. Not a soul was astir. The hush of night lay over everything; it was like a town of the dead, a churchyard with gigantic and grotesque tombstones.

Wondering where all the busy life of the day had so utterly disappeared to, he made his way to a back door that entered the inn by means of the stables, thinking thus to reach his room unob-served. He reached the courtyard safely and crossed it by keeping close to the shadow of the wall. He sidled down it, mincing along on tiptoe, just as the old men did when they entered the *salle à manger*. He was horrified to find himself doing this instinctively. A strange impulse came to him, catching him somehow in the centre of his body—an impulse to drop upon all fours and run swiftly and silently. He glanced upwards and the idea came to him to leap up upon his window-sill overhead instead of going round by the stairs. This occurred to him as the easiest, and most natural way. It was like the beginning of some horrible transformation of himself into something else. He was fearfully strung up.

The moon was higher now, and the shadows very dark along the side of the street where he moved. He kept among the deepest of them, and reached the porch with the glass doors.

But here there was light; the inmates, unfortunately, were still about. Hoping to slip across the hall unobserved and reach the stairs, he opened the door carefully and stole in. Then he saw that the hall was not empty. A large dark thing lay against the wall on his left. At first he thought it must be household articles. Then it moved, and he thought it was an immense cat, distorted in some way by the play of light and shadow. Then it rose straight up before him and he saw that it was the proprietress.

What she had been doing in this position he could only venture a dreadful guess, but the moment she stood up and faced him he was aware of some terrible dignity clothing her about that instantly recalled the girl's strange saying that she was a queen. Huge and sinister she stood there under the little oil lamp; alone with him in the empty hall. Awe stirred in his heart, and the roots of some ancient fear. He felt that he must bow to her and make some kind of obeisance. The impulse was fierce and irresistible, as of long habit. He glanced quickly about him. There was no one there. Then he deliberately inclined his head towards her. He bowed.

"Enfin! M'sieur s'est donc décidé. C'est bien alors. J'en suis contente."

Her words came to him sonorously as through a great open space.

Then the great figure came suddenly across the flagged hall at him and seized his trembling hands. Some overpowering force moved with her and caught him.

"On pourrait faire un p'tit tour ensemble, n'est-ce pas? Nous y allons cette nuit et il faut s'exercer un peu d'avance pour cela. Ilsé, Ilsé, viens donc ici. Viens vite!"

And she whirled him round in the opening steps of some dance that seemed oddly and horribly familiar. They made no sound on the stones, this strangely assorted couple. It was all soft and stealthy. And presently, when the air seemed to thicken like smoke, and a red glare as of flame shot through it, he was aware that some one else had joined them and that his hand the mother had released was now tightly held by the daughter. Ilsé had come in answer to the call, and he saw her with leaves of vervain twined in her dark hair, clothed in tattered vestiges of some curious garment, beautiful as the night, and horribly, odiously, loathsomely seductive.

"To the Sabbath! to the Sabbath!" they cried. "On to the Witches' Sabbath!"

Up and down that narrow hall they danced, the women on each side of him, to the wildest measure he had ever imagined, yet which he dimly, dreadfully remembered, till the lamp on the wall flickered and went out, and they were left in total darkness. And the devil woke in his heart with a thousand vile suggestions and made him afraid.

Suddenly they released his hands and he heard the voice of the mother cry that it was time, and they must go. Which way they went he did not pause to see. He only realised that he was free, and he blundered through the darkness till he found the stairs and then tore up them to his room as though all hell was at his heels.

He flung himself on the sofa, with his face in his hands, and groaned. Swiftly reviewing a dozen ways of immediate escape, all equally impossible, he finally decided that the only thing to do for the moment was to sit quiet and wait. He must see what was going to happen. At least in the privacy of his own bedroom he would be fairly safe. The door was locked. He crossed over and softly opened the window which gave upon the courtyard and also permitted a partial view of the hall through the glass doors.

As he did so the hum and murmur of a great activity reached his ears from the streets beyond—the sound of footsteps and voices muffled by distance. He leaned out cautiously and listened. The moonlight was clear and strong now, but his own window was in shadow, the silver disc being still behind the house. It came to him irresistibly that the inhabitants of the town, who a little while before had all been invisible behind closed doors, were now issuing forth, busy upon some secret and unholy errand. He listened intently.

At first everything about him was silent, but soon he became aware of movements going on in the house itself. Rustlings and cheepings came to him across that still, moonlit yard. A concourse of living beings sent the hum of their activity into the night. Things were on the move everywhere. A biting, pungent odour rose through the air, coming he knew not whence. Presently his eyes became glued to the windows of the opposite wall where the moonshine fell in a soft blaze. The roof overhead, and behind him, was reflected clearly in the panes of glass, and he saw the outlines of dark bodies moving with long footsteps over the tiles and along the coping. They passed swiftly and silently, shaped like immense cats, in an endless procession across the pictured glass, and then appeared to leap down to a lower level, where he lost sight of them. He just caught the soft thudding of their leaps. Sometimes their shadows fell upon the white wall opposite, and then he could not make out whether they were the shadows of human beings or of cats. They seemed to change swiftly from one to the other. The transformation looked horribly real, for they leaped like human beings, yet changed swiftly in the air immediately afterwards, and dropped like animals.

The yard, too, beneath him, was now alive with the creeping movements of dark forms all stealthily drawing towards the porch with the glass doors. They kept so closely to the wall that he could not determine their actual shape, but when he saw that they passed on to the great congregation that was gathering in the hall, he understood that these were the creatures whose leaping shadows he had first seen reflected in the window-panes opposite. They were coming from all parts of the town, reaching the appointed meeting-place across the roofs and tiles, and springing from level to level till they came to the yard.

Then a new sound caught his ear, and he saw that the windows all about him were being softly opened, and that to each window came a face. A moment later figures began dropping hurriedly down into the yard. And these figures, as they lowered themselves down from the windows, were human, he saw; but once safely in the yard they fell upon all fours and changed in the swiftest possible second into—cats—huge, silent cats. They ran in streams to join the main body in the hall beyond.

So, after all, the rooms in the house had not been empty and unoccupied.

Moreover, what he saw no longer filled him with amazement. For he remembered it all. It was familiar. It had all happened before just so, hundreds of times, and he himself had taken part in it and known the wild madness of it all. The outline of the old building changed, the yard grew larger, and he seemed to be staring down upon it from a much greater height through smoky vapours. And, as he looked, half remembering, the old pains of long ago, fierce and sweet, furiously assailed him, and the blood stirred horribly as he heard the Call of the Dance again in his heart and tasted the ancient magic of Ilsé whirling by his side.

Suddenly he started back. A great lithe cat had leaped softly up from the shadows below on to the sill close to his face, and was staring fixedly at him with the eyes of a human. "Come," it seemed to say, "come with us to the Dance! Change as of old! Transform yourself swiftly and come!" Only too well he understood the creature's soundless call.

It was gone again in a flash with scarcely a sound of its padded feet on the stones, and then others dropped by the score down the side of the house, past his very eyes, all changing as they fell and darting away rapidly, softly, towards the gathering point. And again he felt the dreadful desire to do likewise; to murmur the old incantation, and then drop upon hands and knees and run swiftly for the great flying leap into the air. Oh, how the passion of it rose within him like a flood, twisting his very entrails, sending his heart's desire flaming forth into the night for the old, old Dance of the Sorcerers at the Witches' Sabbath! The whirl of the stars was about him; once more he met the magic of the moon. The power of the wind, rushing from precipice and forest, leaping from cliff to cliff across the valleys, tore him away... He heard the cries of the dancers and their wild laughter, and with this savage girl in his embrace he danced furiously about the dim Throne where sate the Figure with the sceptre of majesty...

Then, suddenly, all became hushed and still, and the fever died down a little in his heart. The calm moonlight flooded a courtyard empty and deserted. They had started. The procession was off into the sky. And he was left behind—alone.

Vezin tiptoed softly across the room and unlocked the door. The murmur from the streets, growing momentarily as he advanced, met his ears. He made his way with the utmost caution down the corridor. At the head of the stairs he paused and listened. Below him, the hall where they had gathered was dark and still, but through opened doors and windows on the far side of the building came the sound of a great throng moving farther and farther into the distance.

He made his way down the creaking wooden stairs, dreading yet longing to meet some straggler who should point the way, but finding no one; across the dark hall, so lately thronged with living, moving things, and out through the opened front doors into the street. He could not believe that he was really left behind, really forgotten, that he had been purposely permitted to escape. It perplexed him.

Nervously he peered about him, and up and down the street; then, seeing nothing, advanced slowly down the pavement.

The whole town, as he went, showed itself empty and deserted, as though a great wind had blown everything alive out of it. The doors and windows of the houses stood open to the night; nothing stirred; moonlight and silence lay over all. The night lay about him like a cloak. The air, soft and cool, caressed his cheek like the touch of a great furry paw. He gained confidence and began to walk quickly, though still keeping to the shadowed side. Nowhere could he discover the faintest sign of the great unholy exodus he knew had just taken place. The moon sailed high over all in a sky cloudless and serene.

Hardly realising where he was going, he crossed the open market-place and so came to the ramparts, whence he knew a pathway descended to the high road and along which he could make good his escape to one of the other little towns that lay to the northward, and so to the railway.

But first he paused and gazed out over the scene at his feet where the great plain lay like a silver map of some dream country. The still beauty of it entered his heart, increasing his sense of bewilderment and unreality. No air stirred, the leaves of the plane trees stood motionless, the near details were defined with the sharpness of day against dark shadows, and in the distance the fields and woods melted away into haze and shimmering mistiness.

But the breath caught in his throat and he stood stock-still as though transfixed when his gaze passed from the horizon and fell upon the near prospect in the depth of the valley at his feet. The whole lower slopes of the hill, that lay hid from the brightness of the moon, were aglow, and through the glare he saw countless moving forms, shifting thick and fast between the opening of the trees; while overhead, like leaves driven by the wind, he discerned flying shapes that hovered darkly one moment against the sky and then settled down with cries and weird singing through the branches into the region that was aflame.

Spellbound, he stood and stared for a time that he could not measure. And then, moved by one of the terrible impulses that seemed to control the whole adventure, he climbed swiftly upon the top of the broad coping, and balanced a moment where the valley gaped at his feet. But in that very instant, as he stood hovering, a sudden movement among the shadows of the houses caught his eye, and he turned to see the outline of a large animal dart swiftly across the open space behind him, and land with a flying leap upon the top of the wall a little lower down. It ran like the wind to his feet and then rose up beside him upon the ramparts. A shiver seemed to run through the moonlight, and his sight trembled for a second. His heart pulsed fearfully. Ilsé stood beside him, peering into his face.

Some dark substance, he saw, stained the girl's face and skin, shining in the moonlight as she stretched her hands towards him; she was dressed in wretched tattered garments that yet became her mightily; rue and vervain twined about her temples; her eyes glittered with unholy light. He only just controlled the wild impulse to take her in his arms and leap with her from their giddy perch into the valley below.

"See!" she cried, pointing with an arm on which the rags fluttered in the rising wind towards the forest aglow in the distance. "See where they await us! The woods are alive! Already the Great Ones are there, and the dance will soon begin! The salve is here! Anoint yourself and come!"

Though a moment before the sky was clear and cloudless, yet even while she spoke the face of the moon grew dark and the wind began to toss in the crests of the plane trees at his feet. Stray gusts brought the sounds of hoarse singing and crying from the lower slopes of the hill, and the pungent odour he had already noticed about the courtyard of the inn rose about him in the air.

"Transform, transform!" she cried again, her voice rising like a song. "Rub well your skin before you fly. Come! Come with me to the Sabbath, to the madness of its furious delight, to the sweet abandonment of its evil worship! See! the Great Ones are there, and the terrible Sacraments prepared. The Throne is occupied. Anoint and come! Anoint and come!"

She grew to the height of a tree beside him, leaping upon the wall with flaming eyes and hair strewn upon the night. He too began to change swiftly. Her hands touched the skin of his face and neck, streaking him with the burning salve that sent the old magic into his blood with the power before which fades all that is good.

A wild roar came up to his ears from the heart of the wood, and the girl, when she heard it, leaped upon the wall in the frenzy of her wicked joy.

"Satan is there!" she screamed, rushing upon him and striving to draw him with her to the edge of the wall. "Satan has come! The Sacraments call us! Come, with your dear apostate soul, and we will worship and dance till the moon dies and the world is forgotten!"

Just saving himself from the dreadful plunge, Vezin struggled to release himself from her grasp, while the passion tore at his reins and all but mastered him. He shrieked aloud, not knowing what he said, and then he shrieked again. It was the old impulses, the old awful habits instinctively finding voice; for though it seemed to him that he merely shrieked nonsense, the words he uttered really had meaning in them, and were intelligible. It was the ancient call. And it was heard below. It was answered.

The wind whistled at the skirts of his coat as the air round him darkened with many flying forms crowding upwards out of the valley. The crying of hoarse voices smote upon his ears, coming closer. Strokes of wind buffeted him, tearing him this way and that along the crumbling top of the stone wall; and Ilsé clung to him with her long shining arms, smooth and bare, holding him fast about the neck. But not Ilsé alone, for a dozen of them surrounded him, dropping out of the air. The pungent odour of the anointed bodies stifled him, exciting him to the old madness of the Sabbath, the dance of the witches and sorcerers doing honour to the personified Evil of the world.

"Anoint and away! Anoint and away!" they cried in wild chorus about him. "To the Dance that never dies! To the sweet and fearful fantasy of evil!"

Another moment and he would have yielded and gone, for his will turned soft and the flood of passionate memory all but overwhelmed him, when—so can a small thing alter the whole course of an adventure—he caught his foot upon a loose stone in the edge of the wall, and then fell with a sudden crash on to the ground below. But he fell towards the houses, in the open space of dust and cobble stones, and fortunately not into the gaping depth of the valley on the farther side.

And they, too, came in a tumbling heap about him, like flies upon a piece of food, but as they fell he was released for a moment from the power of their touch, and in that brief instant of freedom there flashed into his mind the sudden intuition that saved him. Before he could regain his feet he saw them scrabbling awkwardly back upon the wall, as though bat-like they could only fly by dropping from a height, and had no hold upon him in the open. Then, seeing them perched there in a row like cats upon a roof, all dark and singularly shapeless, their eyes like lamps, the sudden memory came back to him of Ilsé's terror at the sight of fire.

Quick as a flash he found his matches and lit the dead leaves that lay under the wall.

Dry and withered, they caught fire at once, and the wind carried the flame in a long line down the length of the wall, licking upwards as it ran; and with shrieks and wailings, the crowded row of forms upon the top melted away into the air on the other side, and were gone with a great rush and whirring of their bodies down into the heart of the haunted valley, leaving Vezin breathless and shaken in the middle of the deserted ground.

"Ilsé!" he called feebly; "Ilsé!" for his heart ached to think that she was really gone to the great Dance without him, and that he had lost the opportunity of its fearful joy. Yet at the same time his relief was so great, and he was so dazed and troubled in mind with the whole thing, that he hardly knew what he was saying, and only cried aloud in the fierce storm of his emotion…

The fire under the wall ran its course, and the moonlight came out again, soft and clear, from its temporary eclipse. With one last shuddering look at the ruined ramparts, and a feeling of horrid wonder for the haunted valley beyond, where the shapes still crowded and flew, he turned his face towards the town and slowly made his way in the direction of the hotel.

And as he went, a great wailing of cries, and a sound of howling, followed him from the gleaming forest below, growing fainter and fainter with the bursts of wind as he disappeared between the houses.

VI

"It may seem rather abrupt to you, this sudden tame ending," said Arthur Vezin, glancing with flushed face and timid eyes at Dr. Silence sitting there with his notebook, "but the fact is—er—from that moment my memory seems to have failed rather. I have no distinct recollection of how I got home or what precisely I did.

"It appears I never went back to the inn at all. I only dimly recollect racing down a long white road in the moonlight, past woods and villages, still and deserted, and then the dawn came up, and I saw the towers of a biggish town and so came to a station.

"But, long before that, I remember pausing somewhere on the road and looking back to where the hill-town of my adventure stood up in the moonlight, and thinking how exactly like a great monstrous cat it lay there upon the plain, its huge front paws lying down the two main streets, and the twin and broken towers of the cathedral marking its torn ears against the sky. That picture stays in my mind with the utmost vividness to this day.

"Another thing remains in my mind from that escape—namely, the sudden sharp reminder that I had not paid my bill, and the decision I made, standing there on the dusty highroad, that the small baggage I had left behind would more than settle for my indebtedness.

"For the rest, I can only tell you that I got coffee and bread at a café on the outskirts of this town I had come to, and soon after found my way to the station and caught a train later in the day. That same evening I reached London."

"And how long altogether," asked John Silence quietly, "do you think you stayed in the town of the adventure?"

Vezin looked up sheepishly.

"I was coming to that," he resumed, with apologetic wrigglings of his body. "In London I found that I was a whole week out in my reckoning of time. I had stayed over a week in the town, and it ought to have been September 15th,—instead of which it was only September 10th!"

"So that, in reality, you had only stayed a night or two in the inn?" queried the doctor.

Vezin hesitated before replying. He shuffled upon the mat.

"I must have gained time somewhere," he said at length— "somewhere or somehow. I certainly had a week to my credit. I can't explain it. I can only give you the fact."

"And this happened to you last year, since when you have never been back to the place?"

"Last autumn, yes," murmured Vezin; "and I have never dared to go back. I think I never want to."

"And, tell me," asked Dr. Silence at length, when he saw that the little man had evidently come to the end of his words and had nothing more to say, "had you ever read up the subject of the old witchcraft practices during the Middle Ages, or been at all interested in the subject?"

"Never!" declared Vezin emphatically. "I had never given a thought to such matters so far as I know—"

"Or to the question of reincarnation, perhaps?"

"Never—before my adventure; but I have since," he replied significantly.

There was, however, something still on the man's mind that he wished to relieve himself of by confession, yet could with difficulty bring himself to mention; and it was only after the sympathetic tactfulness of the doctor had provided numerous openings that he at length availed himself of one of them, and stammered that he would like to show him the marks he still had on his neck where, he said, the girl had touched him with her anointed hands.

He took off his collar after infinite fumbling hesitation, and lowered his shirt a little for the doctor to see. And there, on the surface of the skin, lay a faint reddish line across the shoulder and extending a little way down the back towards the spine. It certainly indicated exactly the position an arm might have taken in the act of embracing. And on the other side of the neck, slightly higher up, was a similar mark, though not quite so clearly defined.

"That was where she held me that night on the ramparts," he whispered, a strange light coming and going in his eyes.

*

It was some weeks later when I again found occasion to consult John Silence concerning another extraordinary case that had come under my notice, and we fell to discussing Vezin's story. Since hearing it, the doctor had made investigations on his own account, and one of his secretaries had discovered that Vezin's ancestors had actually lived for generations in the very town where the adventure came to him. Two of them, both women, had been tried and convicted as witches, and had been burned alive at the stake. Moreover, it had not been difficult to prove that the very inn where Vezin stayed was built about 1700 upon the spot where the funeral pyres stood and the executions took place. The town was a sort of headquarters for all the sorcerers and witches of the entire region, and after conviction they were burnt there literally by scores.

"It seems strange," continued the doctor, "that Vezin should have remained ignorant of all this; but, on the other hand, it was not the kind of history that successive generations would have been anxious to keep alive, or to repeat to their children. Therefore I am inclined to think he still knows nothing about it.

"The whole adventure seems to have been a very vivid revival of the memories of an earlier life, caused by coming directly into contact with the living forces still intense enough to hang about the place, and, by a most singular chance too, with the very souls who had taken part with him in the events of that particular life. For the mother and daughter who impressed him so strangely must have been leading actors, with himself, in the scenes and practices of witchcraft which at that period dominated the imaginations of the whole country.

"One has only to read the histories of the times to know that these witches claimed the power of transforming themselves into various animals, both for the purposes of disguise and also to convey themselves swiftly to the scenes of their imaginary orgies. Lycanthropy, or the power to change themselves into wolves, was everywhere believed in, and the ability to transform themselves into cats by rubbing their bodies with a special salve or ointment provided by Satan himself, found equal credence. The witchcraft trials abound in evidences of such universal beliefs."

Dr. Silence quoted chapter and verse from many writers on the subject, and showed how every detail of Vezin's adventure had a basis in the practices of those dark days.

"But that the entire affair took place subjectively in the man's own consciousness, I have no doubt," he went on, in reply to my questions; "for my secretary, who has been to the town to investigate, discovered his signature in the visitors' book, and proved by it that he had arrived on September 8th, and left suddenly without paying his bill. He left two days later, and they still were in possession of his dirty brown bag and some tourist clothes. I paid a few francs in settlement of his debt, and have sent his luggage on to him. The daughter was absent from home, but the proprietress, a large woman very much as he described her, told my secretary that he had seemed a very strange, absent-minded kind of gentleman, and after his disappearance she had feared for a long time that he had met with a violent end in the neighbouring forest, where he used to roam about alone.

"I should like to have obtained a personal interview with the daughter so as to ascertain how much was subjective and how much actually took place with her as Vezin told it. For her dread of fire and the sight of burning must, of course, have been the intuitive memory of her former painful death at the stake, and have thus explained why he fancied more than once that he saw her through smoke and flame."

"And that mark on his skin, for instance?" I inquired.

"Merely the marks produced by hysterical brooding," he replied, "like the stigmata of the *religieuses*, and the bruises which appear on the bodies of hypnotised subjects who have been told to expect them. This is very common and easily explained. Only it seems curious that these marks should have remained so long in Vezin's case. Usually they disappear quickly."

"Obviously he is still thinking about it all, brooding, and living it all over again," I ventured.

"Probably. And this makes me fear that the end of his trouble is not yet. We shall hear of him again. It is a case, alas! I can do little to alleviate."

Dr. Silence spoke gravely and with sadness in his voice.

"And what do you make of the Frenchman in the train?" I asked further—"the man who warned him against the place, *à cause du sommeil et à cause des chats?* Surely a very singular incident?"

"A *very* singular incident indeed," he made answer slowly, "and one I can only explain on the basis of a highly improbable coincidence—"

"Namely?"

"That the man was one who had himself stayed in the town and undergone there a similar experience. I should like to find this man and ask him. But the crystal is useless here, for I have no slightest clue to go upon, and I can only conclude that some singular psychic affinity, some force still active in his being out of the same past life, drew him thus to the personality of Vezin, and enabled him to fear what might happen to him, and thus to warn him as he did.

"Yes," he presently continued, half talking to himself, "I suspect in this case that Vezin was swept into the vortex of forces arising out of the intense activities of a past life, and that he lived over again a scene in which he had often played a leading part centuries before. For strong actions set up forces that are so slow to exhaust themselves, they may be said in a sense never to die. In this case they were not vital enough to render the illusion complete, so that the little man found himself caught in a very distressing confusion of the present and the past; yet he was sufficiently sensitive to recognise that it was true, and to fight against the degradation of returning, even in memory, to a former and lower state of development.

"Ah yes!" he continued, crossing the floor to gaze at the darkening sky, and seemingly quite oblivious of my presence, "subliminal up-rushes of memory like this can be exceedingly painful, and sometimes exceedingly dangerous. I only trust that this gentle soul may soon escape from this obsession of a passionate and tempestuous past. But I doubt it, I doubt it."

His voice was hushed with sadness as he spoke, and when he turned back into the room again there was an expression of profound yearning upon his face, the yearning of a soul whose desire to help is sometimes greater than his power.

The Wendigo

—1910—

A CONSIDERABLE NUMBER OF HUNTING PARTIES WERE OUT that year without finding so much as a fresh trail; for the moose were uncommonly shy, and the various Nimrods returned to the bosoms of their respective families with the best excuses the facts or their imaginations could suggest. Dr. Cathcart, among others, came back without a trophy; but he brought instead the memory of an experience which he declares was worth all the bull-moose that had ever been shot. But then Cathcart, of Aberdeen, was interested in other things besides moose—amongst them the vagaries of the human mind. This particular story, however, found no mention in his book on *Collective Hallucination* for the simple reason (so he confided once to a fellow colleague) that he himself played too intimate a part in it to form a competent judgment of the affair as a whole...

Besides himself and his guide, Hank Davis, there was young Simpson, his nephew, a divinity student destined for the "Wee Kirk" (then on his first visit to Canadian backwoods), and the latter's guide, Défago. Joseph Défago was a French "Canuck," who had strayed from his native Province of Quebec years before, and had got caught in Rat Portage when the Canadian Pacific Railway was a-building; a man who, in addition to his unparalleled knowledge of woodcraft and bush-lore, could also sing the old *voyageur* songs and tell a capital hunting yarn into the bargain. He was deeply susceptible, moreover, to that singular spell which the wilderness lays upon certain lonely natures, and he loved the wild solitudes with a kind of romantic passion that amounted almost to an obsession. The life of the backwoods fascinated him—whence, doubtless, his surpassing efficiency in dealing with their mysteries.

On this particular expedition he was Hank's choice. Hank knew him and swore by him. He also swore at him, "jest as a pal might," and since he had a vocabulary of picturesque, if utterly meaningless, oaths, the conversation between the two stalwart and hardy woodsmen was often of a rather lively description. This river of expletives, however, Hank agreed to dam a little out of respect for his old "hunting boss," Dr. Cathcart, whom of course he addressed after the fashion of the country as "Doc"; and also because he understood that young Simpson was already a "bit of a parson." He had, however, one objection to Défago, and one only—which was, that the French Canadian sometimes exhibited what Hank described as "the output of a cursed and dismal mind," meaning apparently that he sometimes was true to type, Latin type, and suffered fits of a kind of silent moroseness when nothing could induce him to utter speech. Défago, that is to say, was imaginative and melancholy. And, as a rule, it was too long a spell of "civilisation" that induced the attacks, for a few days of the wilderness invariably cured them.

This, then, was the party of four that found themselves in camp the last week in October of that "shy moose year" 'way up in the wilderness north of Rat Portage—a forsaken and desolate country. There was also Punk, an Indian, who had accompanied Dr. Cathcart and Hank on their hunting trips in previous years, and who acted as cook. His duty was merely to stay in camp, catch fish, and prepare venison steaks and coffee at a few minutes' notice. He dressed in the worn-out clothes bequeathed to him by former patrons, and, except for his coarse black hair and dark skin, he looked in these city garments no more like a real redskin than a stage negro looks like a real African. For all that, however, Punk had in him still the instincts of his dying race; his taciturn silence and his endurance survived; also his superstition.

The party round the blazing fire that night were despondent, for a week had passed without a single sign of recent moose discovering itself. Défago had sung his song and plunged into a story, but Hank, in bad humour, reminded him so often that "he kep' mussing-up the fac's so, that it was 'most all nothin' but a petred-out lie," that the Frenchman had finally subsided into a sulky silence which nothing seemed likely to break. Dr. Cathcart and his nephew were fairly done after an exhausting day. Punk was washing up the dishes, grunting to himself under the lean-to of branches, where he later also slept. No one troubled to stir the slowly dying fire. Overhead the stars were brilliant in a sky quite wintry, and there was so little wind that ice was already forming stealthily along the shores of the still lake behind them. The silence of the vast listening forest stole forward and enveloped them.

Hank broke in suddenly with his nasal voice.

"I'm in favour of breaking new ground to-morrow, Doc," he observed with energy, looking across at his employer. "We don't stand a dead Dago's chance about here."

"Agreed," said Cathcart, always a man of few words. "Think the idea's good."

"Sure pop, it's good," Hank resumed with confidence. "S'pose, now, you and I strike west, up Garden Lake way for a change! None of us ain't touched that quiet bit o' land yet—"

"I'm with you."

"And you, Défago, take Mr. Simpson along in the small canoe, skip across the lake, portage over into Fifty Island Water, and take a good squint down that thar southern shore. The moose 'yarded' there like hell last year, and for all we know they may be doin' it agin this year jest to spite us."

Défago, keeping his eyes on the fire, said nothing by way of reply. He was still offended, possibly, about his interrupted story.

"No one's been up that way this year, an' I'll lay my bottom dollar on *that!*" Hank added with emphasis, as though he had a reason for knowing. He looked over at his partner sharply. "Better take the little silk tent and stay away a couple o' nights," he concluded, as though the matter were definitely settled. For Hank was recognised as general organiser of the hunt, and in charge of the party.

It was obvious to any one that Défago did not jump at the plan, but his silence seemed to convey something more than ordinary disapproval, and across his sensitive dark face there passed a curious expression like a flash of firelight—not so quickly, however, that the three men had not time to catch it. "He funked for some reason, *I* thought," Simpson said afterwards in the tent he shared with his uncle. Dr. Cathcart made no immediate reply, although the look had interested him enough at the time for him to make a mental note of it. The expression had caused him a passing uneasiness he could not quite account for at the moment.

But Hank, of course, had been the first to notice it, and the odd thing was that instead of becoming explosive or angry over the other's reluctance, he at once began to humour him a bit.

"But there ain't no *speshul* reason why no one's been up there this year," he said, with a perceptible hush in his tone; "not the reason *you* mean, anyway! Las' year it was the fires that kep' folks out, and this year I guess—I guess it jest happened so, that's all!" His manner was clearly meant to be encouraging.

Joseph Défago raised his eyes a moment, then dropped them again. A breath of wind stole out of the forest and stirred the embers into a passing blaze. Dr. Cathcart again noticed the expression in the guide's face, and again he did not like it. But this time the nature of the look betrayed itself. In those eyes, for an instant, he caught the gleam of a man scared in his very soul. It disquieted him more than he cared to admit.

"Bad Indians up that way?" he asked, with a laugh to ease matters a little, while Simpson, too sleepy to notice this subtle by-play, moved off to bed with a prodigious yawn; "or—or anything wrong with the country?" he added, when his nephew was out of hearing.

Hank met his eye with something less than his usual frankness.

"He's jest skeered," he replied good-humouredly, "skeered stiff about some ole feery tale! That's all, ain't it, ole pard?" And he gave Défago a friendly kick on the moccasined foot that lay nearest the fire.

Défago looked up quickly, as from an interrupted reverie, a reverie, however, that had not prevented his seeing all that went on about him.

"Skeered—*nuthin'!*" he answered, with a flush of defiance. "There's nuthin' in the Bush that can skeer Joseph Défago, and don't you forget it!" And the natural energy with which he spoke made it impossible to know whether he told the whole truth or only a part of it.

Hank turned towards the doctor. He was just going to add something when he stopped abruptly and looked round. A sound close behind them in the darkness made all three start. It was old Punk, who had moved up from his lean-to while they talked and now stood there just beyond the circle of firelight—listening.

"'Nother time, Doc!" Hank whispered, with a wink, "when the gallery ain't stepped down into the stalls!" And, springing to his feet, he slapped the Indian on the back and cried noisily, "Come up t' the fire an' warm yer dirty red skin a bit." He dragged him towards the blaze and threw more wood on. "That was a mighty good feed you give us an hour or two back," he continued heartily, as though to set the man's thoughts on another scent, "and it ain't Christian to let you stand out there freezin' yer ole soul to hell while we're gettin' all good an' toasted!" Punk moved in and warmed his feet, smiling darkly at the other's volubility which he only half understood, but saying nothing. And presently Dr. Cathcart, seeing that further conversation was impossible, followed his nephew's example and moved off to the tent, leaving the three men smoking over the now blazing fire.

It is not easy to undress in a small tent without waking one's companion, and Cathcart, hardened and warm-blooded as he was in spite of his fifty odd years, did what Hank would have described as "considerable of his twilight" in the open. He noticed, during the process, that Punk had meanwhile gone back to his lean-to, and that Hank and Défago were at it hammer and tongs, or, rather, hammer and anvil, the little French Canadian being the anvil. It was all very like the conventional stage picture of Western melodrama: the fire lighting up their faces with patches of alternate red and black; Défago, in slouch hat and moccasins in the part of the "badlands'" villain; Hank, open-faced and hatless, with that reckless fling of his shoulders, the honest and deceived hero; and old Punk, eavesdropping in the background, supplying the atmosphere of mystery. The doctor smiled as he noticed the details; but at the same time something deep within him—he hardly knew what—shrank a little, as though an almost imperceptible breath of warning had touched the surface of his soul and was gone again before he could seize it. Probably it was traceable to that "scared expression" he had seen in the eyes of Défago; "probably"—for this hint of fugitive emotion otherwise escaped his usually so keen analysis. Défago, he was vaguely aware, might cause trouble somehow... He was not as steady a guide as Hank, for instance... Further than that he could not get...

He watched the men a moment longer before diving into the stuffy tent where Simpson already slept soundly. Hank, he saw, was swearing like a mad African in a New York n—— saloon; but it was the swearing of "affection." The ridiculous oaths flew freely now that the cause of their obstruction was asleep. Presently he put his arm almost tenderly upon his comrade's shoulder, and they moved off together into the shadows where their tent stood faintly glimmering. Punk, too, a moment later followed their example and disappeared between his odorous blankets in the opposite direction.

Dr. Cathcart then likewise turned in, weariness and sleep still fighting in his mind with an obscure curiosity to know what it was had scared Défago about the country up Fifty Island Water way,—wondering, too, why Punk's presence had prevented the completion of what Hank had to say. Then sleep overtook him. He would know to-morrow. Hank would tell him the story while they trudged after the elusive moose.

Deep silence fell about the little camp, planted there so audaciously in the jaws of the wilderness. The lake gleamed like a sheet of black glass beneath the stars. The cold air pricked. In the draughts of night that poured their silent tide from the depths of the forest, with messages from distant ridges and from lakes just beginning to freeze, there lay already the faint, bleak odours of coming winter. White men, with their dull scent, might never have divined them;

the fragrance of the wood-fire would have concealed from them these almost electrical hints of moss and bark and hardening swamp a hundred miles away. Even Hank and Défago, subtly in league with the soul of the woods as they were, would probably have spread their delicate nostrils in vain...

But an hour later, when all slept like the dead, old Punk crept from his blankets and went down to the shore of the lake like a shadow—silently, as only Indian blood can move. He raised his head and looked about him. The thick darkness rendered sight of small avail, but, like the animals, he possessed other senses that darkness could not mute. He listened—then sniffed the air. Motionless as a hemlock-stem he stood there. After five minutes again he lifted his head and sniffed, and yet once again. A tingling of the wonderful nerves that betrayed itself by no outer sign, ran through him as he tasted the keen air. Then, merging his figure into the surrounding blackness in a way that only wild men and animals understand, he turned, still moving like a shadow, and went stealthily back to his lean-to and his bed.

And soon after he slept, the change of wind he had divined stirred gently the reflection of the stars within the lake. Rising among the far ridges of the country beyond Fifty Island Water, it came from the direction in which he had stared, and it passed over the sleeping camp with a faint and sighing murmur through the tops of the big trees that was almost too delicate to be audible. With it, down the desert paths of night, though too faint, too high even for the Indian's hair-like nerves, there passed a curious, thin odour, strangely disquieting, an odour of something that seemed unfamiliar—utterly unknown.

The French Canadian and the man of Indian blood each stirred uneasily in his sleep just about this time, though neither of them woke. Then the ghost of that unforgettably strange odour passed away and was lost among the leagues of tenantless forest beyond.

II

In the morning the camp was astir before the sun. There had been a light fall of snow during the night and the air was sharp. Punk had done his duty betimes, for the odours of coffee and fried bacon reached every tent. All were in good spirits.

"Wind's shifted!" cried Hank vigorously, watching Simpson and his guide already loading the small canoe. "It's across the lake—dead right for you fellers. And the snow'll make bully trails! If there's any moose mussing around up thar, they'll not get so much as a tail-end scent of you with the wind as it is. Good luck, Monsieur Défago!" he added, facetiously giving the name its French pronunciation for once, *"bonne chance!"*

Défago returned the good wishes, apparently in the best of spirits, the silent mood gone. Before eight o'clock old Punk had the camp to himself, Cathcart and Hank were far along the trail that led westwards, while the canoe that carried Défago and Simpson, with silk tent and grub for two days, was already a dark speck bobbing on the bosom of the lake, going due east.

The wintry sharpness of the air was tempered now by a sun that topped the wooded ridges and blazed with a luxurious warmth upon the world of lake and forest below; loons flew skimming through the sparkling spray that the wind lifted; divers shook their dripping heads to the sun and popped smartly out of sight again; and as far as eye could reach rose the leagues of endless, crowding

Bush, desolate in its lonely sweep and grandeur, untrodden by foot of man, and stretching its mighty and unbroken carpet right up to the frozen shores of Hudson Bay.

Simpson, who saw it all for the first time as he paddled hard in the bows of the dancing canoe, was enchanted by its austere beauty. His heart drank in the sense of freedom and great spaces just as his lungs drank in the cool and perfumed wind. Behind him in the stern seat, singing fragments of his native chanties, Défago steered the craft of birchbark like a thing of life, answering cheerfully all his companion's questions. Both were gay and light-hearted. On such occasions men lose the superficial, worldly distinctions; they become human beings working together for a common end. Simpson, the employer, and Défago the employed, among these primitive forces, were simply—two men, the "guider" and the "guided." Superior knowledge, of course, assumed control, and the younger man fell without a second thought into the quasi-subordinate position. He never dreamed of objecting when Défago dropped the "Mr.," and addressed him as "Say, Simpson," or "Simpson, boss," which was invariably the case before they reached the farther shore after a stiff paddle of twelve miles against a head wind. He only laughed, and liked it; then ceased to notice it at all.

For this "divinity student" was a young man of parts and character, though as yet, of course, untravelled; and on this trip—the first time he had seen any country but his own and little Switzerland— the huge scale of things somewhat bewildered him. It was one thing, he realised, to hear about primeval forests, but quite another to see them. While to dwell in them and seek acquaintance with their wild life was, again, an initiation that no intelligent man could undergo without a certain shifting of personal values hitherto held for permanent and sacred.

Simpson knew the first faint indication of this emotion when he held the new 303 rifle in his hands and looked along its pair of faultless, gleaming barrels. The three days' journey to their headquarters, by lake and portage, had carried the process a stage farther. And now that he was about to plunge beyond even the fringe of wilderness where they were camped into the virgin heart of uninhabited regions as vast as Europe itself, the true nature of the situation stole upon him with an effect of delight and awe that his imagination was fully capable of appreciating. It was himself and Défago against a multitude—at least, against a Titan!

The bleak splendours of these remote and lonely forests rather overwhelmed him with the sense of his own littleness. That stern quality of the tangled backwoods which can only be described as merciless and terrible, rose out of these far blue woods swimming upon the horizon, and revealed itself. He understood the silent warning. He realised his own utter helplessness. Only Défago, as a symbol of a distant civilisation where man was master, stood between him and a pitiless death by exhaustion and starvation.

It was thrilling to him, therefore, to watch Défago turn over the canoe upon the shore, pack the paddles carefully underneath, and then proceed to "blaze" the spruce stems for some distance on either side of an almost invisible trail, with the careless remark thrown in, "Say, Simpson, if anything happens to me, you'll find the canoe all correc' by these marks;—then strike doo west into the sun to hit the home camp agin, see?"

It was the most natural thing in the world to say, and he said it without any noticeable inflexion of the voice, only it happened to express the youth's emotions at the moment with an utterance that was symbolic of the situation and of his own helplessness as a factor in it. He was alone with Défago in a primitive world: that was all. The canoe, another symbol of man's ascendancy, was now to be left behind. Those small yellow patches, made on the trees by the axe, were the only indications of its hiding-place.

Meanwhile, shouldering the packs between them, each man carrying his own rifle, they followed the slender trail over rocks and fallen trunks and across half-frozen swamps; skirting numerous lakes that fairly gemmed the forest, their borders fringed with mist; and towards five o'clock found themselves suddenly on the edge of the woods, looking out across a large sheet of water in front of them, dotted with pine-clad islands of all describable shapes and sizes.

"Fifty Island Water," announced Défago wearily, "and the sun jest goin' to dip his bald old head into it!" he added, with unconscious poetry; and immediately they set about pitching camp for the night.

In a very few minutes, under those skilful hands that never made a movement too much or a movement too little, the silk tent stood taut and cosy, the beds of balsam boughs ready laid, and a brisk cooking-fire burned with the minimum of smoke. While the young Scotchman cleaned the fish they had caught trolling behind the canoe, Défago "guessed" he would "jest as soon" take a turn through the Bush for indications of moose. "May come across a trunk where they bin and rubbed horns," he said, as he moved off, "or feedin' on the last of the maple leaves,"—and he was gone.

His small figure melted away like a shadow in the dusk, while Simpson noted with a kind of admiration how easily the forest absorbed him into herself. A few steps, it seemed, and he was no longer visible.

Yet there was little underbrush hereabouts; the trees stood somewhat apart, well spaced; and in the clearings grew silver-birch and maple, spear-like and slender, against the immense stems of spruce and hemlock. But for occasional prostrate monsters, and the boulders of grey rock that thrust uncouth shoulders here and there out of the ground, it might well have been a bit of park in the Old Country. Almost, one might have seen in it the hand of man. A little to the right, however, began the great burnt section, miles in extent, proclaiming its real character—*brulé*, as it is called, where the fires of the previous year had raged for weeks, and the blackened stumps now rose gaunt and ugly, bereft of branches, like gigantic match-heads stuck into the ground, savage and desolate beyond words. The perfume of charcoal and rain-soaked ashes still hung faintly about it.

The dusk rapidly deepened; the glades grew dark; the crackling of the fire and the wash of little waves along the rocky lake shore were the only sounds audible. The wind had dropped with the sun, and in all that vast world of branches nothing stirred. Any moment, it seemed, the woodland gods, who are to be worshipped in silence and loneliness, might sketch their mighty and terrific outlines among the trees. In front, through doorways pillared by huge straight stems, lay the stretch of Fifty Island Water, a crescent-shaped lake some fifteen miles from tip to tip, and perhaps five miles across where they were camped. A sky of rose and saffron, more clear than any atmosphere Simpson had ever known, still dropped its pale streaming fires across the waves, where the islands—a hundred, surely, rather than fifty—floated like the fairy barques of some enchanted fleet. Fringed with pines, whose crests fingered most delicately the sky, they almost seemed to move upwards as the light faded—about to weigh anchor and navigate the pathways of the heavens instead of the currents of their native and desolate lake.

And strips of coloured cloud, like flaunting pennons, signalled their departure to the stars...

The beauty of the scene was strangely uplifting. Simpson smoked the fish and burnt his fingers into the bargain in his efforts to enjoy it and at the same time tend the frying-pan and the fire. Yet, ever at the back of his thoughts, lay that other aspect of the wilderness: the indifference to human life, the merciless spirit of desolation which took no note of man. The sense of his utter loneliness, now that even Défago had gone, came close as he looked about him and listened for the sound of his companion's returning footsteps.

There was pleasure in the sensation, yet with it a perfectly comprehensible alarm. And instinctively the thought stirred in him: "What should I—*could* I, do—if anything happened and he did not come back—?"

They enjoyed their well-earned supper, eating untold quantities of fish, and drinking unmilked tea strong enough to kill men who had not covered thirty miles of hard "going," eating little on the way. And when it was over, they smoked and told stories round the blazing fire, laughing, stretching weary limbs, and discussing plans for the morrow. Défago was in excellent spirits, though disappointed at having no signs of moose to report. But it was dark and he had not gone far. The *brulé*, too, was bad. His clothes and hands were smeared with charcoal. Simpson, watching him, realised with renewed vividness their position—alone together in the wilderness.

"Défago," he said presently, "these woods, you know, are a bit too big to feel quite at home in—to feel comfortable in, I mean!... Eh?" He merely gave expression to the mood of the moment; he was hardly prepared for the earnestness, the solemnity even, with which the guide took him up.

"You've hit it right, Simpson, boss," he replied, fixing his searching brown eyes on his face, "and that's the truth, sure. There's no end to 'em—no end at all." Then he added in a lowered tone as if to himself, "There's lots found out *that*, and gone plumb to pieces!"

But the man's gravity of manner was not quite to the other's liking; it was a little too suggestive for this scenery and setting; he was sorry he had broached the subject. He remembered suddenly how his uncle had told him that men were sometimes stricken with a strange fever of the wilderness, when the seduction of the uninhabited wastes caught them so fiercely that they went forth, half fascinated, half deluded, to their death. And he had a shrewd idea that his companion held something in sympathy with that queer type. He led the conversation on to other topics, on to Hank and the doctor, for instance, and the natural rivalry as to who should get the first sight of moose.

"If they went doo west," observed Défago carelessly, "there's sixty miles between us now—with ole Punk at halfway house eatin' himself full to bustin' with fish and corfee." They laughed together over the picture. But the casual mention of those sixty miles again made Simpson realise the prodigious scale of this land where they hunted; sixty miles was a mere step; two hundred little more than a step. Stories of lost hunters rose persistently before his memory. The passion and mystery of homeless and wandering men, seduced by the beauty of great forests, swept his soul in a way too vivid to be quite pleasant. He wondered vaguely whether it was the mood of his companion that invited the unwelcome suggestion with such persistence.

"Sing us a song, Défago, if you're not too tired," he asked; "one of those old *voyageur* songs you sang the other night." He handed his tobacco pouch to the guide and then filled his own pipe, while the Canadian, nothing loth, sent his light voice across the lake in one of those plaintive, almost melancholy chanties with which lumbermen and trappers lessen the burden of their labour. There was an appealing and romantic flavour about it, something that recalled the atmosphere of the old pioneer days when Indians and wilderness were leagued together, battles frequent, and the Old Country farther off than it is to-day. The sound travelled pleasantly over the water, but the forest at their backs seemed to swallow it down with a single gulp that permitted neither echo nor resonance.

It was in the middle of the third verse that Simpson noticed something unusual—something that brought his thoughts back with a rush from far-away scenes. A curious change had come into the man's voice. Even before he knew what it was, uneasiness caught him, and looking up quickly, he saw that Défago, though still singing, was peering about him into the Bush, as though he heard or saw something. His voice grew fainter—dropped to a hush—then ceased altogether. The same instant, with a movement amazingly alert, he started to his feet and stood upright—*sniffing the air*. Like a dog scenting game, he drew the air into his nostrils in short, sharp breaths, turning quickly as he did so in all directions, and finally "pointing" down the lake shore, eastwards. It was a performance unpleasantly suggestive and at the same time singularly dramatic. Simpson's heart fluttered disagreeably as he watched it.

"Lord, man! How you made me jump!" he exclaimed, on his feet beside him the same instant, and peering over his shoulder into the sea of darkness. "What's up? Are you frightened—?"

Even before the question was out of his mouth he knew it was foolish, for any man with a pair of eyes in his head could see that the Canadian had turned white down to his very gills. Not even sunburn and the glare of the fire could hide that.

The student felt himself trembling a little, weakish in the knees. "What's up?" he repeated quickly. "D'you smell moose? Or anything queer, anything—wrong?" He lowered his voice instinctively.

The forest pressed round them with its encircling wall; the nearer tree-stems gleamed like bronze in the firelight; beyond that—blackness, and, so far as he could tell, a silence of death. Just behind them a passing puff of wind lifted a single leaf, looked at it, then laid it softly down again without disturbing the rest of the covey. It seemed as if a million invisible causes had combined just to produce that single visible effect. *Other* life pulsed about them—and was gone.

Défago turned abruptly; the livid hue of his face had turned to a dirty grey.

"I never said I heered—or smelt—nuthin'," he said slowly and emphatically, in an oddly altered voice that conveyed somehow a touch of defiance. "I was only—takin' a look round—so to speak. It's always a mistake to be too previous with yer questions." Then he added suddenly with obvious effort, in his more natural voice, "Have you got the matches, Boss Simpson?" and proceeded to light the pipe he had half filled just before he began to sing.

Without speaking another word they sat down again by the fire, Défago changing his side so that he could face the direction the wind came from. For even a tenderfoot could tell that. Défago changed his position in order to hear and smell—all there was to be heard and smelt. And, since he now faced the lake with his back to the trees it was evidently nothing in the forest that had sent so strange and sudden a warning to his marvellously trained nerves.

"Guess now I don't feel like singing any," he explained presently of his own accord. "That song kinder brings back memories that's troublesome to me; I never oughter've begun it. It sets me on t' imagining things, see?"

Clearly the man was still fighting with some profoundly moving emotion. He wished to excuse himself in the eyes of the other. But the explanation, in that it was only a part of the truth, was a lie, and he knew perfectly well that Simpson was not deceived by it. For nothing could explain away the livid terror that had dropped over his face while he stood there sniffing the air. And nothing—no amount of blazing fire, or chatting on ordinary subjects—could make that camp exactly as it had been before. The shadow of an unknown horror, naked if unguessed, that had flashed for an instant in the face and gestures of the guide, had also communicated itself, vaguely and therefore more potently, to his companion. The guide's visible efforts to dissemble the truth only made things worse. Moreover, to add to the younger man's uneasiness, was the difficulty, nay, the impossibility he felt of asking questions, and also his complete ignorance as to the cause... Indians, wild animals, forest fires—all these, he knew, were wholly out of the question. His imagination searched vigorously, but in vain...

Yet, somehow or other, after another long spell of smoking, talking and roasting themselves before the great fire, the shadow that had so suddenly invaded their peaceful camp began to lift. Perhaps Défago's efforts, or the return of his quiet and normal attitude accomplished this; perhaps Simpson himself had exaggerated the affair out of all proportion to the truth; or possibly the vigorous air of the wilderness brought its own powers of healing. Whatever the cause, the feeling of immediate horror seemed to have passed away as mysteriously as it had come, for nothing occurred to feed it. Simpson began to feel that he had permitted himself the unreasoning terror of a child. He put it down partly to a certain subconscious excitement that this wild and immense scenery generated in his blood, partly to the spell of solitude, and partly to over fatigue. That pallor in the guide's face was, of course, uncommonly hard to explain, yet it *might* have been due in some way to an effect of firelight, or his own imagination... He gave it the benefit of the doubt; he was Scotch.

When a somewhat unordinary emotion has disappeared, the mind always finds a dozen ways of explaining away its causes... Simpson lit a last pipe and tried to laugh to himself. On getting home to Scotland it would make quite a good story. He did not realise that this laughter was a sign that terror still lurked in the recesses of his soul—that, in fact, it was merely one of the conventional signs by which a man, seriously alarmed, tries to persuade himself that he is *not* so.

Défago, however, heard that low laughter and looked up with surprise on his face. The two men stood, side by side, kicking the embers about before going to bed. It was ten o'clock—a late hour for hunters to be still awake.

"What's ticklin' yer?" he asked in his ordinary tone, yet gravely.

"I—I was thinking of our little toy woods at home, just at that moment," stammered Simpson, coming back to what really dominated his mind, and startled by the question, "and comparing them to—to all this," and he swept his arm round to indicate the Bush.

A pause followed in which neither of them said anything.

"All the same I wouldn't laugh about it, if I was you," Défago added, looking over Simpson's shoulder into the shadows. "There's places in there nobody won't never see into—nobody knows what lives in there either."

"Too big—too far off?" The suggestion in the guide's manner was immense and horrible.

Défago nodded. The expression on his face was dark. He, too, felt uneasy. The younger man understood that in a *hinterland* of this size there might well be depths of wood that would never in the life of the world be known or trodden. The thought was not exactly the sort he welcomed. In a loud voice, cheerfully, he suggested that it was time for bed. But the guide lingered, tinkering with the fire, arranging the stones needlessly, doing a dozen things that did not really need doing. Evidently there was something he wanted to say, yet found it difficult to "get at."

"Say, you, Boss Simpson," he began suddenly, as the last shower of sparks went up into the air, "you don't—smell nothing, do you—nothing pertickler, I mean?" The commonplace question, Simpson realised, veiled a dreadfully serious thought in his mind. A shiver ran down his back.

"Nothing but this burning wood," he replied firmly, kicking again at the embers. The sound of his own foot made him start.

"And all the evenin' you ain't smelt—nothing?" persisted the guide, peering at him through the gloom; "nothing extrordiny, and different to anything else you ever smelt before?"

"No, no, man; nothing at all!" he replied aggressively, half angrily.

Défago's face cleared. "That's good!" he exclaimed, with evident relief. "That's good to hear."

"Have *you*?" asked Simpson sharply, and the same instant regretted the question.

The Canadian came closer in the darkness. He shook his head. "I guess not," he said, though without overwhelming conviction. "It must 've been jest that song of mine that did it. It's the song they sing in lumber-camps and god-forsaken places like that, when they're skeered the Wendigo's somewheres around, doin' a bit of swift travellin'—"

"And what's the Wendigo, pray?" Simpson asked quickly, irritated because again he could not prevent that sudden shiver of the nerves. He knew that he was close upon the man's terror and the cause of it. Yet a rushing passionate curiosity overcame his better judgment, *and* his fear.

Défago turned swiftly and looked at him as though he were suddenly about to shriek. His eyes shone, his mouth was wide open. Yet all he said, or whispered rather, for his voice sank very low, was—

"It's nuthin'—nuthin' but what those lousy fellers believe when they've bin hittin' the bottle too long—a sort of great animal that lives up yonder," he jerked his head northwards, "quick as lightning in its tracks, an' bigger'n anything else in the Bush, an' ain't supposed to be very good to look at—*that's all!*"

"A backwoods' superstition—" began Simpson, moving hastily towards the tent in order to shake off the hand of the guide that clutched his arm. "Come, come, hurry up for God's sake, and get the lantern going! It's time we were in bed and asleep if we're to be up with the sun to-morrow…"

The guide was close on his heels. "I'm coming," he answered out of the darkness, "I'm coming." And after a slight delay he appeared with the lantern and hung it from a nail in the front pole of the tent. The shadows of a hundred trees shifted their places quickly as he did so, and when he stumbled over the rope, diving swiftly inside, the whole tent trembled as though a gust of wind struck it.

The two men lay down, without undressing, upon their beds of soft balsam boughs, cunningly arranged. Inside, all was warm and cosy, but outside the world of crowding trees pressed close about them, marshalling their million shadows, and smothering the little tent that stood there like a wee white shell facing the ocean of tremendous forest.

Between the two lonely figures within, however, there pressed another shadow that was *not* a shadow from the night. It was the Shadow cast by the strange Fear, never wholly exorcised, that had leaped suddenly upon Défago in the middle of his singing. And Simpson, as he lay there, watching the darkness through the open flap of the tent, ready to plunge into the fragrant abyss of sleep, knew first that unique and profound stillness of a primeval forest when no wind stirs... and when the night has weight and substance that enters into the soul to bind a veil about it... Then sleep took him...

III

Thus it seemed to him, at least. Yet it was true that the lap of the water, just beyond the tent door, still beat time with his lessening pulses when he realised that he was lying with his eyes open and that another sound had recently introduced itself with cunning softness between the splash and murmur of the little waves.

And, long before he understood what this sound was, it had stirred in him the centres of pity and alarm. He listened intently, though at first in vain, for the running blood beat all its drums too noisily in his ears. Did it come, he wondered, from the lake, or from the woods?...

Then, suddenly, with a rush and a flutter of the heart, he knew that it was close beside him in the tent; and, when he turned over for a better hearing, it focussed itself unmistakably not two feet away. It was a sound of weeping: Défago upon his bed of branches was sobbing in the darkness as though his heart would break, the blankets evidently stuffed against his mouth to stifle it.

And his first feeling, before he could think or reflect, was the rush of a poignant and searching tenderness. This intimate, human sound, heard amid the desolation about them, woke pity. It was so incongruous, so pitifully incongruous—and so vain! Tears—in this vast and cruel wilderness: of what avail? He thought of a little child crying in mid-Atlantic... Then, of course, with fuller realisation, and the memory of what had gone before, came the descent of the terror upon him, and his blood ran cold.

"Défago," he whispered quickly, "what's the matter?" He tried to make his voice very gentle. "Are you in pain—unhappy—?" There was no reply, but the sounds ceased abruptly. He stretched his hand out and touched him. The body did not stir.

"Are you awake?" for it occurred to him that the man was crying in his sleep. "Are you cold?" He noticed that his feet, which were uncovered, projected beyond the mouth of the tent. He spread an extra fold of his own blankets over them. The guide had slipped down in his bed, and the branches seemed to have been dragged with him. He was afraid to pull the body back again, for fear of waking him.

One or two tentative questions he ventured softly, but though he waited for several minutes there came no reply, nor any sign of movement. Presently he heard his regular and quiet breathing, and putting his hand again gently on the breast, felt the steady rise and fall beneath.

"Let me know if anything's wrong," he whispered, "or if I can do anything. Wake me at once if you feel—queer."

He hardly knew quite what to say. He lay down again, thinking and wondering what it all meant. Défago, of course, had been crying in his sleep. Some dream or other had afflicted him. Yet never in his life would he forget that pitiful sound of sobbing, and the feeling that the whole awful wilderness of woods listened...

His own mind busied itself for a long time with the recent events, of which *this* took its mysterious place as one, and though his reason successfully argued away all unwelcome suggestions, a sensation of uneasiness remained, resisting ejection, very deep-seated—peculiar beyond ordinary.

IV

But sleep, in the long run, proves greater than all emotions. His thoughts soon wandered again; he lay there, warm as a toast, exceedingly weary; the night soothed and comforted, blunting the edges of memory and alarm. Half-an-hour later he was oblivious of everything in the outer world about him.

Yet sleep, in this case, was his great enemy, concealing all approaches, smothering the warning of his nerves.

As, sometimes, in a nightmare events crowd upon each others' heels with a conviction of dreadfullest reality, yet some inconsistent detail accuses the whole display of incompleteness and disguise, so the events that now followed, though they actually happened, persuaded the mind somehow that the detail which could explain them had been overlooked in the confusion, and that therefore they were but partly true, the rest delusion. At the back of the sleeper's mind something remains awake, ready to let slip the judgment, "All this is not *quite* real; when you wake up you'll understand."

And thus, in a way, it was with Simpson. The events, not wholly inexplicable or incredible in themselves, yet remain for the man who saw and heard them a sequence of separate acts of cold horror, because the little piece that might have made the puzzle clear lay concealed or overlooked.

So far as he can recall, it was a violent movement, running downwards through the tent towards the door, that first woke him and made him aware that his companion was sitting bolt upright beside him—quivering. Hours must have passed, for it was the pale gleam of the dawn that revealed his outline against the canvas. This time the man was not crying; he was quaking like a leaf; the trembling he felt plainly through the blankets down the entire length of his own body. Défago had huddled down against him for protection, shrinking away from something that apparently concealed itself near the door-flaps of the little tent.

Simpson thereupon called out in a loud voice some question or other—in the first bewilderment of waking he does not remember exactly what—and the man made no reply. The atmosphere and feeling of true nightmare lay horribly about him, making movement and speech both difficult. At first, indeed, he was not sure where he was—whether in one of the earlier camps, or at home in his bed at Aberdeen. The sense of confusion was very troubling.

And next—almost simultaneous with his waking, it seemed—the profound stillness of the dawn outside was shattered by a most uncommon sound. It came without warning, or audible approach; and it was unspeakably dreadful. It was a voice, Simpson declares, possibly a human voice; hoarse yet plaintive—a soft, roaring voice close outside the tent, overhead rather than upon the ground, of immense volume, while in some strange way most penetratingly and seductively sweet. It rang out, too, in three separate and distinct notes, or cries, that bore in some odd fashion a resemblance, far-fetched yet recognisable, to the name of the guide: "Dé—fa—go!"

The student admits he is unable to describe it quite intelligently, for it was unlike any sound he had ever heard in his life, and combined a blending of such contrary qualities. "A sort of windy, crying voice," he calls it, "as of something lonely and untamed, wild and of abominable power..."

And, even before it ceased, dropping back into the great gulfs of silence, the guide beside him had sprung to his feet with an answering though unintelligible cry. He blundered against the tent-pole with violence, shaking the whole structure, spreading his arms out frantically for more room, and kicking his legs impetuously free of the clinging blankets. For a second, perhaps two, he stood upright by the door, his outline dark against the pallor of the dawn; then, with a furious, rushing speed, before his companion could move a hand to stop him, he shot with a plunge through the flaps of canvas—and was gone. And as he went—so astonishingly fast that the voice could actually be heard dying in the distance—he called aloud in tones of anguished terror that at the same time held something strangely like the frenzied exultation of delight—

"Oh! oh! My feet of fire! My burning feet of fire! Oh! oh! This height and fiery speed!"

And then the distance quickly buried it, and the deep silence of very early morning descended upon the forest as before.

It had all come about with such rapidity that, but for the evidence of the empty bed beside him, Simpson could almost have believed it to have been the memory of a nightmare carried over from sleep. He still felt the warm pressure of that vanished body against his side; there lay the twisted blankets in a heap; the very tent yet trembled with the vehemence of the impetuous departure. The strange words rang in his ears, as though he still heard them in the distance—wild language of a suddenly stricken mind. Moreover, it was not only the senses of sight and hearing that reported uncommon things to his brain, for even while the man cried and ran, he had become aware that a strange perfume, faint yet pungent, pervaded the interior of the tent. And it was at this point, it seems, brought to himself by the consciousness that his nostrils were taking this distressing odour down into his throat, that he found his courage, sprang quickly to his feet—and went out.

The grey light of dawn that dropped, cold and glimmering, between the trees revealed the scene tolerably well. There stood the tent behind him, soaked with dew; the dark ashes of the fire, still warm; the lake, white beneath a coating of mist, the islands rising darkly out of it like objects packed in wool; and patches of snow beyond among the clearer spaces of the Bush—everything cold, still, waiting for the sun. But nowhere a sign of the vanished guide—still, doubtless, flying at frantic speed through the frozen woods. There was not even the sound of disappearing footsteps, nor the echoes of the dying voice. He had gone—utterly.

There was nothing; nothing but the sense of his recent presence, so strongly left behind about the camp; and—this penetrating, all-pervading odour.

And even this was now rapidly disappearing in its turn. In spite of his exceeding mental perturbation, Simpson struggled hard to detect its nature, and define it, but the ascertaining of an elusive scent, not recognised subconsciously and at once, is a very subtle operation of the mind. And he failed. It was gone before he could properly seize or name it. Approximate description, even, seems to have been difficult, for it was unlike any smell he knew. Acrid rather, not unlike the odour of a lion, he thinks, yet softer and not wholly unpleasing, with something almost sweet in it that reminded him of the scent of decaying garden leaves, earth, and the myriad, nameless perfumes that make up the odour of a big forest. Yet the "odour of lions" is the phrase with which he usually sums it all up.

Then—it was wholly gone, and he found himself standing by the ashes of the fire in a state of amazement and stupid terror that left him the helpless prey of anything that chose to happen. Had a musk-rat poked its pointed muzzle over a rock, or a squirrel scuttled in that instant down the bark of a tree, he would most likely have collapsed without more ado and fainted. For he felt about the whole affair the touch somewhere of a great Outer Horror... and his scattered powers had not as yet had time to collect themselves into a definite attitude of fighting self-control.

Nothing did happen, however. A great kiss of wind ran softly through the awakening forest, and a few maple leaves here and there rustled tremblingly to earth. The sky seemed to grow suddenly much lighter. Simpson felt the cool air upon his cheek and uncovered head; realised that he was shivering with the cold; and, making a great effort, realised next that he was alone in the Bush—*and* that he was called upon to take immediate steps to find and succour his vanished companion.

Make an effort, accordingly, he did, though an ill-calculated and futile one. With that wilderness of trees about him, the sheet of water cutting him off behind, and the horror of that wild cry in his blood, he did what any other inexperienced man would have done in similar bewilderment: he ran about, without any sense of direction, like a frantic child, and called loudly without ceasing the name of the guide—

"Défago! Défago! Défago!" he yelled, and the trees gave him back the name as often as he shouted, only a little softened—"Défago! Défago! Défago!"

He followed the trail that lay for a short distance across the patches of snow, and then lost it again where the trees grew too thickly for snow to lie. He shouted till he was hoarse, and till the sound of his own voice in all that unanswering and listening world began to frighten him. His confusion increased in direct ratio to the violence of his efforts. His distress became formidably acute, till at length his exertions defeated their own object, and from sheer exhaustion he headed back to the camp again. It remains a wonder that he ever found his way. It was with great difficulty, and only after numberless false clues, that he at last saw the white tent between the trees, and so reached safety.

Exhaustion then applied its own remedy, and he grew calmer. He made the fire and breakfasted. Hot coffee and bacon put a little sense and judgment into him again, and he realised that he had been behaving like a boy. He now made another, and more successful attempt to face the situation collectedly, and, a nature naturally plucky coming to his assistance, he decided that he must first make as thorough a search as possible, failing success in which, he must find his way to the home camp as best he could and bring help.

And this was what he did. Taking food, matches and rifle with him, and a small axe to blaze the trees against his return journey, he set forth. It was eight o'clock when he started, the sun shining over the tops of the trees in a sky without clouds. Pinned to a stake by the fire he left a note in case Défago returned while he was away.

This time, according to a careful plan, he took a new direction, intending to make a wide sweep that must sooner or later cut into indications of the guide's trail; and, before he had gone a quarter of a mile he came across the tracks of a large animal in the snow, and beside it the light and smaller tracks of what were beyond question human feet—the feet of Défago. The relief he at once experienced was natural, though brief; for at first sight he saw in these tracks a simple explanation of the whole matter: these big marks had surely been left by a bull moose that, wind against it, had blundered upon the camp, and uttered its singular cry of warning and alarm the moment its mistake was apparent. Défago, in whom the hunting instinct was developed to the point of uncanny perfection, had scented the brute coming down the wind hours before. His excitement and disappearance were due, of course, to—to his—

Then the impossible explanation at which he grasp faded, as common sense showed him mercilessly that none of this was true. No guide, much less a guide like Défago, could have acted in so irrational a way, going off even without his rifle...! The whole affair demanded a far more complicated elucidation, when he remembered the details of it all—the cry of terror, the amazing language, the grey face of horror when his nostrils first caught the new odour; that muffled sobbing in the darkness, and—for this, too, now came back to him dimly—the man's original aversion for this particular bit of country...

Besides, now that he examined them closer, these were not the tracks of a moose at all! Hank had explained to him the outline of a bull's hoofs, of a cow's or calf's, too, for that matter; he had drawn them clearly on a strip of birch bark. And these were wholly different. They were big, round, ample, and with no pointed outline as of sharp hoofs. He wondered for a moment whether bear-tracks were like that. There was no other animal he could think of, for caribou did not come so far south at this season, and, even if they did, would leave hoof-marks.

They were ominous signs—these mysterious writings left in the snow by the unknown creature that had lured a human being away from safety—and when he coupled them in his imagination with that haunting sound that broke the stillness of the dawn, a momentary dizziness shook his mind, distressing him again beyond belief. He felt the *threatening* aspect of it all. And, stooping down to examine the marks more closely, he caught a faint whiff of that sweet yet pungent odour that made him instantly straighten up again, fighting a sensation almost of nausea.

Then his memory played him another evil trick. He suddenly recalled those uncovered feet projecting beyond the edge of the tent, and the body's appearance of having been dragged towards the opening; the man's shrinking from something by the door when he woke later. The details now beat against his trembling mind with concerted attack. They seemed to gather in those deep spaces of the silent forest about him, where the host of trees stood waiting, listening, watching to see what he would do. The woods were closing round him.

With the persistence of true pluck, however, Simpson went forward, following the tracks as best he could, smothering these ugly emotions that sought to weaken his will. He blazed innumerable trees as he went, ever fearful of being unable to find the way back, and calling aloud at intervals of a few seconds the name of the guide. The dull tapping of the axe upon the massive trunks, and the unnatural accents of his own voice became at length sounds that he even dreaded to make, dreaded to hear. For they drew attention without ceasing to his presence and exact whereabouts, and if it were really the case that something was hunting himself down in the same way that he was hunting down another—

With a strong effort, he crushed the thought out the instant it rose. It was the beginning, he realised, of a bewilderment utterly diabolical in kind that would speedily destroy him.

*

Although the snow was not continuous, lying merely in shallow flur-
ries over the more open spaces, he found no difficulty in following
the tracks for the first few miles. They went straight as a ruled line
wherever the trees permitted. The stride soon began to increase in
length, till it finally assumed proportions that seemed absolutely
impossible for any ordinary animal to have made. Like huge flying
leaps they became. One of these he measured, and though he knew
that "stretch" of eighteen feet must be somehow wrong, he was at
a complete loss to understand why he found no signs on the snow
between the extreme points. But what perplexed him even more,
making him feel his vision had gone utterly awry, was that Défago's
stride increased in the same manner, and finally covered the same
incredible distances. It looked as if the great beast had lifted him
with it and carried him across these astonishing intervals. Simpson,
who was much longer in the limb, found that he could not compass
even half the stretch by taking a running jump.

And the sight of these huge tracks, running side by side, silent
evidence of a dreadful journey in which terror or madness had
urged to impossible results, was profoundly moving. It shocked him
in the secret depths of his soul. It was the most horrible thing his
eyes had ever looked upon. He began to follow them mechanically,
absent-mindedly almost, ever peering over his shoulder to see if
he, too, were being followed by something with a gigantic tread...
And soon it came about that he no longer quite realised what it was
they signified—these impressions left upon the snow by something
nameless and untamed, always accompanied by the footmarks of
the little French Canadian, his guide, his comrade, the man who
had shared his tent a few hours before, chatting, laughing, even
singing by his side...

V

For a man of his years and inexperience, only a canny Scot, perhaps, grounded in common sense and established in logic, could have preserved even that measure of balance that this youth somehow or other did manage to preserve through the whole adventure. Otherwise, two things he presently noticed, while forging pluckily ahead, must have sent him headlong back to the comparative safety of his tent, instead of only making his hands close more tightly upon the rifle-stock, while his heart, trained for the Wee Kirk, sent a wordless prayer winging its way to heaven. Both tracks, he saw, had undergone a change, and this change, so far as it concerned the foot-steps of the man, was in some undecipherable manner—appalling.

It was in the bigger tracks he first noticed this, and for a long time he could not quite believe his eyes. Was it the blown leaves that produced odd effects of light and shade, or that the dry snow, drift-ing like finely-ground rice about the edges, cast shadows and high lights? Or was it actually the fact that the great marks had become faintly coloured? For round about the deep, plunging holes of the animal there now appeared a mysterious, reddish tinge that was more like an effect of light than of anything that dyed the substance of the snow itself. Every mark had it, and had it increasingly—this indistinct fiery tinge that painted a new touch of ghastliness into the picture.

But when, wholly unable to explain or credit it, he turned his attention to the other tracks to discover if they, too, bore similar witness, he noticed that these had meanwhile undergone a change that was infinitely worse, and charged with far more horrible sugges-tion. For, in the last hundred yards or so, he saw that they had grown gradually into the semblance of the parent tread. Imperceptibly the change had come about, yet unmistakably. It was hard to see where the change first began. The result, however, was beyond question. Smaller, neater, more cleanly modelled, they formed now an exact and careful duplicate of the larger tracks beside them. The feet that produced them had, therefore, also changed. And something in his mind reared up with loathing and with terror as he saw it.

Simpson, for the first time, hesitated; then, ashamed of his alarm and indecision, took a few hurried steps ahead; the next instant stopped dead in his tracks. Immediately in front of him all signs of the trail ceased; both tracks came to an abrupt end. On all sides, for a hundred yards and more, he searched in vain for the least indication of their continuance. There was—nothing.

The trees were very thick just there, big trees all of them, spruce, cedar, hemlock; there was no underbrush. He stood, looking about him, all distraught; bereft of any power of judgment. Then he set to work to search again, and again, and yet again, but always with the same result: *nothing*. The feet that printed the surface of the snow thus far had now, apparently, left the ground!

And it was in that moment of distress and confusion that the whip of terror laid its most nicely calculated lash about his heart. It dropped with deadly effect upon the sorest spot of all, completely unnerving him. He had been secretly dreading all the time that it would come—and come it did.

Far overhead, muted by great height and distance, strangely thinned and wailing, he heard the crying voice of Défago, the guide.

The sound dropped upon him out of that still, wintry sky with an effect of dismay and terror unsurpassed. The rifle fell to his feet. He stood motionless an instant, listening as it were with his whole body, then staggered back against the nearest tree for support, disorganised hopelessly in mind and spirit. To him, in that moment, it seemed the most shattering and dislocating experience he had ever known, so that his heart emptied itself of all feeling whatsoever as by a sudden draught.

"Oh! oh! This fiery height! Oh, my feet of fire! My burning feet of fire…!" ran in far, beseeching accents of indescribable appeal this voice of anguish down the sky. Once it called—then silence through all the listening wilderness of trees.

And Simpson, scarcely knowing what he did, presently found himself running wildly to and fro, searching, calling, tripping over roots and boulders, and flinging himself in a frenzy of undirected pursuit after the Caller. Behind the screen of memory and emotion with which experience veils events, he plunged, distracted and half-deranged, picking up false lights like a ship at sea, terror in his eyes and heart and soul. For the Panic of the Wilderness had called to him in that far voice—the Power of untamed Distance— the Enticement of the Desolation that destroys. He knew in that moment all the pains of some one hopelessly and irretrievably lost, suffering the lust and travail of a soul in the final Loneliness. A vision of Défago, eternally hunted, driven and pursued across the skiey vastness of those ancient forests, fled like a flame across the dark ruin of his thoughts…

It seemed ages before he could find anything in the chaos of his disorganised sensations to which he could anchor himself steady for a moment, and think…

The cry was not repeated; his own hoarse calling brought no response; the inscrutable forces of the Wild had summoned their victim beyond recall—and held him fast.

Yet he searched and called, it seems, for hours afterwards, for it was late in the afternoon when at length he decided to abandon a useless pursuit and return to his camp on the shores of Fifty Island Water. Even then he went with reluctance, that crying voice still echoing in his ears. With difficulty he found his rifle and the homeward trail. The concentration necessary to follow the badly blazed trees, and a biting hunger that gnawed, helped to keep his mind steady. Otherwise, he admits, the temporary aberration he had suffered might have been prolonged to the point of positive disaster. Gradually the ballast shifted back again, and he regained something that approached his normal equilibrium.

But for all that the journey through the gathering dusk was miserably haunted. He heard innumerable following footsteps; voices that laughed and whispered; and saw figures crouching behind trees and boulders, making signs to one another for a concerted attack the moment he had passed. The creeping murmur of the wind made him start and listen. He went stealthily, trying to hide where possible, and making as little sound as he could. The shadows of the woods, hitherto protective or covering merely, had now become menacing, challenging; and the pageantry in his frightened mind masked a host of possibilities that were all the more ominous for being obscure. The presentiment of a nameless doom lurked ill-concealed behind every detail of what had happened.

It was really admirable how he emerged victor in the end; men of riper powers and experience might have come through the ordeal with less success. He had himself tolerably well in hand, all things considered, and his plan of action proves it. Sleep being absolutely out of the question, and travelling an unknown trail in the darkness equally impracticable, he sat up the whole of that night, rifle in hand, before a fire he never for a single moment allowed to die down. The severity of the haunted vigil marked his soul for life; but it was successfully accomplished; and with the very first signs of dawn he set forth upon the long return journey to the home-camp to get help. As before, he left a written note to explain his absence, and to indicate where he had left a plentiful *cache* of food and matches—though he had no expectation that any human hands would find them!

How Simpson found his way alone by lake and forest might well make a story in itself, for to hear him tell it is to *know* the passionate loneliness of soul that a man can feel when the Wilderness holds him in the hollow of its illimitable hand—and laughs. It is also to admire his indomitable pluck.

He claims no skill, declaring that he followed the almost invisible trail mechanically, and without thinking. And this, doubtless, is the truth. He relied upon the guiding of the unconscious mind, which is instinct. Perhaps, too, some sense of orientation, known to animals and primitive men, may have helped as well, for through all that tangled region he succeeded in reaching the exact spot where Défago had hidden the canoe nearly three days before with the remark, "Strike doo west across the lake into the sun to find the camp."

There was not much sun left to guide him, but he used his compass to the best of his ability, embarking in the frail craft for the last twelve miles of his journey with a sensation of immense relief that the forest was at last behind him. And, fortunately, the water was calm; he took his line across the centre of the lake instead of coasting round the shores for another twenty miles. Fortunately, too, the other hunters were back. The light of their fires furnished a steering-point without which he might have searched all night long for the actual position of the camp.

It was close upon midnight all the same when his canoe grated on the sandy cove, and Hank, Punk and his uncle, disturbed in their sleep by his cries, ran quickly down and helped a very exhausted

and broken specimen of Scotch humanity over the rocks towards
a dying fire.

VI

The sudden entrance of his prosaic uncle into this world of wiz-
ardry and horror that had haunted him without interruption now
for two days and two nights, had the immediate effect of giving to
the affair an entirely new aspect. The sound of that crisp "Hulloa,
my boy! And what's up *now*?" and the grasp of that dry and vigorous hand introduced another standard of judgment. A revulsion of
feeling washed through him. He realised that he had let himself
"go" rather badly. He even felt vaguely ashamed of himself. The
native hard-headedness of his race reclaimed him.

And this doubtless explains why he found it so hard to tell that
group round the fire—everything. He told enough, however, for the
immediate decision to be arrived at that a relief party must start at
the earliest possible moment, and that Simpson, in order to guide
it capably, must first have food and, above all, sleep. Dr. Cathcart
observing the lad's condition more shrewdly than his patient knew,
gave him a very slight injection of morphine. For six hours he slept
like the dead.

From the description carefully written out afterwards by this
student of divinity, it appears that the account he gave to the aston-
ished group omitted sundry vital and important details. He declares
that, with his uncle's wholesome, matter-of-fact countenance staring
him in the face, he simply had not the courage to mention them.
Thus, all the search-party gathered, it would seem, was that Défago
had suffered in the night an acute and inexplicable attack of mania,

had imagined himself "called" by some one or something, and had plunged into the Bush after it without food or rifle, where he must die a horrible and lingering death by cold and starvation unless he could be found and rescued in time. "In time," moreover, meant "at once."

In the course of the following day, however—they were off by seven, leaving Punk in charge with instructions to have food and fire always ready—Simpson found it possible to tell his uncle a good deal more of the story's true inwardness, without divining that it was drawn out of him as a matter of fact by a very subtle form of cross-examination. By the time they reached the beginning of the trail, where the canoe was laid up against the return journey, he had mentioned how Défago spoke vaguely of "something he called a 'Wendigo'"; how he cried in his sleep; how he imagined an unusual scent about the camp; and had betrayed other symptoms of mental excitement. He also admitted the bewildering effect of "that extraordinary odour" upon himself, "pungent and acrid like the odour of lions." And by the time they were within an easy hour of Fifty Island Water he had let slip the further fact—a foolish avowal of his own hysterical condition, as he felt afterwards—that he had heard the vanished guide call "for help." He omitted the singular phrases used, for he simply could not bring himself to repeat the preposterous language. Also, while describing how the man's footsteps in the snow had gradually assumed an exact miniature likeness of the animal's plunging tracks, he left out the fact that they measured a *wholly* incredible distance. It seemed a question, nicely balanced between individual pride and honesty, what he should reveal and what suppress. He mentioned the fiery tinge in the snow, for instance, yet shrank from telling that body and bed had been partly dragged out of the tent...

With the net result that Dr. Cathcart, adroit psychologist that he fancied himself to be, had assured him clearly enough exactly where his mind, influenced by loneliness, bewilderment and terror, had yielded to the strain and invited delusion. While praising his conduct, he managed at the same time to point out where, when, and how his mind had gone astray. He made his nephew think himself finer than he was by judicious praise, yet more foolish than he was by minimising the value of his evidence. Like many another materialist, that is, he lied cleverly on the basis of insufficient knowledge, *because* the knowledge supplied seemed to his own particular intelligence inadmissible.

"The spell of these terrible solitudes," he said, "cannot leave any mind untouched, any mind, that is, possessed of the higher imaginative qualities. It has worked upon yours exactly as it worked upon my own when I was your age. The animal that haunted your little camp was undoubtedly a moose, for the 'belling' of a moose may have, sometimes, a very peculiar quality of sound. The coloured appearance of the big tracks was obviously a defect of vision in your own eyes produced by excitement. The size and stretch of the tracks we shall prove when we come to them. But the hallucination of an audible voice, of course, is one of the commonest forms of delusion due to mental excitement—an excitement, my dear boy, perfectly excusable, and, let me add, wonderfully controlled by you under the circumstances. For the rest, I am bound to say, you have acted with a splendid courage, for the terror of feeling oneself lost in this wilderness is nothing short of awful, and, had I been in your place, I don't for a moment believe I could have behaved with one quarter of your wisdom and decision. The only thing I find it uncommonly difficult to explain is—that—damned odour."

"It made me feel sick, I assure you," declared his nephew, "positively dizzy!" His uncle's attitude of calm omniscience, merely because he knew more psychological formulæ, made him slightly defiant. It was so easy to be wise in the explanation of an experience one has not personally witnessed. "A kind of desolate and terrible odour is the only way I can describe it," he concluded, glancing at the features of the quiet, unemotional man beside him.

"I can only marvel," was the reply, "that under the circumstances it did not seem to you even worse." The dry words, Simpson knew, hovered between the truth, and his uncle's interpretation of "the truth."

And so at last they came to the little camp and found the tent still standing, the remains of the fire, and the piece of paper pinned to a stake beside it—untouched. The *cache*, poorly contrived by inexperienced hands, however, had been discovered and opened—by musk rats, mink and squirrel. The matches lay scattered about the opening, but the food had been taken to the last crumb.

"Well, fellers, he ain't here," exclaimed Hank loudly after his fashion, "and that's as sartain as the coal supply down below! But whar he's got to by this time is 'bout as onsartain as the trade in crowns in t'other place." The presence of a divinity student was no barrier to his language at such a time, though for the reader's sake it may be severely edited. "I propose," he added, "that we start out at once an' hunt for'm like hell!"

The gloom of Défago's probable fate oppressed the whole party with a sense of dreadful gravity the moment they saw the familiar signs of recent occupancy. Especially the tent, with the bed of balsam branches still smoothed and flattened by the pressure of his body, seemed to bring his presence near to them. Simpson, feeling vaguely as if his word were somehow at stake, went about explaining particulars in a hushed tone. He was much calmer now, though overwearied with the strain of his many journeys. His uncle's method of explaining—"explaining away," rather—the details still fresh in his haunted memory helped, too, to put ice upon his emotions.

"And that's the direction he ran off in," he said to his two companions, pointing in the direction where the guide had vanished that morning in the grey dawn. "Straight down there he ran like a deer, in between the birch and the hemlock…"

Hank and Dr. Cathcart exchanged glances.

"And it was about two miles down there, in a straight line," continued the other, speaking with something of the former terror in his voice, "that I followed his trail to the place where—it stopped—dead!"

"And where you heered him callin' an' caught the stench, an' all the rest of the wicked entertainment," cried Hank, with a volubility that betrayed his keen distress.

"And where your excitement overcame you to the point of producing illusions," added Dr. Cathcart under his breath, yet not so low that his nephew did not hear it.

It was early in the afternoon, for they had travelled quickly, and there were still a good two hours of daylight left. Dr. Cathcart and Hank lost no time in beginning the search, but Simpson was too exhausted to accompany them. They would follow the blazed marks on the trees, and where possible, his footsteps. Meanwhile the best thing he could do was to keep a good fire going, and rest.

But after something like three hours' search, the darkness already down, the two men returned to camp with nothing to report. Fresh snow had covered all signs, and though they had followed the blazed trees to the spot where Simpson had turned back, they had not discovered the smallest indications of a human being—or, for that matter, of an animal. There were no fresh tracks of any kind; the snow lay undisturbed.

It was difficult to know what was best to do, though in reality there was nothing more they *could* do. They might stay and search for weeks without much chance of success. The fresh snow destroyed their only hope, and they gathered round the fire for supper, a gloomy and despondent party. The facts, indeed, were sad enough, for Défago had a wife at Rat Portage, and his earnings were the family's sole means of support.

Now that the whole truth in all its ugliness was out, it seemed useless to deal in further disguise or pretence. They talked openly of the facts and probabilities. It was not the first time, even in the experience of Dr. Cathcart, that a man had yielded to the singular seduction of the Solitudes and gone out of his mind; Défago, moreover, was predisposed to something of the sort, for he already had the touch of melancholia in his blood, and his fibre was weakened by bouts of drinking that often lasted for weeks at a time. Something on this trip—one might never know precisely what—had sufficed to push him over the line, that was all. And he had gone, gone off into the great wilderness of trees and lakes to die by starvation and exhaustion. The chances against his finding camp again were overwhelming; the delirium that was upon him would also doubtless have increased, and it was quite likely he might do violence to himself and so hasten his cruel fate. Even while they talked, indeed, the end had probably come. On the suggestion of Hank, his old pal, however, they proposed to wait a little longer and devote the whole of the following day, from dawn to darkness, to the most

systematic search they could devise. They would divide the territory between them. They discussed their plan in great detail. All
that men could do they would do.

    And, meanwhile, they talked about the particular form in which
the singular Panic of the Wilderness had made its attack upon
the mind of the unfortunate guide. Hank, though familiar with
the legend in its general outline, obviously did not welcome the
turn the conversation had taken. He contributed little, though
that little was illuminating. For he admitted that a story ran over
all this section of country to the effect that several Indians had
"seen the Wendigo" along the shores of Fifty Island Water in the
"fall" of last year, and that this was the true reason of Défago's
disinclination to hunt there. Hank doubtless felt that he had in a
sense helped his old pal to death by over-persuading him. "When
an Indian goes crazy," he explained, talking to himself more
than to the others, it seemed, "it's always put that he's 'seen the
Wendigo.' An' pore old Défaygo was superstitious down to his
very heels…!"

    And then Simpson, feeling the atmosphere more sympathetic,
told over again the full story of his astonishing tale; he left out no
details this time; he mentioned his own sensations and gripping
fears. He only omitted the strange language used.

    "But Défago surely had already told you all these details of the
Wendigo legend, my dear fellow," insisted the doctor. "I mean, he
had talked about it, and thus put into your mind the ideas which
your own excitement afterwards developed?"

    Whereupon Simpson again repeated the facts. Défago, he
declared, had barely mentioned the beast. He, Simpson, knew
nothing of the story, and, so far as he remembered, had never even
read about it. Even the word was unfamiliar.

Of course he was telling the truth, and Dr. Cathcart was reluctantly compelled to admit the singular character of the whole affair. He did not do this in words so much as in manner, however. He kept his back against a good, stout tree; he poked the fire into a blaze the moment it showed signs of dying down; he was quicker than any of them to notice the least sound in the night about them—a fish jumping in the lake, a twig snapping in the Bush, the dropping of occasional fragments of frozen snow from the branches overhead where the heat loosened them. His voice, too, changed a little in quality, becoming a shade less confident, lower also in tone. Fear, to put it plainly, hovered close about that little camp, and though all three would have been glad to speak of other matters, the only thing they seemed able to discuss was this—the source of their fear. They tried other subjects in vain; there was nothing to say about them. Hank was the most honest of the group; he said next to nothing. He never once, however, turned his back to the darkness. His face was always to the forest, and when wood was needed he didn't go farther than was necessary to get it.

VII

A wall of silence wrapped them in, for the snow, though not thick, was sufficient to deaden any noise, and the frost held things pretty tight besides. No sound but their voices and the soft roar of the flames made itself heard. Only, from time to time, something soft as the flutter of a pine-moth's wings went past them through the air. No one seemed anxious to go to bed. The hours slipped towards midnight.

"The legend is picturesque enough," observed the doctor after one of the longer pauses, speaking to break it rather than because he had anything to say, "for the Wendigo is simply the Call of the Wild personified, which some natures hear to their own destruction."

"That's about it," Hank said presently. "An' there's no misunderstandin' when you hear it. It calls you by name right 'nough."

Another pause followed. Then Dr. Cathcart came back to the forbidden subject with a rush that made the others jump.

"The allegory *is* significant," he remarked, looking about him into the darkness, "for the Voice, they say, resembles all the minor sounds of the Bush—wind, falling water, cries of animals, and so forth. And, once the victim hears *that*—he's off for good, of course! His most vulnerable points, moreover, are said to be the feet and the eyes; the feet, you see, for the lust of wandering, and the eyes for the lust of beauty. The poor beggar goes at such a dreadful speed that he bleeds beneath the eyes, and his feet burn."

Dr. Cathcart, as he spoke, continued to peer uneasily into the surrounding gloom. His voice sank to a hushed tone.

"The Wendigo," he added, "is said to burn his feet—owing to the friction, apparently caused by its tremendous velocity—till they drop off, and new ones form exactly like its own."

Simpson listened in horrified amazement; but it was the pallor on Hank's face that fascinated him most. He would willingly have stopped his ears and closed his eyes, had he dared.

"It don't always keep to the ground neither," came in Hank's slow, heavy drawl, "for it goes so high that he thinks the stars have set him all a-fire. An' it'll take great thumpin' jumps sometimes, an' run along the tops of the trees, carrying its partner with it, an' then droppin' him jest as a fish-hawk 'll drop a pickerel to kill it before eatin'. An' its food, of all the muck in the whole Bush is—moss!" And he laughed a short, unnatural laugh. "It's a moss-eater, is the Wendigo," he added, looking up excitedly into the faces of his companions, "moss-eater," he repeated, with a string of the most outlandish oaths he could invent.

But Simpson now understood the true purpose of all this talk. What these two men, each strong and "experienced" in his own way, dreaded more than anything else was—silence. They were talking against time. They were also talking against darkness, against the invasion of panic, against the admission reflection might bring that they were in an enemy's country—against anything, in fact, rather than allow their inmost thoughts to assume control. He himself, already initiated by the awful vigil with terror, was beyond both of them in this respect. He had reached the stage where he was immune. But these two, the scoffing, analytical doctor, and the honest, dogged backwoodsman, each sat trembling in the depths of his being.

Thus the hours passed; and thus, with lowered voices and a kind of taut inner resistance of spirit, this little group of humanity sat in the jaws of the wilderness and talked foolishly of the terrible and haunting legend. It was an unequal contest, all things considered, for the wilderness had already the advantage of first attack—and of a hostage. The fate of their comrade hung over them with a steadily increasing weight of oppression that finally became insupportable.

It was Hank, after a pause longer than the preceding ones that no one seemed able to break, who first let loose all this pent-up emotion in very unexpected fashion, by springing suddenly to his feet and letting out the most ear-shattering yell imaginable into the night. He could not contain himself any longer, it seemed. To make it carry even beyond an ordinary cry he interrupted its rhythm by shaking the palm of his hand before his mouth.

"That's for Défago," he said, looking down at the other two with a queer, defiant laugh, "for it's my belief"—the sandwiched oaths may be omitted—"that my ole partner's not far from us at this very minute."

There was a vehemence and recklessness about his performance that made Simpson, too, start to his feet in amazement, and betrayed even the doctor into letting the pipe slip from between his lips. Hank's face was ghastly, but Cathcart's showed a sudden weakness— a loosening of all his faculties, as it were. Then a momentary anger blazed into his eyes, and he too, though with deliberation born of habitual self-control, got upon his feet and faced the excited guide. For this was unpermissible, foolish, dangerous, and he meant to stop it in the bud.

What might have happened in the next minute or two one may speculate about, yet never definitely know, for in the instant of profound silence that followed Hank's roaring voice, and as though in answer to it, something went past through the darkness of the sky overhead at terrific speed—something of necessity very large, for it displaced much air, while down between the trees there fell a faint and windy cry of a human voice, calling in tones of indescribable anguish and appeal—

"Oh, oh! this fiery height! Oh, oh! My feet of fire! My burning feet of fire!"

White to the very edge of his shirt, Hank looked stupidly about him like a child. Dr. Cathcart uttered some kind of unintelligible cry, turning as he did so with an instinctive movement of blind terror towards the protection of the tent, then halting in the act as though frozen. Simpson, alone of the three, retained his presence of mind a little. His own horror was too deep to allow of any immediate reaction. He had heard that cry before.

Turning to his stricken companions, he said almost calmly—

"That's exactly the cry I heard—the very words he used!"

Then, lifting his face to the sky, he cried aloud, "Défago, Défago! Come down here to us! Come down—!"

And before there was time for anybody to take definite action one way or another, there came the sound of something dropping heavily between the trees, striking the branches on the way down, and landing with a dreadful thud upon the frozen earth below. The crash and thunder of it was really terrific.

"That's him, s'help me the good Gawd!" came from Hank in a whispering cry half choked, his hand going automatically towards the hunting-knife in his belt. "And he's coming! He's coming!" he added, with an irrational laugh of terror, as the sounds of heavy footsteps crunching over the snow became distinctly audible, approaching through the blackness towards the circle of light.

And while the steps, with their stumbling motion, moved nearer and nearer upon them, the three men stood round that fire, motionless and dumb. Dr. Cathcart had the appearance as of a man suddenly withered; even his eyes did not move. Hank, suffering shockingly, seemed on the verge again of violent action; yet did nothing. He, too, was hewn of stone. Like stricken children they seemed. The picture was hideous. And, meanwhile, their owner still invisible, the footsteps came closer, crunching the frozen snow. It was endless—too prolonged to be quite real—this measured and pitiless approach. It was accursed.

VIII

Then at length the darkness, having this laboriously conceived, brought forth—a figure. It drew forward into the zone of uncertain light where fire and shadows mingled, not ten feet away; then halted, staring at them fixedly. The same instant it started forward again with the spasmodic motion as of a thing moved by wires, and coming up closer to them, full into the glare of the fire, they perceived then that—it was a man; and apparently that this man was—Défago.

Something like a skin of horror almost perceptibly drew down in that moment over every face, and three pairs of eyes shone through it as though they saw across the frontiers of normal vision into the Unknown.

Défago advanced, his tread faltering and uncertain; he made his way straight up to them as a group first, then turned sharply and peered close into the face of Simpson. The sound of a voice issued from his lips—

"Here I am, Boss Simpson. I heered some one calling me." It was a faint, dried-up voice, made wheezy and breathless as by immense exertion. "I'm havin' a reg'lar hell-fire kind of a trip, I am." And he laughed, thrusting his head forward into the other's face.

But that laugh started the machinery of the group of wax-work figures with the wax-white skins. Hank immediately sprang forward with a stream of oaths so far-fetched that Simpson did not recognise them as English at all, but thought he had lapsed into Indian or some other lingo. He only realised that Hank's presence, thrust thus between them, was welcome—uncommonly welcome. Dr. Cathcart, though more calmly and leisurely, advanced behind him, heavily stumbling.

Simpson seems hazy as to what was actually said and done in those next few seconds, for the eyes of that detestable and blasted visage peering at such close quarters into his own utterly bewildered his senses at first. He merely stood still. He said nothing. He had not the trained will of the older men that forced them into action in defiance of all emotional stress. He watched them moving as behind a glass, that half destroyed their reality: it was dream-like, perverted. Yet, through the torrent of Hank's meaningless phrases, he remembers hearing his uncle's tone of authority—hard and forced—saying several things about food and warmth, blankets, whisky and the rest;… and, further, that whiffs of that penetrating, unaccustomed odour, vile, yet sweetly bewildering, assailed his nostrils during all that followed.

It was no less a person than himself, however—less experienced and adroit than the others though he was—who gave instinctive utterance to the sentence that brought a measure of relief into the ghastly situation by expressing the doubt and thought in each one's heart.

"It *is*—YOU, isn't it, Défago?" he asked under his breath, horror breaking his speech.

And at once Cathcart burst out with the loud answer before the other had time to move his lips. "Of course it is! Of course it is! Only—can't you see—he's nearly dead with exhaustion, cold and terror? Isn't *that* enough to change a man beyond all recognition?" It was said in order to convince himself as much as to convince the others. The overemphasis alone proved that. And continually, while he spoke and acted, he held a handkerchief to his nose. That odour pervaded the whole camp.

For the "Défago" who sat huddled by the big fire, wrapped in blankets, drinking hot whisky and holding food in wasted hands, was no more like the guide they had last seen alive than the picture of a man of sixty is like the daguerreotype of his early youth in the costume of another generation. Nothing really can describe that ghastly caricature, that parody, masquerading there in the firelight as Défago. From the ruins of the dark and awful memories he still retains, Simpson declares that the face was more animal than human, the features drawn about into wrong proportions, the skin loose and hanging, as though he had been subjected to extraordinary pressures and tensions. It made him think vaguely of those bladder-faces blown up by the hawkers on Ludgate Hill, that change their expression as they swell, and as they collapse emit a faint and wailing imitation of a voice. Both face and voice suggested some such abominable resemblance. But Cathcart long afterwards, seeking to describe the indescribable, asserts that thus might have looked a face and body that had been in air so rarefied that, the weight of atmosphere being removed, the entire structure threatened to fly asunder and become—*incoherent*...

It was Hank, though all distraught and shaking with a tear-ing volume of emotion he could neither handle nor understand, who brought things to a head without more ado. He went off to a little distance from the fire, apparently so that the light should not dazzle him too much, and shading his eyes for a moment with both hands, shouted in a loud voice that held anger and affection dreadfully mingled—

"You ain't Défaygo! You ain't Défago at all! I don't give a—damn, but that ain't you, my ole pal of twenty years!" He glared upon the huddled figure as though he would destroy him with his eyes. "An' if it is I'll swab the floor of hell with a wad of cotton-wool on a toothpick, s'help me the good Gawd!" he added, with a violent fling of horror and disgust.

It was impossible to silence him. He stood there shouting like one possessed, horrible to see, horrible to hear—*because it was the truth*. He repeated himself in fifty different ways, each more outlandish than the last. The woods rang with echoes. At one time it looked as if he meant to fling himself upon "the intruder," for his hand continually jerked towards the long hunting-knife in his belt.

But in the end he did nothing, and the whole tempest completed itself very nearly with tears. Hank's voice suddenly broke, he collapsed on the ground, and Cathcart somehow or other persuaded him at last to go into the tent and lie quiet. The remainder of the affair, indeed, was witnessed by him from behind the canvas, his white and terrified face peeping through the crack of the tent door-flap.

Then Dr. Cathcart, closely followed by his nephew who so far had kept his courage better than all of them, went up with a determined air and stood opposite to the figure of Défago huddled over the fire. He looked him squarely in the face and spoke. At first his voice was firm.

"Défago, tell us what's happened—just a little, so that we can know how best to help you?" he asked in a tone of authority, almost of command. And at that point, it *was* command. At once afterwards, however, it changed in quality, for the figure turned up to him a face so piteous, so terrible and so little like humanity, that the doctor shrank back from him as from something spiritually unclean. Simpson, watching close behind him, says he got the impression of a mask that was on the verge of dropping off, and that underneath they would discover something black and diabolical, revealed in utter nakedness. "Out with it, man, out with it!" Cathcart cried, terror running neck and neck with entreaty. "None of us can stand this much longer...!" It was the cry of instinct over reason.

And then "Défago," smiling *whitely*, answered in that thin and fading voice that already seemed passing over into a sound of quite another character—

"I seen that great Wendigo thing," he whispered, sniffing the air about him exactly like an animal. "I been with it too—"

Whether the poor devil would have said more, or whether Dr. Cathcart would have continued the impossible cross-examination cannot be known, for at that moment the voice of Hank was heard yelling at the top of his shout from behind the canvas that concealed all but his terrified eyes. Such a howling was never heard.

"His feet! Oh, Gawd, his feet! Look at his great changed—feet!"

Défago, shuffling where he sat, had moved in such a way that for the first time his legs were in full light and his feet were visible. Yet Simpson had no time, himself, to see properly what Hank had seen. And Hank has never seen fit to tell. That same instant, with a leap like that of a frightened tiger, Cathcart was upon him, bundling the folds of blanket about his legs with such speed that the young student caught little more than a passing glimpse of something dark and oddly massed where moccasined feet ought to have been, and saw even that but with uncertain vision.

Then, before the doctor had time to do more, or Simpson time to even think a question, much less ask it, Défago was standing upright in front of them, balancing with pain and difficulty, and upon his shapeless and twisted visage an expression so dark and so malicious that it was, in the true sense, monstrous.

"Now *you* seen it too," he wheezed, "you seen my fiery, burning feet! And now—that is, unless you kin save me an' prevent—it's 'bout time for—"

His piteous and beseeching voice was interrupted by a sound that was like the roar of wind coming across the lake. The trees overhead shook their tangled branches. The blazing fire bent its flames as before a blast. And something swept with a terrific, rushing noise about the little camp and seemed to surround it entirely in a single moment of time. Défago shook the clinging blankets from his body, turned towards the woods behind, and with the same stumbling motion that had brought him—was gone: gone, before any one could move muscle to prevent him, gone with an amazing, blundering swiftness that left no time to act. The darkness positively swallowed him; and less than a dozen seconds later, above the roar of the swaying trees and the shout of the sudden wind, all three men, watching and listening with stricken hearts, heard a cry that seemed to drop down upon them from a great height of sky and distance—

"Oh, oh! This fiery height! Oh, oh! My feet of fire! My burning feet of fire…!" then died away, into untold space and silence.

Dr. Cathcart—suddenly master of himself, and therefore of the others—was just able to seize Hank violently by the arm as he tried to dash headlong into the Bush.

"But I want ter know,—you!" shrieked the guide. "I want ter see! That ain't him at all, but some—devil that's shunted into his place…!"

Somehow or other—he admits he never quite knew how he accomplished it—he managed to keep him in the tent and pacify him. The doctor, apparently, had reached the stage where reaction had set in and allowed his own innate force to conquer. Certainly he "managed" Hank admirably. It was his nephew, however, hitherto so wonderfully controlled, who gave him most cause for anxiety, for the cumulative strain had now produced a condition of lachrymose hysteria which made it necessary to isolate him upon a bed of boughs and blankets as far removed from Hank as was possible under the circumstances.

And there he lay, as the watches of that haunted night passed over the lonely camp, crying startled sentences, and fragments of sentences, into the folds of his blankets. A quantity of gibberish about speed and height and fire mingled oddly with biblical memories of the class-room. "People with broken faces all on fire are coming at a most awful, awful, pace towards the camp!" he would moan one minute; and the next would sit up and stare into the woods, intently listening, and whisper, "How terrible in the wilderness are—are the feet of them that—" until his uncle came across to change the direction of his thoughts and comfort him.

The hysteria, fortunately, proved but temporary. Sleep cured him, just as it cured Hank.

Till the first signs of daylight came, soon after five o'clock, Dr. Cathcart kept his vigil. His face was the colour of chalk, and there were strange flushes beneath the eyes. An appalling terror of the soul battled with his will all through those silent hours. These were some of the outer signs...

At dawn he lit the fire himself, made breakfast, and woke the others, and by seven they were well on their way back to the home camp—three perplexed and afflicted men, but each in his own way having reduced his inner turmoil to a condition of more or less systematised order again.

IX

They talked little, and then only of the most wholesome and common things, for their minds were charged with painful thoughts that clamoured for explanation, though no one dared refer to them. Hank, being nearest to primitive conditions, was the first to find himself, for he was also less complex. In Dr. Cathcart "civilisation" championed his forces against an attack singular enough. To this day, perhaps, he is not *quite* sure of certain things. Anyhow, he took longer to "find himself."

Simpson, the student of divinity, it was who arranged his conclusions probably with the best, though not most scientific, appearance of order. Out there, in the heart of unreclaimed wilderness, they had surely witnessed something crudely and essentially primitive. Something that had survived somehow the advance of humanity had emerged terrifically, betraying a scale of life still monstrous and immature. He envisaged it rather as a glimpse into prehistoric ages, when superstitions, gigantic and uncouth, still oppressed the hearts of men; when the forces of nature were still untamed, the Powers that may have haunted a primeval universe not yet withdrawn. To this day he thinks of what he termed years later in a sermon "savage and formidable Potencies lurking behind the souls of men, not evil perhaps in themselves, yet instinctively hostile to humanity as it exists."

With his uncle he never discussed the matter in detail, for the barrier between the two types of mind made it difficult. Only once, years later, something led them to the frontier of the subject—of a single detail of the subject, rather—

"Can't you even tell me what—*they* were like?" he asked; and the reply, though conceived in wisdom, was not encouraging, "It is far better you should not try to know, or to find out."

"Well—that odour...?" persisted the nephew. "What do you make of that?"

Dr. Cathcart looked at him and raised his eyebrows.

"Odours," he replied, "are not so easy as sounds and sights of telepathic communication. I make as much, or as little, probably, as you do yourself."

He was not quite so glib as usual with his explanations. That was all.

At the fall of day, cold, exhausted, famished, the party came to the end of the long portage and dragged themselves into a camp that at first glimpse seemed empty. Fire there was none, and no Punk came forward to welcome them. The emotional capacity of all three was too over-spent to recognise either surprise or annoyance; but the cry of spontaneous affection that burst from the lips of Hank, as he rushed ahead of them towards the fire-place, came probably as a warning that the end of the amazing affair was not quite yet. And both Cathcart and his nephew confessed afterwards that when they saw him kneel down in his excitement and embrace something that reclined, gently moving, beside the extinguished ashes, they felt in their very bones that this "something" would prove to be Défago—the true Défago, returned.

And so, indeed, it was.

It is soon told. Exhausted to the point of emaciation, the French Canadian—what was left of him, that is—fumbled among the ashes, trying to make a fire. His body crouched there, the weak fingers obeying feebly the instinctive habit of a lifetime with twigs and matches. But there was no longer any mind to direct the simple operation. The mind had fled beyond recall. And with it, too, had fled memory. Not only recent events, but all previous life was a blank.

This time it was the real man, though incredibly and horribly shrunken. On his face was no expression of any kind whatever—fear, welcome, or recognition. He did not seem to know who it was that embraced him, or who it was that fed, warmed and spoke to him the words of comfort and relief. Forlorn and broken beyond all reach of

human aid, the little man did meekly as he was bidden. The "something" that had constituted him "individual" had vanished for ever.

In some ways it was more terribly moving than anything they
had yet seen—that idiot smile as he drew wads of coarse moss
from his swollen cheeks and told them that he was "a damned
moss eater"; the continued vomiting of even the simplest food; and,
worst of all, the piteous and childish voice of complaint in which
he told them that his feet pained him—"burn like fire"—which was
natural enough when Dr. Cathcart examined them and found that
both were dreadfully frozen. Beneath the eyes there were faint
indications of recent bleeding.

The details of how he survived the prolonged exposure, of
where he had been, or of how he covered the great distance from
one camp to the other, including an immense detour of the lake
on foot since he had no canoe—all this remains unknown. His
memory had vanished completely. And before the end of the winter
whose beginning witnessed this strange occurrence, Défago, bereft
of mind, memory and soul, had gone with it. He lingered only a
few weeks.

And what Punk was able to contribute to the story throws no
further light upon it. He was cleaning fish by the lake shore about
five o'clock in the evening—an hour, that is, before the search party
returned—when he saw this shadow of the guide picking its way
weakly into camp. In advance of him, he declares, came the faint
whiff of a certain singular odour.

That same instant old Punk started for home. He covered the
entire journey of three days as only Indian blood could have covered it. The terror of a whole race drove him. He knew what it all
meant. Défago had "seen the Wendigo."

The Man Whom the Trees Loved

—1912—

I

H E PAINTED TREES AS BY SOME SPECIAL DIVINING INSTINCT
of their essential qualities. He understood them. He knew
why in an oak forest, for instance, each individual was utterly
distinct from its fellows, and why no two beeches in the whole
world were alike. People asked him down to paint a favourite lime
or silver birch, for he caught the individuality of a tree as some
catch the individuality of a horse. How he managed it was something of a puzzle, for he never had painting lessons, his drawing
was often wildly inaccurate, and, while his perception of a Tree
Personality was true and vivid, his rendering of it might almost
approach the ludicrous. Yet the character and personality of that
particular tree stood there alive beneath his brush—shining, frowning, dreaming, as the case might be, friendly or hostile, good or
evil. It emerged.

There was nothing else in the wide world that he could paint;
flowers and landscapes he only muddled away into a smudge; with
people he was helpless and hopeless; also with animals. Skies he
could sometimes manage, or effects of wind in foliage, but as a rule
he left these all severely alone. He kept to trees, wisely following an
instinct that was guided by love. It was quite arresting, this way he
had of making a tree look almost like a being—alive. It approached
the uncanny.

"Yes, Sanderson knows what he's doing when he paints a tree!"
thought old David Bittacy, C.B., late of the Woods and Forests.

"Why, you can almost hear it rustle. You can smell the thing. You can hear the rain drip through its leaves. You can almost see the branches move. It grows." For in this way somewhat he expressed his satisfaction, half to persuade himself that the twenty guineas were well spent (since his wife thought otherwise), and half to explain this uncanny reality of life that lay in the fine old cedar framed above his study table.

Yet in the general view the mind of Mr. Bittacy was held to be austere, not to say morose. Few divined in him the secretly tenacious love of nature that had been fostered by years spent in the forests and jungles of the eastern world. It was odd for an Englishman, due possibly to that Eurasian ancestor. Surreptitiously, as though half ashamed of it, he had kept alive a sense of beauty that hardly belonged to his type, and was unusual for its vitality. Trees, in particular, nourished it. He, also, understood trees, felt a subtle sense of communion with them, born perhaps of those years he had lived in caring for them, guarding, protecting, nursing, years of solitude among their great shadowy presences. He kept it largely to himself, of course, because he knew the world he lived in. He also kept it from his wife—to some extent. He knew it came between them, knew that she feared it, was opposed. But what he did not know, or realise at any rate, was the extent to which she grasped the power which they wielded over his life. Her fear, he judged, was simply due to those years in India, when for weeks at a time his calling took him away from her into the jungle forests, while she remained at home dreading all manner of evils that might befall him. This, of course, explained her instinctive opposition to the passion for woods that still influenced and clung to him. It was a natural survival of those anxious days of waiting in solitude for his safe return.

For Mrs. Bittacy, daughter of an evangelical clergyman, was a self-sacrificing woman, who in most things found a happy duty in sharing her husband's joys and sorrows to the point of self-obliteration. Only in this matter of the trees she was less successful than in others. It remained a problem difficult of compromise.

He knew, for instance, that what she objected to in this portrait of the cedar on their lawn was really not the price he had given for it, but the unpleasant way in which the transaction emphasised this breach between their common interests—the only one they had, but deep.

Sanderson, the artist, earned little enough money by his strange talent; such cheques were few and far between. The owners of fine or interesting trees who cared to have them painted singly were rare indeed; and the "studies" that he made for his own delight he also kept for his own delight. Even were there buyers, he would not sell them. Only a few, and these peculiarly intimate friends, might even see them, for he disliked to hear the undiscerning criticisms of those who did not understand. Not that he minded laughter at his craftsmanship—he admitted it with scorn—but that remarks about the personality of the tree itself could easily wound or anger him. He resented slighting observations concerning them, as though insults offered to personal friends who could not answer for themselves. He was instantly up in arms.

"It really *is* extraordinary," said a Woman who Understood, "that you can make that cypress seem an individual, when in reality all cypresses are so *exactly* alike."

And though the bit of calculated flattery had come so near to saying the right, true thing, Sanderson flushed as though she had slighted a friend beneath his very nose. Abruptly he passed in front of her and turned the picture to the wall.

"Almost as queer," he answered rudely, copying her silly emphasis, "as that *you* should have imagined individuality in your husband, Madame, when in reality all men are so *exactly* alike!"

Since the only thing that differentiated her husband from the mob was the money for which she had married him, Sanderson's relations with that particular family terminated on the spot, chance of prospective "orders" with it. His sensitiveness, perhaps, was morbid. At any rate the way to reach his heart lay through his trees. He might be said to love trees. He certainly drew a splendid inspiration from them, and the source of a man's inspiration, be it music, religion, or a woman, is never a safe thing to criticise.

"I do think, perhaps, it was just a little extravagant, dear," said Mrs. Bittacy, referring to the cedar cheque, "when we want a lawn-mower so badly too. But, as it gives you such pleasure—"

"It reminds me of a certain day, Sophia," replied the old gentleman, looking first proudly at herself, then fondly at the picture, "now long gone by. It reminds me of another tree—that Kentish lawn in the spring, birds singing in the lilacs, and some one in a muslin frock waiting patiently beneath a certain cedar—not the one in the picture, I know, but—"

"I was not waiting," she said indignantly, "I was picking fir-cones for the schoolroom fire—"

"Fir-cones, my dear, do not grow on cedars, and schoolroom fires were not made in June in my young days."

"And anyhow it isn't the same cedar."

"It has made me fond of all cedars for its sake," he answered, "and it reminds me that you are the same young girl still—"

She crossed the room to his side, and together they looked out of the window where, upon the lawn of their Hampshire cottage, a ragged Lebanon stood in solitary state.

"You're as full of dreams as ever," she said gently, "and I don't regret the cheque a bit—really. Only it would have been more real if it had been the original tree, wouldn't it?"

"That was blown down long ago. I passed the place last year, and there's not a sign of it left," he replied tenderly. And presently, when he released her from his side, she went up to the wall and carefully dusted the picture Sanderson had made of the cedar on their present lawn. She went all round the frame with her tiny handkerchief, standing on tiptoe to reach the top rim.

"What I like about it," said the old fellow to himself when his wife had left the room, "is the way he has made it live. All trees have it, of course, but a cedar taught it to me first—the 'something' trees possess that make them know I'm there when I stand close and watch. I suppose I felt it then because I was in love, and love reveals life everywhere." He glanced a moment at the Lebanon looming gaunt and sombre through the gathering dusk. A curious wistful expression danced a moment through his eyes. "Yes, Sanderson has seen it as it is," he murmured, "solemnly dreaming there its dim hidden life against the Forest edge, and as different from that other tree in Kent as I am from—from the vicar, say. It's quite a stranger, too. I don't know anything about it really. That other cedar I loved; this old fellow I respect. Friendly though—yes, on the whole quite friendly. He's painted the friendliness right enough. He saw that. I'd like to know that man better," he added. "I'd like to ask him how he saw so clearly that it stands there between this cottage and the Forest—yet somehow more in sympathy with us than with the mass of woods behind—a sort of go-between. *That* I never noticed before. I see it now—through his eyes. It stands there like a sentinel—protective rather."

He turned away abruptly to look through the window. He saw

the great encircling mass of gloom that was the Forest, fringing their little lawn. It pressed up closer in the darkness. The prim garden with its formal beds of flowers seemed an impertinence almost—some little coloured insect that sought to settle on a sleeping monster—some gaudy fly that danced impudently down the edge of a great river that could engulf it with a toss of its smallest wave. That Forest with its thousand years of growth and its deep spreading being was some such slumbering monster, yes. Their cottage and garden stood too near its running lip. When the winds were strong and lifted its shadowy skirts of black and purple... He loved this feeling of the Forest Personality; he had always loved it.

"Queer," he reflected, "awfully queer, that trees should bring me such a sense of dim, vast living! I used to feel it particularly, I remember, in India; in Canadian woods as well; but never in little English woods till here. And Sanderson's the only man I ever knew who felt it too. He's never said so, but there's the proof," and he turned again to the picture that he loved. A thrill of unaccustomed life ran through him as he looked. "I wonder, by Jove, I wonder," his thoughts ran on, "whether a tree—er—in any lawful meaning of the term can be—alive. I remember some writing fellow telling me long ago that trees had once been moving things, animal organisms of some sort, that had stood so long feeding, sleeping, dreaming, or something, in the same place, that they had lost the power to get away...!"

Fancies flew pell-mell about his mind, and, lighting a cheroot, he dropped into an armchair beside the open window and let them play. Outside the blackbirds whistled in the shrubberies across the lawn. He smelt the earth and trees and flowers, the perfume of mown grass, and the bits of open heath-land far away in the heart of the woods. The summer wind stirred very faintly through the leaves. But the great New Forest hardly raised her sweeping skirts of black and purple shadow.

Mr. Bittacy, however, knew intimately every detail of that wilderness of trees within. He knew all the purple coombs splashed with yellow waves of gorse; sweet with juniper and myrtle, and gleaming with clear and dark-eyed pools that watched the sky. There hawks hovered, circling hour by hour, and the flicker of the peewit's flight with its melancholy, petulant cry, deepened the sense of stillness. He knew the solitary pines, dwarfed, tufted, vigorous, that sang to every lost wind, travellers like the gipsies who pitched their bush-like tents beneath them; he knew the shaggy ponies, with foals like baby centaurs; the chattering jays, the milky call of cuckoos in the spring, and the boom of the bittern from the lonely marshes. The undergrowth of watching hollies, he knew too, strange and mysterious, with their dark, suggestive beauty, and the yellow shimmer of their pale dropped leaves.

Here all the Forest lived and breathed in safety, secure from mutilation. No terror of the axe could haunt the peace of its vast subconscious life, no terror of devastating Man afflict it with the dread of premature death. It knew itself supreme; it spread and preened itself without concealment. It set no spires to carry warnings, for no wind brought messages of alarm as it bulged outwards to the sun and stars.

But, once its leafy portals left behind, the trees of the countryside were otherwise. The houses threatened them; they knew themselves in danger. The roads were no longer glades of silent turf, but noisy, cruel ways by which men came to attack them. They were civilised, cared for—but cared for in order that some day they might be put to death. Even in the villages, where the solemn and immemorial repose of giant chestnuts aped security, the tossing of a silver birch against their mass, impatient in the littlest wind, brought warning. Dust clogged their leaves. The inner humming of their quiet life became inaudible beneath the scream and shriek of clattering traffic. They longed and prayed to enter the great Peace of the Forest yonder, but they could not move. They knew, moreover, that the Forest with its august, deep splendour despised and pitied them. They were a thing of artificial gardens, and belonged to beds of flowers all forced to grow one way...

"I'd like to know that artist fellow better," was the thought upon which he returned at length to the things of practical life. "I wonder if Sophia would mind him here for a bit—?" He rose with the sound of the gong, brushing the ashes from his speckled waistcoat. He pulled the waistcoat down. He was slim and spare in figure, active in his movements. In the dim light, but for that silvery moustache, he might easily have passed for a man of forty. "I'll suggest it to her anyhow," he decided on his way upstairs to dress. His thought really was that Sanderson could probably explain this world of things he had always felt about—trees. A man who could paint the soul of a cedar in that way must know it all.

"Why not?" she gave her verdict later over the bread-and-butter pudding; "unless you think he'd find it dull without companions."

"He would paint all day in the Forest, dear. I'd like to pick his brains a bit, too, if I could manage it."

"You can manage anything, David," was what she answered, for this elderly childless couple used an affectionate politeness long since deemed old-fashioned. The remark, however, displeased her, making her feel uneasy, and she did not notice his rejoinder, smiling his pleasure and content—"Except yourself and our bank account, my dear." This passion of his for trees was of old a bone of contention, though very mild contention. It frightened her. That was the truth. The Bible, her Baedeker for earth and heaven, did not mention it. Her husband, while humouring her, could never alter that instinctive dread she had. He soothed, but never changed her. She liked the woods, perhaps as spots for shade and picnics, but she could not, as he did, love them.

And after dinner, with a lamp beside the open window, he read aloud from *The Times* the evening post had brought, such fragments as he thought might interest her. The custom was invariable, except on Sundays, when, to please his wife, he dozed over Tennyson or Farrar as their mood might be. She knitted while he read, asked gentle questions, told him his voice was a "lovely reading voice," and enjoyed the little discussions that occasions prompted because he always let her win them with "Ah, Sophia, I had never thought of it quite in *that* way before; but now you mention it I must say I think there's something in it…"

For David Bittacy was wise. It was long after marriage, during his months of loneliness spent with trees and forests in India, his wife waiting at home in the Bungalow, that his other, deeper side had developed the strange passion that she could not understand. And after one or two serious attempts to let her share it with him, he had given up and learned to hide it from her. He learned, that is, to speak of it only casually; for since she knew it was there, to keep silence altogether would only increase her pain. So from time to time he skimmed the surface just to let her show him where he was wrong and think she won the day. It remained a debatable land of compromise. He listened with patience to her criticisms, her excursions and alarms, knowing that while it gave her satisfaction, it could not change himself. The thing lay in him too deep and true for change. But, for peace' sake, some meeting-place was desirable, and he found it thus.

It was her one fault in his eyes, this religious mania carried over from her up-bringing, and it did no serious harm. Great emotion could shake it sometimes out of her. She clung to it because her father taught it her and not because she had thought it out for herself. Indeed, like many women, she never really *thought* at all, but merely reflected the images of others' thinking which she had learned to see. So, wise in his knowledge of human nature, old David Bittacy accepted the pain of being obliged to keep a portion of his inner life shut off from the woman he deeply loved. He regarded her little biblical phrases as oddities that still clung to a rather fine, big soul—like horns and little useless things some animals have not yet lost in the course of evolution while they have outgrown their use.

"My dear, what is it? You frightened me!" She asked it suddenly, sitting up so abruptly that her cap dropped sideways almost to her ear. For David Bittacy behind his crackling paper had uttered a sharp exclamation of surprise. He had lowered the sheet and was staring at her over the tops of his gold glasses.

"Listen to this, if you please," he said, a note of eagerness in his voice, "listen to this, my dear Sophia. It's from an address by Francis Darwin before the Royal Society. He is president, you know, and son of the great Darwin. Listen carefully, I beg you. It is *most* significant."

"I *am* listening, David," she said with some astonishment, looking up. She stopped her knitting. For a second she glanced behind her. Something had suddenly changed in the room, and it made her feel wide awake, though before she had been almost dozing. Her husband's voice and manner had introduced this new thing. Her instincts rose in warning. *"Do* read it, dear." He took a deep breath, looking first again over the rims of his glasses to make quite sure of her attention. He had evidently come across something of genuine interest, although herself she often found the passages from these "Addresses" somewhat heavy.

In a deep, emphatic voice he read aloud:

"'It is impossible to know whether or not plants are conscious; but it is consistent with the doctrine of continuity that in all living things there is something psychic, and if we accept this point of view—'"

"If," she interrupted, scenting danger.

He ignored the interruption as a thing of slight value he was accustomed to.

"'If we accept this point of view,'" he continued, "'we must believe that in plants there exists a faint copy of *what we know as consciousness in ourselves.*'"

He laid the paper down and steadily stared at her. Their eyes met. He had italicised the last phrase.

For a minute or two his wife made no reply or comment. They stared at one another in silence. He waited for the meaning of the words to reach her understanding with full import. Then he turned and read them again in part, while she, released from that curious driving look in his eyes, instinctively again glanced over her shoulder round the room. It was almost as if she felt some one had come in to them unnoticed.

"We must believe that in plants there exists a faint copy of what we know as consciousness in ourselves."

"If," she repeated lamely, feeling before the stare of those questioning eyes she must say something, but not yet having gathered her wits together quite.

"*Consciousness*," he rejoined. And then he added gravely: "That, my dear, is the statement of a scientific man of the Twentieth Century."

Mrs. Bittacy sat forward in her chair so that her silk flounces crackled louder than the newspaper. She made a characteristic little sound between sniffing and snorting. She put her shoes closely together, with her hands upon her knees.

"David," she said quietly, "I think these scientific men are simply losing their heads. There is nothing in the Bible that I can remember about any such thing whatsoever."

"Nothing, Sophia, that I can remember either," he answered patiently. Then, after a pause, he added, half to himself perhaps more than to her: "And, now that I come to think about it, it seems that Sanderson once said something to me that was similar."

"Then Mr. Sanderson is a wise and thoughtful man, and a safe man," she quickly took him up, "if he said that."

For she thought her husband referred to her remark about the Bible, and not to her judgment of the scientific men. And he did not correct her mistake.

"And plants, you see, dear, are not the same thing as trees," she drove her advantage home, "not quite, that is."

"I agree," said David quietly; "but both belong to the great vegetable kingdom."

There was a moment's pause before she answered.

"Pah! the vegetable kingdom, indeed!" She tossed her pretty old head. And into the words she put a degree of contempt that, could the vegetable kingdom have heard it, might have made it feel ashamed for covering a third of the world with its wonderful tangled network of roots and branches, delicate shaking leaves, and its millions of spires that caught the sun and wind and rain. Its very right to existence seemed in question.

II

Sanderson accordingly came down, and on the whole his short visit was a success. Why he came at all was a mystery to those who heard of it, for he never paid visits and was certainly not the kind of man to court a customer. There must have been something in Bittacy he liked.

Mrs. Bittacy was glad when he left. He brought no dress-suit for one thing, not even a dinner-jacket, and he wore very low collars with big balloon ties like a Frenchman, and let his hair grow longer than was nice, she felt. Not that these things were important, but that she considered them symptoms of something a little disordered. The ties were unnecessarily flowing.

For all that he was an interesting man, and, in spite of his eccentricities of dress and so forth, a gentleman. "Perhaps," she reflected in her genuinely charitable heart, "he had other uses for the twenty guineas, an invalid sister or an old mother to support!" She had no notion of the cost of brushes, frames, paints, and canvases. Also she forgave him much for the sake of his beautiful eyes and his eager enthusiasm of manner. So many men of thirty were already blasé.

Still, when the visit was over, she felt relieved. She said nothing about his coming a second time, and her husband, she was glad to notice, had likewise made no suggestion. For, truth to tell, the way the younger man engrossed the older, keeping him out for hours in the Forest, talking on the lawn in the blazing sun, and in the evenings when the damp of dusk came creeping out from the surrounding woods, all regardless of his age and usual habits, was not quite to her taste. Of course, Mr. Sanderson did not know how easily those attacks of Indian fever came back, but David surely might have told him.

They talked trees from morning till night. It stirred in her the old subconscious trail of dread, a trail that led ever into the darkness of big woods; and such feelings, as her early evangelical training taught her, were temptings. To regard them in any other way was to play with danger.

Her mind, as she watched these two, was charged with curious thoughts of dread she could not understand, yet feared the more on that account. The way they studied that old mangy cedar was a trifle unnecessary, unwise, she felt. It was disregarding the sense of proportion which deity had set upon the world for men's safe guidance.

Even after dinner they smoked their cigars upon the low branches that swept down and touched the lawn, until at length she insisted on their coming in. Cedars, she had somewhere heard, were not safe after sundown; it was not wholesome to be too near them; to sleep beneath them was even dangerous, though what the precise danger was she had forgotten. The upas was the tree she really meant.

At any rate she summoned David in, and Sanderson came presently after him.

For a long time, before deciding on this peremptory step, she had watched them surreptitiously from the drawing-room window—her husband and her guest. The dusk enveloped them with its damp veil of gauze. She saw the glowing tips of their cigars, and heard the drone of voices. Bats flitted overhead, and big, silent moths whirred softly over the rhododendron blossoms. And it came suddenly to her, while she watched, that her husband had somehow altered these last few days—since Mr. Sanderson's arrival in fact. A change had come over him, though what it was she could not say. She hesitated, indeed, to search. That was the instinctive dread operating in her. Provided it passed she would rather not know. Small things, of course, she noticed; small outward signs. He had neglected *The Times* for one thing, left off his speckled waistcoats for another. He was absent-minded sometimes; showed vagueness in practical details where hitherto he showed decision. And—he had begun to talk in his sleep again.

These and a dozen other small peculiarities came suddenly upon her with the rush of a combined attack. They brought with them a faint distress that made her shiver. Momentarily her mind was startled, then confused, as her eyes picked out the shadowy figures in the dusk, the cedar covering them, the Forest close at their backs. And then, before she could think, or seek internal guidance as her habit was, this whisper, muffled and very hurried, ran across her brain: "It's Mr. Sanderson. Call David in at once!"

And she had done so. Her shrill voice crossed the lawn and died away into the Forest, quickly smothered. No echo followed it. The sound fell dead against the rampart of a thousand listening trees.

"The damp is so very penetrating, even in summer," she murmured when they came obediently. She was half surprised at her own audacity, half repentant. They came so meekly at her call. "And my husband is sensitive to fever from the East. No, *please* do not throw away your cigars. We can sit by the open window and enjoy the evening while you smoke."

She was very talkative for a moment; subconscious excitement was the cause.

"It is so still—so wonderfully still," she went on, as no one spoke, "so peaceful, and the air so very sweet… and God is always near to those who need His aid." The words slipped out before she realised quite what she was saying, yet fortunately, in time to lower her voice, for no one heard them. They were, perhaps, an instinctive expression of relief. It flustered her that she could have said the thing at all.

Sanderson brought her shawl and helped to arrange the chairs; she thanked him in her old-fashioned, gentle way, declining the lamps which he had offered to light. "They attract the moths and insects so, I think!"

The three of them sat there in the gloaming, Mr. Bittacy's white moustache and his wife's yellow shawl gleaming at either end of the little horseshoe, Sanderson with his wild black hair and shining eyes midway between them. The painter went on talking softly, continuing evidently the conversation begun with his host beneath the cedar. Mrs. Bittacy, on her guard, listened—uneasily.

"For trees, you see, rather conceal themselves in daylight. They reveal themselves fully only after sunset. I never *know* a tree," he bowed here slightly towards the lady as though to apologise for something he felt she would not quite understand or like, "until I've seen it in the night. Your cedar, for instance," looking towards her husband again so that Mrs. Bittacy caught the gleaming of his turned eyes, "I failed with badly at first, because I did it in the morning. You shall see to-morrow what I mean—that first sketch is upstairs in my portfolio; it's quite another tree to the one you bought. That view"—he leaned forward, lowering his voice—"I caught one morning about two o'clock in very faint moonlight and the stars. I saw the naked being of the thing—"

"You mean that you went out, Mr. Sanderson, at that hour?" the old lady asked with astonishment and mild rebuke. She did not care particularly for his choice of adjectives either.

"I fear it was rather a liberty to take in another's house, perhaps," he answered courteously. "But, having chanced to wake, I saw the tree from my window, and made my way downstairs."

"It's a wonder Boxer didn't bite you; he sleeps loose in the hall," she said.

"On the contrary. The dog came out with me. I hope," he added, "the noise didn't disturb you, though it's rather late to say so. I feel quite guilty." His white teeth showed in the dusk as he smiled. A smell of earth and flowers stole in through the window on a breath of wandering air.

Mrs. Bittacy said nothing at the moment. "We both sleep like tops," put in her husband, laughing. "You're a courageous man, though, Sanderson; and, by Jove, the picture justifies you. Few artists would have taken so much trouble, though I read once that Holman Hunt, Rossetti, or some one of that lot, painted all night in his orchard to get an effect of moonlight that he wanted."

He chattered on. His wife was glad to hear his voice; it made her feel more easy in her mind. But presently the other held the floor again, and her thoughts grew darkened and afraid. Instinctively she feared the influence on her husband. The mystery and wonder that lie in woods, in forests, in great gatherings of trees everywhere, seemed so real and present while he talked.

"The Night transfigures all things in a way," he was saying; "but nothing so searchingly as trees. From behind a veil that sunlight hangs before them in the day they emerge and show themselves. Even buildings do that—in a measure—but trees particularly. In the daytime they sleep; at night they wake, they manifest, turn active—live. You remember," turning politely again in the direction of his hostess, "how clearly Henley understood that?"

"That socialist person, you mean?" asked the lady. Her tone and accent made the substantive sound criminal. It almost hissed, the way she uttered it.

"The poet, yes," replied the artist tactfully, "the friend of Stevenson, you remember, Stevenson who wrote those charming children's verses."

He quoted in a low voice the lines he meant. It was, for once, the time, the place, and the setting all together. The words floated out across the lawn towards the wall of blue darkness where the big Forest swept the little garden with its league-long curve that was like the shore-line of a sea. A wave of distant sound that was like surf accompanied his voice, as though the wind was fain to listen too:

> Not to the staring Day,
> For all the importunate questionings he pursues
> In his big, violent voice,
> Shall those mild things of bulk and multitude,
> The trees—God's sentinels...
> Yield of their huge, unutterable selves.

> *   *   *   *   *

> But at the word
> Of the ancient, sacerdotal Night,
> Night of the many secrets, whose effect—
> Transfiguring, hierophantic, dread—
> Themselves alone may fully apprehend,
> They tremble and are changed:
> In each the uncouth, individual soul
> Looms forth and glooms
> Essential, and, their bodily presences
> Touched with inordinate significance,
> Wearing the darkness like a livery

Of some mysterious and tremendous guild,
They brood—they menace—they appal.

The voice of Mrs. Bittacy presently broke the silence that followed.

"I like that part about God's sentinels," she murmured. There was no sharpness in her tone; it was hushed and quiet. The truth, so musically uttered, muted her shrill objections though it had not lessened her alarm. Her husband made no comment; his cigar, she noticed, had gone out.

"And old trees in particular," continued the artist, as though to himself, "have very definite personalities. You can offend, wound, please them; the moment you stand within their shade you feel whether they come out to you, or whether they withdraw." He turned abruptly towards his host. "You know that singular essay of Prentice Mulford's, no doubt, 'God in the Trees'—extravagant perhaps, but yet with a fine true beauty in it? You've never read it, no?" he asked.

But it was Mrs. Bittacy who answered; her husband keeping his curious deep silence.

"I never did!" It fell like a drip of cold water from the face muffled in the yellow shawl; even a child could have supplied the remainder of the unspoken thought.

"Ah," said Sanderson gently, "but there is 'God' in the trees, God in a very subtle aspect and sometimes—I have known the trees express it too—that which is *not* God—dark and terrible. Have you ever noticed, too, how clearly trees show what they want—choose their companions, at least? How beeches, for instance, allow no life too near them—birds or squirrels in their boughs, nor any growth beneath? The silence in the beech wood is quite terrifying often! And how pines like bilberry bushes at their feet and sometimes little oaks—all trees making a clear, deliberate choice, and holding firmly to it? Some trees obviously—it's very strange and marked—seem to prefer the human."

The old lady sat up crackling, for this was more than she could permit. Her stiff silk dress emitted little sharp reports.

"We know," she answered, "that He was said to have walked in the garden in the cool of the evening"—the gulp betrayed the effort that it cost her—"but we are nowhere told that He hid in the trees, or anything like that. Trees, after all, we must remember, are only large vegetables."

"True," was the soft answer, "but in everything that grows, has life, that is, there's mystery past all finding out. The wonder that lies hidden in our own souls lies also hidden, I venture to assert, in the stupidity and silence of a mere potato."

The observation was not meant to be amusing. It was *not* amusing. No one laughed. On the contrary, the words conveyed in too literal a sense the feeling that haunted all that conversation. Each one in his own way realised—with beauty, with wonder, with alarm—that the talk had somehow brought the whole vegetable kingdom nearer to that of man. Some link had been established between the two. It was not wise, with that great Forest listening at their very doors, to speak so plainly. The Forest edged up closer while they did so.

And Mrs. Bittacy, anxious to interrupt the horrid spell, broke suddenly in upon it with a matter-of-fact suggestion. She did not like her husband's prolonged silence, stillness. He seemed so negative—so changed.

"David," she said, raising her voice, "I think you're feeling the dampness. It's grown chilly. The fever comes so suddenly, you know, and it might be wise to take the tincture. I'll go and get it, dear, at once. It's better." And before he could object she had left the room to bring the homoeopathic dose that she believed in, and that, to please her, he swallowed by the tumbler-full from week to week.

And the moment the door closed behind her, Sanderson began again, though now in quite a different tone. Mr. Bittacy sat up in his chair. The two men obviously resumed the conversation—the real conversation interrupted beneath the cedar—and left aside the sham one which was so much dust merely thrown in the old lady's eyes.

"Trees love you, that's the fact," he said earnestly. "Your service to them all these years abroad has made them know you."

"Know me?"

"Made them, yes,"—he paused a moment, then added,—"made them *aware of your presence*; aware of a force outside themselves that deliberately seeks their welfare, don't you see?"

"By Jove, Sanderson—!" This put into plain language actual sensations he had felt, yet had never dared to phrase in words before. "They get into touch with me, as it were?" he ventured, laughing at his own sentence, yet laughing only with his lips.

"Exactly," was the quick, emphatic reply. "They seek to blend with something they feel instinctively to be good for them, helpful to their essential beings, encouraging to their best expression—their life."

"Good Lord, Sir!" Bittacy heard himself saying, "but you're putting my own thoughts into words. D'you know, I've felt something like that for years. As though—" he looked round to make sure his wife was not there, then finished the sentence—"as though the trees were after me!"

"'Amalgamate' seems the best word, perhaps," said Sanderson slowly. "They would draw you to themselves. Good forces, you see, always seek to merge; evil to separate; that's why Good in the end must always win the day—everywhere. The accumulation in the long run becomes overwhelming. Evil tends to separation, dissolution, death. The comradeship of trees, their instinct to run together, is a vital symbol. Trees in a mass are good; alone, you may take it generally, are—well, dangerous. Look at a monkey-puzzler, or better still, a holly. Look at it, watch it, understand it. Did you ever see more plainly an evil thought made visible? They're wicked. Beautiful too, oh yes! There's a strange, miscalculated beauty often in evil—"

"That cedar, then—?"

"Not evil, no; but alien, rather. Cedars grow in forests all together. The poor thing has drifted, that is all."

They were getting rather deep. Sanderson, talking against time, spoke so fast. It was too condensed. Bittacy hardly followed that last bit. His mind floundered among his own less definite, less sorted thoughts, till presently another sentence from the artist startled him into attention again.

"That cedar will protect you here, though, because you both have humanised it by your thinking so lovingly of its presence. The others can't get past it, as it were."

"Protect me!" he exclaimed. "Protect me from their love?"

Sanderson laughed. "We're getting rather mixed," he said; "we're talking of one thing in the terms of another really. But what I mean is—you see—that their love for you, their 'awareness' of your personality and presence involves the idea of winning you—across the border—into themselves—into their world of living. It means, in a way, taking you over."

The ideas the artist started in his mind ran furious wild races to and fro. It was like a maze sprung suddenly into movement. The whirling of the intricate lines bewildered him. They went so fast, leaving but half an explanation of their goal. He followed first one, then another, but a new one always dashed across to intercept before he could get anywhere.

"But India," he said, presently in a lower voice, "India is so far away—from this little English forest. The trees, too, are utterly different for one thing?"

The rustle of skirts warned of Mrs. Bittacy's approach. This was a sentence he could turn round another way in case she came up and pressed for explanation.

"There is communion among trees all the world over," was the strange quick reply. "They always know."

"They always know! You think then—?"

"The winds, you see—the great, swift carriers! They have their ancient rights of way about the world. An easterly wind, for instance, carrying on stage by stage as it were—linking dropped messages and meanings from land to land like the birds—an easterly wind—"

Mrs. Bittacy swept in upon them with the tumbler—

"There, David," she said, "that will ward off any beginnings of attack. Just a spoonful, dear. Oh, oh! not *all*!" for he had swallowed half the contents at a single gulp as usual; "another dose before you go to bed, and the balance in the morning, first thing when you wake."

She turned to her guest, who put the tumbler down for her upon a table at his elbow. She had heard them speak of the east wind. She emphasised the warning she had misinterpreted. The private part of the conversation came to an abrupt end.

"It is the one thing that upsets him more than any other—an east wind," she said, "and I am glad, Mr. Sanderson, to hear you think so too."

III

A deep hush followed, in the middle of which an owl was heard calling its muffled note in the forest. A big moth whirred with a soft collision against one of the windows. Mrs. Bittacy started slightly, but no one spoke. Above the trees the stars were faintly visible. From the distance came the barking of a dog.

Bittacy, relighting his cigar, broke the little spell of silence that had caught all three.

"It's rather a comforting thought," he said, throwing the match out of the window, "that life is about us everywhere, and that there is really no dividing line between what we call organic and inorganic."

"The universe, yes," said Sanderson, "is all one, really. We're puzzled by the gaps we cannot see across, but as a fact, I suppose, there are no gaps at all."

Mrs. Bittacy rustled ominously, holding her peace meanwhile. She feared long words she did not understand. Beelzebub lay hid among too many syllables.

"In trees and plants especially, there dreams an exquisite life that no one yet has proved unconscious."

"Or conscious either, Mr. Sanderson," she neatly interjected. "It's only man that was made after His image, not shrubberies and things…"

Her husband interposed without delay.

"It is not necessary," he explained suavely, "to say that they're alive in the sense that we are alive. At the same time," with an eye to his wife, "I see no harm in holding, dear, that all created things contain some measure of His life Who made them. It's only beautiful to hold that He created nothing dead. We are not pantheists for all that!" he added soothingly.

"Oh, no! Not that, I hope!" The word alarmed her. It was worse than pope. Through her puzzled mind stole a stealthy, dangerous thing... like a panther.

"I like to think that even in decay there's life," the painter murmured. "The falling apart of rotten wood breeds sentiency; there's force and motion in the falling of a dying leaf, in the breaking up and crumbling of everything indeed. And take an inert stone: it's crammed with heat and weight and potencies of all sorts. What holds its particles together indeed? We understand it as little as gravity or why a needle always turns to the 'North.' Both things may be a mode of life..."

"You think a compass has a soul, Mr. Sanderson?" exclaimed the lady with a crackling of her silk flounces that conveyed a sense of outrage even more plainly than her tone. The artist smiled to himself in the darkness, but it was Bittacy who hastened to reply.

"Our friend merely suggests that these mysterious agencies," he said quietly, "may be due to some kind of life we cannot understand. Why should water only run downhill? Why should trees grow at right angles to the surface of the ground and towards the sun? Why should the worlds spin for ever on their axes? Why should fire change the form of every thing it touches without really destroying them? To say these things follow the law of their being explains nothing. Mr. Sanderson merely suggests—poetically, my dear, of course—that these may be manifestations of life, though life at a different stage to ours."

"The '*breath* of life,' we read, 'He breathed into them.' These things do not breathe." She said it with triumph.

Then Sanderson put in a word. But he spoke rather to himself or to his host than by way of serious rejoinder to the ruffled lady.

"But plants do breathe too, you know," he said. "They breathe, they eat, they digest, they move about, and they adapt themselves to their environment as men and animals do. They have a nervous system too… at least a complex system of nuclei which have some of the qualities of nerve cells. They may have memory too. Certainly, they know definite action in response to stimulus. And though this may be physiological, no one has proved that it is only that, and not—psychological."

He did not notice, apparently, the little gasp that was audible behind the yellow shawl. Bittacy cleared his throat, threw his extinguished cigar upon the lawn, crossed and recrossed his legs.

"And in trees," continued the other, "behind a great forest, for instance," pointing towards the woods, "may stand a rather splendid Entity that manifests through all the thousand individual trees—some huge collective life, quite as minutely and delicately organised as our own. It might merge and blend with ours under certain conditions, so that we could understand it by *being* it, for a time at least. It might even engulf human vitality into the immense whirlpool of its own vast dreaming life. The pull of a big forest on a man can be tremendous and utterly overwhelming."

The mouth of Mrs. Bittacy was heard to close with a snap. Her shawl, and particularly her crackling dress, exhaled the protest that burned within her like a pain. She was too distressed to be overawed, but at the same time too confused 'mid the litter of words and meanings half understood, to find immediate phrases she could use. Whatever the actual meaning of his language might be, however, and whatever subtle dangers lay concealed behind them meanwhile, they certainly wove a kind of gentle spell with the glimmering darkness that held all three delicately enmeshed there by that open window. The odours of dewy lawn, flowers, trees, and earth formed part of it.

"The moods," he continued, "that people waken in us are due to their hidden life affecting our own. Deep calls to deep. A person, for instance, joins you in an empty room: you both instantly change. The new arrival, though in silence, has caused a change of mood. May not the moods of Nature touch and stir us in virtue of a similar prerogative? The sea, the hills, the desert, wake passion, joy, terror, as the case may be; for a few, perhaps," he glanced significantly at his host so that Mrs. Bittacy again caught the turning of his eyes, "emotions of a curious, flaming splendour that are quite nameless. Well… whence come these powers? Surely from nothing that is… dead! Does not the influence of a forest, its sway and strange ascendancy over certain minds, betray a direct manifestation of life? It lies otherwise beyond all explanation, this mysterious emanation of big woods. Some natures, of course, deliberately invite it. The authority of a host of trees,"—his voice grew almost solemn as he said the words—"is something not to be denied. One feels it here, I think, particularly."

There was considerable tension in the air as he ceased speaking. Mr. Bittacy had not intended that the talk should go so far. They had drifted. He did not wish to see his wife unhappy or afraid, and he was aware—acutely so—that her feelings were stirred to a point he did not care about. Something in her, as he put it, was "working up" towards explosion.

He sought to generalise the conversation, diluting this accumulated emotion by spreading it.

"The sea is His and He made it," he suggested vaguely, hoping Sanderson would take the hint, "and with the trees it is the same…"

"The whole gigantic vegetable kingdom, yes," the artist took him up, "all at the service of man, for food, for shelter and for a thousand purposes of his daily life. Is it not striking what a lot of the globe they cover... exquisitely organised life, yet stationary, always ready to our hand when we want them, never running away? But the taking them, for all that, not so easy. One man shrinks from picking flowers, another from cutting down trees. And, it's curious that most of the forest tales and legends are dark, mysterious, and somewhat ill-omened. The forest-beings are rarely gay and harmless. The forest life was felt as terrible. Tree-worship still survives to-day. Woodcutters... those who take the life of trees... you see, a race of haunted men..."

He stopped abruptly, a singular catch in his voice. Bittacy felt something even before the sentences were over. His wife, he knew, felt it still more strongly. For it was in the middle of the heavy silence following upon these last remarks, that Mrs. Bittacy, rising with a violent abruptness from her chair, drew the attention of the others to something moving towards them across the lawn. It came silently. In outline it was large and curiously spread. It rose high, too, for the sky above the shrubberies, still pale gold from the sunset, was dimmed by its passage. She declared afterwards that it moved in "looping circles," but what she perhaps meant to convey was "spirals."

She screamed faintly. "It's come at last! And it's you that brought it!"

She turned excitedly, half afraid, half angry, to Sanderson. With a breathless sort of gasp she said it, politeness all forgotten. "I knew it... if you went on. I knew it. Oh! Oh!" And she cried again, "Your talking has brought it out!" The terror that shook her voice was rather dreadful.

But the confusion of her vehement words passed unnoticed in the first surprise they caused. For a moment nothing happened.

"What is it you think you see, my dear?" asked her husband, startled. Sanderson said nothing. All three leaned forward, the men still sitting, but Mrs. Bittacy had rushed hurriedly to the window, placing herself of a purpose, as it seemed, between her husband and the lawn. She pointed. Her little hand made a silhouette against the sky, the yellow shawl hanging from the arm like a cloud.

"Beyond the cedar—between it and the lilacs." The voice had lost its shrillness; it was thin and hushed. "There... now you see it going round upon itself again—going back, thank God!... going back to the Forest." It sank to a whisper, shaking. She repeated, with a great dropping sigh of relief—"Thank God! I thought... at first... it was coming here... to us!... David... to *you*!"

She stepped back from the window, her movements confused, feeling in the darkness for the support of a chair, and finding her husband's outstretched hand instead. "Hold me, dear, hold me, please... tight. Do not let me go." She was in what he called afterwards "a regular state." He drew her firmly down upon her chair again.

"Smoke, Sophie, my dear," he said quickly, trying to make his voice calm and natural. "I see it, yes. It's smoke blowing over from the gardener's cottage..."

"But, David,"—and there was new horror in her whisper now—"it made a noise. It makes it still. I hear it swishing." Some such word she used—swishing, sishing, rushing, or something of the kind. "David, I'm very frightened. It's something awful! That man has called it out...!"

"Hush, hush," whispered her husband. He stroked her trembling hand beside him.

"It is in the wind," said Sanderson, speaking for the first time, very quietly. The expression on his face was not visible in the gloom, but his voice was soft and unafraid. At the sound of it, Mrs. Bittacy started violently again. Bittacy drew his chair a little forward to obstruct her view of him. He felt bewildered himself, a little, hardly knowing quite what to say or do. It was all so very curious and sudden.

But Mrs. Bittacy was badly frightened. It seemed to her that what she saw came from the enveloping forest just beyond their little garden. It emerged in a sort of secret way, moving towards them as with a purpose, stealthily, difficultly. Then something stopped it. It could not advance beyond the cedar. The cedar—this impression remained with her afterwards too—prevented, kept it back. Like a rising sea the Forest had surged a moment in their direction through the covering darkness, and this visible movement was its first wave. Thus to her mind it seemed... like that mysterious turn of the tide that used to frighten and mystify her in childhood on the sands. The outward surge of some enormous Power was what she felt... something to which every instinct in her being rose in opposition because it threatened her and hers. In that moment she realised the Personality of the Forest... menacing.

In the stumbling movement that she made away from the window and towards the bell she barely caught the sentence Sanderson—or was it her husband?—murmured to himself: "It came because we talked of it; our thinking made it aware of us and brought it out. But the cedar stops it. It cannot cross the lawn, you see..."

All three were standing now, and her husband's voice broke in with authority while his wife's fingers touched the bell.

"My dear, I should *not* say anything to Thompson." The anxiety he felt was manifest in his voice, but his outward composure had returned. "The gardener can go..."

Then Sanderson cut him short. "Allow me," he said quickly. "I'll see if anything's wrong." And before either of them could answer or object, he was gone, leaping out by the open window. They saw his figure vanish with a run across the lawn into the darkness.

A moment later the maid entered, in answer to the bell, and with her came the loud barking of the terrier from the hall.

"The lamps," said her master shortly, and as she softly closed the door behind her, they heard the wind pass with a mournful sound of singing round the outer walls. A rustle of foliage from the distance passed within it.

"You see, the wind *is* rising. It *was* the wind!" He put a comforting arm about her, distressed to feel that she was trembling. But he knew that he was trembling too, though with a kind of odd elation rather than alarm. "And it *was* smoke that you saw coming from Stride's cottage, or from the rubbish heaps he's been burning in the kitchen garden. The noise we heard was the branches rustling in the wind. Why should you be so nervous?"

A thin whispering voice answered him:

"I was afraid for *you*, dear. Something frightened me for you. That man makes me feel so uneasy and uncomfortable for his influence upon you. It's very foolish, I know. I think... I'm tired; I feel so overwrought and restless." The words poured out in a hurried jumble and she kept turning to the window while she spoke.

"The strain of having a visitor," he said soothingly, "has taxed you. We're so unused to having people in the house. He goes to-morrow." He warmed her cold hands between his own, stroking them tenderly. More, for the life of him, he could not say or do. The joy of a strange, internal excitement made his heart beat faster. He knew not what it was. He knew only, perhaps, whence it came.

She peered close into his face through the gloom, and said a curious thing. "I thought, David, for a moment... you seemed... different. My nerves are all on edge to-night." She made no further reference to her husband's visitor.

A sound of footsteps from the lawn warned of Sanderson's return, as he answered quickly in a lowered tone—"There's no need to be afraid on my account, dear girl. There's nothing wrong with me, I assure you; I never felt so well and happy in my life."

Thompson came in with the lamps and brightness, and scarcely had she gone again when Sanderson in turn was seen climbing through the window.

"There's nothing," he said lightly, as he closed it behind him. "Somebody's been burning leaves, and the smoke is drifting a little through the trees. The wind," he added, glancing at his host a moment significantly, but in so discreet a way that Mrs. Bittacy did not observe it, "the wind, too, has begun to roar... in the Forest... further out."

But Mrs. Bittacy noticed about him two things which increased her uneasiness. She noticed the shining of his eyes, because a similar light had suddenly come into her husband's; and she noticed, too, the apparent depth of meaning he put into those simple words that "the wind had begun to roar in the Forest... further out." Her mind retained the disagreeable impression that he meant more than he said. In his tone lay quite another implication. It was not actually "wind" he spoke of, and it would not remain "further out"... rather, it was coming in. Another impression she got too—still more unwelcome—was that her husband understood his hidden meaning.

IV

"David, dear," she observed gently as soon as they were alone upstairs, "I have a horrible uneasy feeling about that man. I cannot get rid of it." The tremor in her voice caught all his tenderness.

He turned to look at her. "Of what kind, my dear? You're so imaginative sometimes, aren't you?"

"I think," she hesitated, stammering a little, confused, still frightened, "I mean—isn't he a hypnotist, or full of those theofosical ideas, or something of the sort? You know what I mean—"

He was too accustomed to her little confused alarms to explain them away seriously as a rule, or to correct her verbal inaccuracies, but to-night he felt she needed careful, tender treatment. He soothed her as best he could.

"But there's no harm in that, even if he is," he answered quietly. "Those are only new names for very old ideas, you know, dear." There was no trace of impatience in his voice.

"That's what I mean," she replied, the texts he dreaded rising in an unuttered crowd behind the words. "He's one of those things that we are warned would come—one of those Latter-Day things." For her mind still bristled with the bogeys of Antichrist and Prophecy, and she had only escaped the Number of the Beast, as it were, by the skin of her teeth. The Pope drew most of her fire usually, because she could understand him; the target was plain and she could shoot. But this tree-and-forest business was so vague and horrible. It terrified her. "He makes me think," she went on, "of Principalities and Powers in high places, and of things that walk in darkness. I did *not* like the way he spoke of trees getting alive in the night, and all that; it made me think of wolves in sheep's clothing. And when I saw that awful thing in the sky above the lawn—"

But he interrupted her at once, for that was something he had decided it was best to leave unmentioned. Certainly it was better not discussed.

"He only meant, I think, Sophie," he put in gravely, yet with a little smile, "that trees may have a measure of conscious life—rather a nice idea on the whole, surely,—something like that bit we read in *The Times* the other night, you remember—and that a big forest may possess a sort of Collective Personality. Remember, he's an artist, and poetical."

"It's dangerous," she said emphatically. "I feel it's playing with fire, unwise, unsafe—"

"Yet all to the glory of God," he urged gently. "We must not shut our ears and eyes to knowledge—of any kind, must we?"

"With you, David, the wish is always farther than the thought," she rejoined. For, like the child who thought that "suffered under Pontius Pilate" was "suffered under a bunch of violets," she heard her proverbs phonetically and reproduced them thus. She hoped to convey her warning in the quotation. "And we must always try the spirits whether they be of God," she added tentatively.

"Certainly, dear, we can always do that," he assented, getting into bed.

But, after a little pause, during which she blew the light out, David Bittacy settling down to sleep with an excitement in his blood that was new and bewilderingly delightful, realised that perhaps he had not said quite enough to comfort her. She was lying awake by his side, still frightened. He put his head up in the darkness.

"Sophie," he said softly, "you must remember, too, that in any case between us and—and all that sort of thing—there is a great gulf fixed, a gulf that cannot be crossed—er—while we are still in the body."

And hearing no reply, he satisfied himself that she was already asleep and happy. But Mrs. Bittacy was not asleep. She heard the sentence, only she said nothing because she felt her thought was better unexpressed. She was afraid to hear the words in the darkness. The Forest outside was listening and might hear them too—the Forest that was "roaring further out."

And the thought was this: That gulf, of course, existed, but Sanderson had somehow bridged it.

It was much later that night when she awoke out of troubled, uneasy dreams and heard a sound that twisted her very nerves with fear. It passed immediately with full waking, for, listen as she might, there was nothing audible but the inarticulate murmur of the night. It was in her dreams she heard it, and the dreams had vanished with it. But the sound was recognisable, for it was that rushing noise that had come across the lawn; only this time closer. Just above her face while she slept had passed this murmur as of rustling branches in the very room, a sound of foliage whispering. "A going in the tops of the mulberry trees," ran through her mind. She had dreamed that she lay beneath a spreading tree somewhere, a tree that whispered with ten thousand soft lips of green; and the dream continued for a moment even after waking.

She sat up in bed and stared about her. The window was open at the top; she saw the stars; the door, she remembered, was locked as usual; the room, of course, was empty. The deep hush of the summer night lay over all, broken only by another sound that now issued from the shadows close beside the bed, a human sound, yet unnatural, a sound that seized the fear with which she had waked and instantly increased it. And, although it was one she recognised as familiar, at first she could not name it. Some seconds certainly passed—and, they were very long ones—before she understood that it was her husband talking in his sleep.

The direction of the voice confused and puzzled her, moreover, for it was not, as she first supposed, beside her. There was distance in it. The next minute, by the light of the sinking candle flame, she saw his white figure standing out in the middle of the room, half-way towards the window. The candlelight slowly grew. She saw him move then nearer to the window, with arms outstretched. His speech was low and mumbled, the words running together too much to be distinguishable.

And she shivered. To her, sleep-talking was uncanny to the point of horror; it was like the talking of the dead, mere parody of a living voice, unnatural.

"David!" she whispered, dreading the sound of her own voice, and half afraid to interrupt him and see his face. She could not bear the sight of the wide-opened eyes. "David, you're walking in your sleep. Do—come back to bed, dear, *please!*"

Her whisper seemed so dreadfully loud in the still darkness. At the sound of her voice he paused, then turned slowly round to face her. His widely-opened eyes stared into her own without recognition; they looked through her into something beyond; it was as though he knew the direction of the sound, yet could not see her. They were shining, she noticed, as the eyes of Sanderson had shone several hours ago; and his face was flushed, distraught. Anxiety was written upon every feature. And, instantly, recognising that the fever was upon him, she forgot her terror temporarily in practical considerations. He came back to bed without waking. She closed his eyelids. Presently he composed himself quietly to sleep, or rather to deeper sleep. She contrived to make him swallow something from the tumbler beside the bed.

Then she rose very quietly to close the window, feeling the night air blow in too fresh and keen. She put the candle where it could not reach him. The sight of the big Baxter Bible beside it comforted her a little, but all through her under-being ran the warnings of a curious alarm. And it was while in the act of fastening the catch with one hand and pulling the string of the blind with the other, that her husband sat up again in bed and spoke in words this time that were distinctly audible. The eyes had opened wide again. He pointed. She stood stock still and listened, her shadow distorted on the blind. He did not come out towards her as at first she feared.

The whispering voice was very clear, horrible, too, beyond all she had ever known.

"They are roaring in the Forest further out... and I... must go and see." He stared beyond her as he said it, to the woods. "They are needing me. They sent for me..." Then his eyes wandering back again to things within the room, he lay down, his purpose suddenly changed. And that change was horrible as well, more horrible, perhaps, because of its revelation of another detailed world he moved in far away from her.

The singular phrase chilled her blood; for a moment she was utterly terrified. That tone of the somnambulist, differing so slightly yet so distressingly from normal, waking speech, seemed to her somehow wicked. Evil and danger lay waiting thick behind it. She leaned against the window-sill, shaking in every limb. She had an awful feeling for a moment that something was coming in to fetch him.

"Not yet, then," she heard in a much lower voice from the bed, "but later. It will be better so... I shall go later..."

The words expressed some fringe of these alarms that had haunted her so long, and that the arrival and presence of Sanderson seemed to have brought to the very edge of a climax she could not even dare to think about. They gave it form; they brought it closer; they sent her thoughts to her Deity in a wild, deep prayer for help and guidance. For here was a direct, unconscious betrayal of a world of inner purposes and claims her husband recognised while he kept them almost wholly to himself.

By the time she reached his side and knew the comfort of his touch, the eyes had closed again, this time of their own accord, and the head lay calmly back upon the pillows. She gently straightened the bed clothes. She watched him for some minutes, shading the candle carefully with one hand. There was a smile of strangest peace upon the face.

Then, blowing out the candle, she knelt down and prayed before getting back into bed. But no sleep came to her. She lay awake all night thinking, wondering, praying, until at length with the chorus of the birds and the glimmer of the dawn upon the green blind, she fell into a slumber of complete exhaustion.

But while she slept the wind continued roaring in the Forest further out. The sound came closer—sometimes very close indeed.

V

With the departure of Sanderson the significance of the curious incidents waned, because the moods that had produced them passed away. Mrs. Bittacy soon afterwards came to regard them as some growth of disproportion that had been very largely, perhaps, in her own mind. It did not strike her that this change was sudden, for it came about quite naturally. For one thing her husband never spoke of the matter, and for another she remembered how many things

in life that had seemed inexplicable and singular at the time turned
out later to have been quite commonplace.

Most of it, certainly, she put down to the presence of the artist
and to his wild, suggestive talk. With his welcome removal, the
world turned ordinary again and safe. The fever, though it lasted as
usual a short time only, had not allowed of her husband's getting up
to say good-bye, and she had conveyed his regrets and adieux. In the
morning Mr. Sanderson had seemed ordinary enough. In his town
hat and gloves, as she saw him go, he seemed tame and unalarming.

"After all," she thought as she watched the pony-cart bear him
off, "he's only an artist!" What she had thought he might be otherwise her slim imagination did not venture to disclose. Her change
of feeling was wholesome and refreshing. She felt a little ashamed
of her behaviour. She gave him a smile—genuine because the relief
she felt was genuine—as he bent over her hand and kissed it, but
she did not suggest a second visit, and her husband, she noted with
satisfaction and relief had said nothing either.

The little household fell again into the normal and sleepy routine
to which it was accustomed. The name of Arthur Sanderson was
rarely if ever mentioned. Nor, for her part, did she mention to her
husband the incident of his walking in his sleep and the wild words
he used. But to forget it was equally impossible. Thus it lay buried
deep within her like a centre of some unknown disease of which
it was a mysterious symptom, waiting to spread at the first favour-
able opportunity. She prayed against it every night and morning:
prayed that she might forget it—that God would keep her husband
safe from harm.

For in spite of much surface foolishness that many might have
read as weakness, Mrs. Bittacy had balance, sanity, and a fine deep
faith. She was greater than she knew. Her love for her husband and

her God were somehow one, an achievement only possible to a single-hearted nobility of soul.

There followed a summer of great violence and beauty; of beauty, because the refreshing rains at night prolonged the glory of the spring and spread it all across July, keeping the foliage young and sweet; of violence, because the winds that tore about the south of England brushed the whole country into dancing movement. They swept the woods magnificently, and kept them roaring with a perpetual grand voice. Their deepest notes seemed never to leave the sky. They sang and shouted, and torn leaves raced and fluttered through the air long before their usually appointed time. Many a tree, after days of this roaring and dancing, fell exhausted to the ground. The cedar on the lawn gave up two limbs that fell upon successive days, at the same hour too—just before dusk. The wind often makes its most boisterous effort at that time, before it drops with the sun, and these two huge branches lay in dark ruin covering half the lawn. They spread across it and towards the house. They left an ugly gaping space upon the tree, so that the Lebanon looked unfinished, half destroyed, a monster shorn of its old-time comeliness and splendour. Far more of the Forest was now visible than before; it peered through the breach of the broken defences. They could see from the windows of the house now—especially from the drawing-room and bedroom windows—straight out into the glades and depths beyond.

Mrs. Bittacy's niece and nephew, who were staying on a visit at the time, enjoyed themselves immensely helping the gardeners carry off the fragments. It took two days to do this, for Mr. Bittacy insisted on the branches being moved entire. He would not allow them to be chopped; also, he would not consent to their use as firewood. Under his superintendence the unwieldy masses were dragged to the edge of the garden and arranged upon the frontier line between the Forest and the lawn. The children were delighted with the scheme. They entered into it with enthusiasm. At all costs this defence against the inroads of the Forest must be made secure. They caught their uncle's earnestness, felt even something of a hidden motive that he had, and the visit, usually rather dreaded, became the visit of their lives instead. It was Aunt Sophia this time who seemed discouraging and dull.

"She's got so old and funny," opined Stephen.

But Alice, who felt in the silent displeasure of her aunt some secret thing that half alarmed her, said:

"I think she's afraid of the woods. She never comes into them with us, you see."

"All the more reason then for making this wall impreg— all fat and thick and solid," he concluded, unable to manage the longer word. "Then nothing—simply *nothing*—can get through. Can't it, Uncle David?"

And Mr. Bittacy, jacket discarded and working in his speckled waistcoat, went puffing to their aid, arranging the massive limb of the cedar like a hedge.

"Come on," he said, "whatever happens, you know, we must finish before it's dark. Already the wind is roaring in the Forest further out." And Alice caught the phrase and instantly echoed it. "Stevie," she cried below her breath, "look sharp, you lazy lump. Didn't you hear what Uncle David said? It'll come in and catch us before we've done!"

They worked like Trojans, and, sitting beneath the wistaria tree that climbed the southern wall of the cottage, Mrs. Bittacy with her knitting watched them, calling from time to time insignificant messages of counsel and advice. The messages passed, of course, unheeded. Mostly, indeed, they were unheard, for the workers were too absorbed. She warned her husband not to get too hot, Alice not to tear her dress, Stephen not to strain his back with pulling. Her mind hovered between the homoeopathic medicine-chest upstairs and her anxiety to see the business finished.

For this breaking up of the cedar had stirred again her slumbering alarms. It revived memories of the visit of Mr. Sanderson that had been sinking into oblivion; she recalled his queer and odious way of talking, and many things she hoped forgotten drew their heads up from that subconscious region to which all forgetting is impossible. They looked at her and nodded. They were full of life; they had no intention of being pushed aside and buried permanently. "Now look!" they whispered, "didn't we tell you so?" They had been merely waiting the right moment to assert their presence. And all her former vague distress crept over her. Anxiety, uneasiness returned. That dreadful sinking of the heart came too.

This incident of the cedar's breaking up was actually so unimportant, and yet her husband's attitude towards it made it so significant. There was nothing that he said in particular, or did, or left undone that frightened her, but his general air of earnestness seemed so unwarranted. She felt that he deemed the thing important. He was so exercised about it. This evidence of sudden concern and interest, buried all the summer from her sight and knowledge, she realised now had been buried purposely; he had kept it intentionally concealed. Deeply submerged in him there ran this tide of other thoughts, desires, hopes. What were they? Whither did they lead? The accident to the tree betrayed it most unpleasantly; and, doubtless, more than he was aware.

She watched his grave and serious face as he worked there with the children, and as she watched she felt afraid. It vexed her that the children worked so eagerly. They unconsciously supported him. The thing she feared she would not even name. But it was waiting.

Moreover, as far as her puzzled mind could deal with a dread so vague and incoherent, the collapse of the cedar somehow brought it nearer. The fact that, all so ill-explained and formless, the thing yet lay in her consciousness, out of reach but moving and alive, filled her with a kind of puzzled, dreadful wonder. Its presence was so very real, its power so gripping, its partial concealment so abominable. Then, out of the dim confusion, she grasped one thought and saw it stand quite clear before her eyes. She found difficulty in clothing it in words, but its meaning perhaps was this: That cedar stood in their life for something friendly; its downfall meant disaster; a sense of some protective influence about the cottage, and about her husband in particular, was thereby weakened.

"Why do you fear the big winds so?" he had asked her several days before, after a particularly boisterous day; and the answer she gave surprised her while she gave it. One of those heads poked up unconsciously, and let slip the truth:

"Because, David, I feel they—bring the Forest with them," she faltered. "They blow something from the trees—into the mind—into the house."

He looked at her keenly for a moment.

"That must be why I love them then," he answered. "They blow the souls of the trees about the sky like clouds."

The conversation dropped. She had never heard him talk in quite that way before.

And another time, when he had coaxed her to go with him down one of the nearer glades, she asked why he took the small hand-axe with him, and what he wanted it for.

"To cut the ivy that clings to the trunks and takes their life away," he said.

"But can't the verdurers do that?" she asked. "That's what they're paid for, isn't it?"

Whereupon he explained that ivy was a parasite the trees knew not how to fight alone, and that the verdurers were careless and did not do it thoroughly. They gave a chop here and there, leaving the tree to do the rest for itself if it could.

"Besides, I like to do it for them. I love to help them and protect," he added, the foliage rustling all about his quiet words as they went.

And these stray remarks, as his attitude towards the broken cedar, betrayed this curious, subtle change that was going forward in his personality. Slowly and surely all the summer it had increased.

It was growing—the thought startled her horribly—just as a tree grows, the outer evidence from day to day so slight as to be unnoticeable, yet the rising tide so deep and irresistible. The alteration spread all through and over him, was in both mind and actions, sometimes almost in his face as well. Occasionally, thus, it stood up straight outside himself and frightened her. His life was somehow becoming linked so intimately with trees, and with all that trees signified. His interests became more and more their interests, his activity combined with theirs, his thoughts and feelings theirs, his purpose, hope, desire, his fate—

His fate! The darkness of some vague, enormous terror dropped its shadow on her when she thought of it. Some instinct in her heart she dreaded infinitely more than death—for death meant sweet translation for his soul—came gradually to associate the thought of him with the thought of trees, in particular with these Forest trees. Sometimes, before she could face the thing, argue it away, or pray it into silence, she found the thought of him running swiftly through her mind like a thought of the Forest itself, the two most intimately linked and joined together, each a part and complement of the other, one being.

The idea was too dim for her to see it face to face. Its mere possibility dissolved the instant she focussed it to get the truth behind it. It was too utterly elusive, mad, protæan. Under the attack of even a minute's concentration the very meaning of it vanished, melted away. The idea lay really behind any words that she could ever find, beyond the touch of definite thought. Her mind was unable to grapple with it. But, while it vanished, the trail of its approach and disappearance flickered a moment before her shaking vision. The horror certainly remained.

Reduced to the simple human statement that her temperament sought instinctively it stood perhaps at this: Her husband loved her, and he loved the trees as well; but the trees came first, claimed parts of him she did not know. *She* loved her God and him. *He* loved the trees and her.

Thus, in guise of some faint, distressing compromise, the matter shaped itself for her perplexed mind in the terms of conflict. A silent, hidden battle raged, but as yet raged far away. The breaking of the cedar was a visible outward fragment of a distant and mysterious encounter that was coming daily closer to them both. The wind, instead of roaring in the Forest further out, now came nearer, booming in fitful gusts about its edge and frontiers.

Meanwhile the summer dimmed. The autumn winds went sighing through the woods; leaves turned to golden red, and the evenings were drawing in with cosy shadows before the first sign of anything seriously untoward made its appearance. It came then with a flat, decided kind of violence that indicated mature preparation beforehand. It was not impulsive nor ill-considered. In a fashion it seemed expected, and indeed inevitable. For within a fortnight of their annual change to the little village of Seillans above St. Raphael—a change so regular for the past ten years that it was not even discussed between them—David Bittacy abruptly refused to go.

Thompson had laid the tea-table, prepared the spirit lamp beneath the urn, pulled down the blinds in that swift and silent way she had, and left the room. The lamps were still unlit. The firelight shone on the chintz armchairs, and Boxer lay asleep on the black horse-hair rug. Upon the walls the gilt picture frames gleamed faintly, the pictures themselves indistinguishable. Mrs. Bittacy had warmed the teapot and was in the act of pouring the water in to heat the cups when her husband, looking up from his chair across the hearth, made the abrupt announcement:

"My dear," he said, as though following a train of thought of which she only heard this final phrase, "it's really quite impossible for me to go."

And so abrupt, inconsequent, it sounded that she at first misunderstood. She thought he meant go out into the garden or the woods. But her heart leaped all the same. The tone of his voice was ominous.

"Of course not," she answered, "it would be *most* unwise. Why should you—?" She referred to the mist that always spread on autumn nights upon the lawn; but before she finished the sentence she knew that *he* referred to something else. And her heart then gave its second horrible leap.

"David! You mean abroad?" she gasped.

"I mean abroad, dear, yes."

It reminded her of the tone he used when saying good-bye years ago before one of those jungle expeditions she dreaded. His voice then was so serious, so final. It was serious and final now. For several moments she could think of nothing to say. She busied herself with the teapot. She had filled one cup with hot water till it overflowed, and she emptied it slowly into the slop-basin, trying with all her might not to let him see the trembling of her hand. The firelight and the dimness of the room both helped her. But in any case he would hardly have noticed it. His thoughts were far away...

VI

Mrs. Bittacy had never liked their present home. She preferred a flat, more open country that left approaches clear. She liked to see things coming. This cottage on the very edge of the old hunting grounds of William the Conqueror had never satisfied her ideal of a safe and pleasant place to settle down in. The sea-coast, with tree-less downs behind and a clear horizon in front, as at Eastbourne, say, was her ideal of a proper home.

It was curious, this instinctive aversion she felt to being shut in—by trees especially; a kind of claustrophobia almost; probably due, as has been said, to the days in India when the trees took her husband off and surrounded him with dangers. In those weeks of solitude the feeling had matured. She had fought it in her fashion, but never conquered it. Apparently routed, it had a way of creeping back in other forms. In this particular case, yielding to his strong desire, she thought the battle won, but the terror of the trees came back before the first month had passed. They laughed in her face.

She never lost knowledge of the fact that the leagues of forest lay about their cottage like a mighty wall, a crowding, watching, listening presence that shut them in from freedom and escape. Far from morbid naturally, she did her best to deny the thought, and so simple and unartificial was her type of mind that for weeks together she would wholly lose it. Then, suddenly it would return upon her with a rush of bleak reality. It was not only in her mind; it existed apart from any mere mood; a separate fear that walked alone; it came and went, yet when it went—went only to watch her from another point of view. It was in abeyance hidden round the corner.

The Forest never let her go completely. It was ever ready to encroach. All the branches, she sometimes fancied, stretched one way—towards their tiny cottage and garden, as though it sought to draw them in and merge them in itself. Its great, deep-breathing soul resented the mockery, the insolence, the irritation of the prim garden at its very gates. It would absorb and smother them if it could. And every wind that blew its thundering message over the huge sounding-board of the million, shaking trees conveyed the purpose that it had. They had angered its great soul. At its heart was this deep, incessant roaring.

All this she never framed in words; the subtleties of language lay far beyond her reach. But instinctively she felt it; and more besides. It troubled her profoundly. Chiefly, moreover, for her husband. Merely for herself, the nightmare might have left her cold. It was David's peculiar interest in the trees that gave the special invitation.

Jealousy, then, in its most subtle aspect came to strengthen this aversion and dislike, for it came in a form that no reasonable wife could possibly object to. Her husband's passion, she reflected, was natural and inborn. It had decided his vocation, fed his ambition, nourished his dreams, desires, hopes. All his best years of active life had been spent in the care and guardianship of trees. He knew them, understood their secret life and nature, "managed" them intuitively as other men "managed" dogs and horses. He could not live for long away from them without a strange, acute nostalgia that stole his peace of mind and consequently his strength of body. A forest made him happy and at peace; it nursed and fed and soothed his deepest moods. Trees influenced the sources of his life, lowered or raised the very heart-beat in him. Cut off from them he languished as a lover of the sea can droop inland, or a mountaineer may pine in the flat monotony of the plains.

This she could understand, in a fashion at least, and make allowances for. She had yielded gently, even sweetly, to his choice of their English home; for in the little island there is nothing that suggests the woods of wilder countries so nearly as the New Forest. It has the genuine air and mystery, the depth and splendour, the loneliness, and here and there the strong, untamable quality of old-time forests as Bittacy of the Department knew them.

In a single detail only had he yielded to her wishes. He consented to a cottage on the edge, instead of in the heart of it. And for a dozen years now they had dwelt in peace and happiness at the lips of this great spreading thing that covered so many leagues with its tangle of swamps and moors and splendid ancient trees.

Only with the last two years or so—with his own increasing age, and physical decline perhaps—had come this marked growth of passionate interest in the welfare of the Forest. She had watched it grow, at first had laughed at it, then talked sympathetically so far as sincerity permitted, then had argued mildly, and finally come to realise that its treatment lay altogether beyond her powers, and so had come to fear it with all her heart.

★

The six weeks they annually spent away from their English home, each regarded very differently of course. For her husband it meant a painful exile that did his health no good; he yearned for his trees— the sight and sound and smell of them; but for herself it meant release from a haunting dread—escape. To renounce those six weeks by the sea on the sunny, shining coast of France, was almost more than this little woman, even with her unselfishness, could face.

After the first shock of the announcement, she reflected as deeply as her nature permitted, prayed, wept in secret—and made up her mind. Duty, she felt clearly, pointed to renouncement. The discipline would certainly be severe—she did not dream at the moment how severe!—but this fine, consistent little Christian saw it plain; she accepted it, too, without any sighing of the martyr, though the courage she showed was of the martyr order. Her husband should never know the cost. In all but this one passion his unselfishness was ever as great as her own. The love she had borne him all these years, like the love she bore her anthropomorphic deity, was deep and real. She loved to suffer for them both. Besides, the way her husband had put it to her was singular. It did not take the form of a mere selfish predilection. Something higher than two wills in conflict seeking compromise was in it from the beginning.

"I feel, Sophia, it would be really more than I could manage," he said slowly, gazing into the fire over the tops of his stretched-out muddy boots. "My duty and my happiness lie here with the Forest and with you. My life is deeply rooted in this place. Something I can't define connects my inner being with these trees, and separation would make me ill—might even kill me. My hold on life would weaken; here is my source of supply. I cannot explain it better than that." He looked up steadily into her face across the table so that she saw the gravity of his expression and the shining of his steady eyes.

"David, you feel it as strongly as that!" she said, forgetting the tea things altogether.

"Yes," he replied, "I do. And it's not of the body only; I feel it in my soul."

The reality of what he hinted at crept into that shadow-covered room like an actual Presence and stood beside them. It came not by the windows or the door, but it filled the entire space between the walls and ceiling. It took the heat from the fire before her face. She felt suddenly cold, confused a little, frightened. She almost felt the rush of foliage in the wind. It stood between them.

"There are things—some things," she faltered, "we are not intended to know, I think." The words expressed her general attitude to life, not alone to this particular incident.

And after a pause of several minutes, disregarding the criticism as though he had not heard it—"I cannot explain it better than that, you see," his grave voice answered. "There *is* this deep, tremendous link,—some secret power they emanate that keeps me well and happy and—alive. If you cannot understand, I feel at least you may be able to—forgive." His tone grew tender, gentle, soft. "My selfishness, I know, must seem quite unforgivable. I cannot help it somehow; these trees, this ancient Forest, both seem knitted into all that makes me live, and if I go—"

There was a little sound of collapse in his voice. He stopped abruptly, and sank back in his chair. And, at that, a distinct lump came up into her throat which she had great difficulty in managing while she went over and put her arms about him.

"My dear," she murmured, "God will direct. We will accept His guidance. He has always shown the way before."

"My selfishness afflicts me—" he began, but she would not let him finish.

"David, He will direct. Nothing shall harm you. You've never once been selfish, and I cannot bear to hear you say such things. The way will open that is best for you—for both of us." She kissed him; she would not let him speak; her heart was in her throat, and she felt for him far more than for herself.

And then he had suggested that she should go alone perhaps for a shorter time, and stay in her brother's villa with the children, Alice and Stephen. It was always open to her as she well knew.

"You need the change," he said, when the lamps had been lit and the servant had gone out again; "you need it as much as I dread it. I could manage somehow till you returned, and should feel happier that way if you went. I cannot leave this Forest that I love so well. I even feel, Sophie dear"—he sat up straight and faced her as he half whispered it—"that I can *never* leave it again. My life and happiness lie here together."

And even while scorning the idea that she could leave him alone with the Influence of the Forest all about him to have its unimpeded way, she felt the pangs of that subtle jealousy bite keen and close. He loved the Forest better than herself, for he placed it first. Behind the words, moreover, hid the unuttered thought that made her so uneasy. The terror Sanderson had brought revived and shook its wings before her very eyes. For the whole conversation, of which this was a fragment, conveyed the unutterable implication that while he could not spare the trees, they equally could not spare him. The vividness with which he managed to conceal and yet betray the fact brought a profound distress that crossed the border between presentiment and warning into positive alarm.

He clearly felt that the trees would miss him—the trees he tended, guarded, watched over, loved.

"David, I shall stay here with you. I think you need me really,—don't you?" Eagerly, with a touch of heart-felt passion, the words poured out.

"Now more than ever, dear. God bless you for your sweet unselfishness. And your sacrifice," he added, "is all the greater because you cannot understand the thing that makes it necessary for me to stay."

"Perhaps in the spring instead—" she said, with a tremor in the voice.

"In the spring—perhaps," he answered gently, almost beneath his breath. "For they will not need me then. All the world can love them in the spring. It's in the winter that they're lonely and neglected. I wish to stay with them particularly then. I even feel I ought to—and I must."

And in this way, without further speech, the decision was made. Mrs. Bittacy, at least, asked no more questions. Yet she could not bring herself to show more sympathy than was necessary. She felt, for one thing, that if she did, it might lead him to speak freely, and to tell her things she could not possibly bear to know. And she dared not take the risk of that.

VII

This was at the end of summer, but the autumn followed close. The conversation really marked the threshold between the two seasons, and marked at the same time the line between her husband's negative and aggressive state. She almost felt she had done wrong to yield; he grew so bold, concealment all discarded. He went, that is, quite openly to the woods, forgetting all his duties, all his former occupations. He even sought to coax her to go with him. The hidden thing blazed out without disguise. And, while she trembled at his energy, she admired the virile passion he displayed. Her jealousy had long ago retired before her fear, accepting the second place. Her one desire now was to protect. The wife turned wholly mother.

He said so little, but—he hated to come in. From morning to night he wandered in the Forest; often he went out after dinner; his mind was charged with trees—their foliage, growth, development; their wonder, beauty, strength; their loneliness in isolation, their power in a herded mass. He knew the effect of every wind upon them; the danger from the boisterous north, the glory from the west, the eastern dryness, and the soft, moist tenderness that a south wind left upon their thinning boughs. He spoke all day of their sensations: how they drank the fading sunshine, dreamed in the moonlight, thrilled to the kiss of stars. The dew could bring them half the passion of the night, but frost sent them plunging beneath the ground to dwell with hopes of a later coming softness in their roots. They nursed the life they carried—insects, larvae, chrysalis—and when the skies above them melted, he spoke of them standing "motionless in an ecstasy of rain," or in the noon of sunshine "self-poised upon their prodigy of shade."

And once in the middle of the night she woke at the sound of his voice, and heard him—wide awake, not talking in his sleep—but talking towards the window where the shadow of the cedar fell at noon:

O art thou sighing for Lebanon
In the long breeze that streams to thy delicious East?
Sighing for Lebanon,
Dark cedar;

and, when, half charmed, half terrified, she turned and called to him by name, he merely said—

"My dear, I felt the loneliness—suddenly realised it—the alien desolation of that tree, set here upon our little lawn in England when all her Eastern brothers call to her in sleep." And the answer seemed so queer, so "un-evangelical," that she waited in silence till he slept again. The poetry passed her by. It seemed unnecessary and out of place. It made her ache with suspicion, fear, jealousy.

The fear, however, seemed somehow all lapped up and banished soon afterwards by her unwilling admiration of the rushing splendour of her husband's state. Her anxiety, at any rate, shifted from the religious to the medical. She thought he might be losing his steadiness of mind a little. How often in her prayers she offered thanks for the guidance that had made her stay with him to help and watch is impossible to say. It certainly was twice a day.

She even went so far once, when Mr. Mortimer, the vicar, called, and brought with him a more or less distinguished doctor—as to tell the professional man privately some symptoms of her husband's queerness. And his answer that there was "nothing he could prescribe for" added not a little to her sense of unholy bewilderment. No doubt Sir James had never been "consulted" under such unorthodox conditions before. His sense of what was becoming naturally overrode his acquired instincts as a skilled instrument that might help the race.

"No fever, you think?" she asked insistently with hurry, determined to get something from him.

"Nothing that *I* can deal with, as I told you, Madam," replied the offended allopathic Knight.

Evidently he did not care about being invited to examine patients in this surreptitious way before a teapot on the lawn, chance of a fee most problematical. He liked to see a tongue and feel a thumping pulse; to know the pedigree and bank account of his questioner as well. It was most unusual, in abominable taste besides. Of course it was. But the drowning woman seized the only straw she could.

For now the aggressive attitude of her husband overcame her to the point where she found it difficult even to question him. Yet in the house he was so kind and gentle, doing all he could to make her sacrifice as easy as possible.

"David, you really *are* unwise to go out now. The night is damp and very chilly. The ground is soaked in dew. You'll catch your death of cold."

His face lightened. "Won't you come with me, dear,—just for once? I'm only going to the corner of the hollies to see the beech that stands so lonely by itself."

She had been out with him in the short dark afternoon, and they had passed that evil group of hollies where the gipsies camped. Nothing else would grow there, but the hollies throve upon the stony soil.

"David, the beech is all right and safe." She had learned his phraseology a little, made clever out of due season by her love. "There's no wind to-night."

"But it's rising," he answered, "rising in the east. I heard it in the bare and hungry larches. They need the sun and dew, and always cry out when the wind's upon them from the east."

She sent a short unspoken prayer most swiftly to her deity as she heard him say it. For every time now, when he spoke in this familiar, intimate way of the life of the trees, she felt a sheet of cold fasten tight against her very skin and flesh. She shivered. How *could* he possibly know such things?

Yet, in all else, and in the relations of his daily life, he was sane and reasonable, loving, kind and tender. It was only on the subject of the trees he seemed unhinged and queer. Most curiously it seemed that, since the collapse of the cedar they both loved, though in different fashion, his departure from the normal had increased. Why else did he watch them as a man might watch a sickly child? Why did he linger especially in the dusk to catch their "mood of night" as he called it? Why think so carefully upon them when the frost was threatening or the wind appeared to rise?

As she put it so frequently now to herself—How could he possibly *know* such things?

He went. As she closed the front door after him she heard the distant roaring in the Forest...

And then it suddenly struck her: How could she know them too?

It dropped upon her like a blow that she felt at once all over, upon body, heart and mind. The discovery rushed out from its ambush to overwhelm. The truth of it, making all arguing futile, numbed her faculties. But though at first it deadened her, she soon revived, and her being rose into aggressive opposition. A wild yet calculated courage like that which animates the leaders of splendid forlorn hopes flamed in her little person—flamed grandly, and invincible. While knowing herself insignificant and weak, she knew at the same time that power at her back which moves the worlds. The faith that filled her was the weapon in her hands, and the right by which she claimed it; but the spirit of utter, selfless sacrifice that characterised her life was the means by which she mastered its immediate use. For a kind of white and faultless intuition guided her to the attack. Behind her stood her Bible and her God.

How so magnificent a divination came to her at all may well be a matter for astonishment, though some clue of explanation lies, perhaps, in the very simpleness of her nature. At any rate, she saw quite clearly certain things; saw them in moments only—after prayer, in the still silence of the night, or when left alone those long hours in the house with her knitting and her thoughts—and the guidance which then flashed into her remained, even after the manner of its coming was forgotten.

They came to her, these things she saw, formless, wordless; she could not put them into any kind of language; but by the very fact of being uncaught in sentences they retained their original clear vigour.

Hours of patient waiting brought the first, and the others followed easily afterwards, by degrees, on subsequent days, a little and a little. Her husband had been gone since early morning, and had taken his luncheon with him. She was sitting by the tea things, the cups and teapot warmed, the muffins in the fender keeping hot, all ready for his return, when she realised quite abruptly that this thing which took him off, which kept him out so many hours day after day, this thing that was against her own little will and instincts—was enormous as the sea. It was no mere prettiness of single Trees, but something massed and mountainous. About her rose the wall of its huge opposition to the sky, its scale gigantic, its power utterly prodigious. What she knew of it hitherto as green and delicate forms waving and rustling in the winds was but, as it were, the spray of foam that broke into sight upon the nearer edge of viewless depths far, far away. The trees, indeed, were sentinels set visibly about the limits of a camp that itself remained invisible. The awful hum and murmur of the main body in the distance passed into that still room about her with the firelight and hissing kettle. Out yonder—in the

Forest further out—the thing that was ever roaring at the centre was dreadfully increasing.

The sense of definite battle, too—battle between herself and the Forest for his soul—came with it. Its presentment was as clear as though Thompson had come into the room and quietly told her that the cottage was surrounded. "Please, ma'am, there are trees come up about the house," she might have suddenly announced. And equally might have heard her own answer: "It's all right, Thompson. The main body is still far away."

Immediately upon its heels, then, came another truth, with a close reality that shocked her. She saw that jealousy was not confined to the human and animal world alone, but ran through all creation. The Vegetable Kingdom knew it too. So-called inanimate nature shared it with the rest. Trees felt it. This Forest just beyond the window—standing there in the silence of the autumn evening across the little lawn—this Forest understood it equally. The remorseless, branching power that sought to keep exclusively for itself the thing it loved and needed, spread like a running desire through all its million leaves and stems and roots. In humans, of course, it was consciously directed; in animals it acted with frank instinctiveness; but in trees this jealousy rose in some blind tide of impersonal and unconscious wrath that would sweep opposition from its path as the wind sweeps powdered snow from the surface of the ice. Their number was a host with endless reinforcements, and once it realised its passion was returned the power increased... Her husband loved the trees... They had become aware of it... They would take him from her in the end...

Then, while she heard his footsteps in the hall and the closing of the front door, she saw a third thing clearly;—realised the widening of the gap between herself and him. This other love had made it. All these weeks of the summer when she felt so close to him, now especially when she had made the biggest sacrifice of her life to stay by his side and help him, he had been slowly, surely—drawing away. The estrangement was here and now—a fact accomplished. It had been all this time maturing; there yawned this broad deep space between them. Across the empty distance she saw the change in merciless perspective. It revealed his face and figure, dearly-loved, once fondly worshipped, far on the other side in shadowy distance, small, the back turned from her, and moving while she watched— moving away from her.

They had their tea in silence then. She asked no questions, he volunteered no information of his day. The heart was big within her, and the terrible loneliness of age spread through her like a rising icy mist. She watched him, filling all his wants. His hair was untidy and his boots were caked with blackish mud. He moved with a restless, swaying motion that somehow blanched her cheek and sent a miserable shivering down her back. It reminded her of trees. His eyes were very bright.

He brought in with him an odour of the earth and forest that seemed to choke her and make it difficult to breathe; and—what she noticed with a climax of almost uncontrollable alarm—upon his face beneath the lamplight shone traces of a mild, faint glory that made her think of moonlight falling upon a wood through speckled shadows. It was his new-found happiness that shone there, a happiness uncaused by her and in which she had no part.

In his coat was a spray of faded yellow beech leaves. "I brought this from the Forest for you," he said, with all the air that belonged to his little acts of devotion long ago. And she took the spray of leaves mechanically with a smile and a murmured "thank you, dear,"

as though he had unknowingly put into her hands the weapon for
her own destruction and she had accepted it.

And when the tea was over and he left the room, he did not go
to his study, or to change his clothes. She heard the front door softly
shut behind him as he again went out towards the Forest.

A moment later she was in her room upstairs, kneeling beside
the bed—the side he slept on—and praying wildly through a flood
of tears that God would save and keep him to her. Wind brushed
the window panes behind her while she knelt.

VIII

One sunny November morning, when the strain had reached a pitch
that made repression almost unmanageable, she came to an impulsive decision, and obeyed it. Her husband had again gone out with
luncheon for the day. She took adventure in her hands and followed
him. The power of seeing-clear was strong upon her, forcing her
up to some unnatural level of understanding. To stay indoors and
wait inactive for his return seemed suddenly impossible. She meant
to know what he knew, feel what he felt, put herself in his place.
She would dare the fascination of the Forest—share it with him.
It was greatly daring; but it would give her greater understanding
how to help and save him and therefore greater Power. She went
upstairs a moment first to pray.

In a thick, warm skirt, and wearing heavy boots—those walking
boots she used with him upon the mountains about Seillans—she
left the cottage by the back way and turned towards the Forest.
She could not actually follow him, for he had started off an hour
before and she knew not exactly his direction. What was so urgent

in her was the wish to be with him in the woods, to walk beneath
the leafless branches just as he did: to be there when he was there,
even though not together. For it had come to her that she might
thus share with him for once this horrible mighty life and breathing of the trees he loved. In winter, he had said, they needed him
particularly; and winter now was coming. Her love *must* bring her
something of what he felt himself—the huge attraction, the suction
and the pull of all the trees. Thus, in some vicarious fashion, she
might share, though unknown to himself, this very thing that was
taking him away from her. She might thus even lessen its attack
upon himself.

The impulse came to her clairvoyantly, and she obeyed without
a sign of hesitation. Deeper comprehension would come to her of
the whole awful puzzle. And come it did, yet not in the way she
imagined and expected.

The air was very still, the sky a cold pale blue, but cloudless.
The entire Forest stood silent, at attention. It knew perfectly well
that she had come. It knew the moment when she entered; watched
and followed her; and behind her something dropped without a
sound and shut her in. Her feet upon the glades of mossy grass fell
silently, as the oaks and beeches shifted past in rows and took up
their positions at her back. It was not pleasant, this way they grew
so dense behind her the instant she had passed. She realised that
they gathered in an ever-growing army, massed, herded, trooped,
between her and the cottage, shutting off escape. They let her
pass so easily, but to get out again she would know them differently—thick, crowded, branches all drawn and hostile. Already
their increasing numbers bewildered her. In front, they looked so
sparse and scattered, with open spaces where the sunshine fell; but
when she turned it seemed they stood so close together, a serried

army, darkening the sunlight. They blocked the day, collected all the shadows, stood with their leafless and forbidding rampart like the night. They swallowed down into themselves the very glade by which she came. For when she glanced behind her—rarely—the way she had come was shadowy and lost.

Yet the morning sparkled overhead, and a glance of excitement ran quivering through the entire day. It was what she always knew as "children's weather," so clear and harmless, without a sign of danger, nothing ominous to threaten or alarm. Steadfast in her purpose, looking back as little as she dared, Sophia Bittacy marched slowly and deliberately into the heart of the silent woods, deeper, ever deeper...

And then, abruptly, in an open space where the sunshine fell unhindered, she stopped. It was one of the breathing-places of the forest. Dead, withered bracken lay in patches of unsightly grey. There were bits of heather too. All round the trees stood looking on—oak, beech, holly, ash, pine, larch, with here and there small groups of juniper. On the lips of this breathing-space of the woods she stopped to rest, disobeying her instinct for the first time. For the other instinct in her was to go on. She did not really want to rest.

This was the little act that brought it to her—the wireless message from a vast Emitter.

"I've been stopped," she thought to herself with a horrid qualm.

She looked about her in this quiet, ancient place. Nothing stirred. There was no life nor sign of life; no birds sang; no rabbits scuttled off at her approach. The stillness was bewildering, and gravity hung down upon it like a heavy curtain. It hushed the heart in her. Could this be part of what her husband felt—this sense of thick entanglement with stems, boughs, roots, and foliage?

"This has always been as it is now," she thought, yet not knowing why she thought it. "Ever since the Forest grew it has been still and secret here. It has never changed." The curtain of silence drew closer while she said it, thickening round her. "For a thousand years—I'm here with a thousand years. And behind this place stand all the forests of the world!"

So foreign to her temperament were such thoughts, and so alien to all she had been taught to look for in Nature, that she strove against them. She made an effort to oppose. But they clung and haunted just the same; they refused to be dispersed. The curtain hung dense and heavy as though its texture thickened. The air with difficulty came through.

And then she thought that curtain stirred. There was movement somewhere. That obscure dim thing which ever broods behind the visible appearances of trees came nearer to her. She caught her breath and stared about her, listening intently. The trees, perhaps because she saw them more in detail now, it seemed to her had changed. A vague, faint alteration spread over them, at first so slight she scarcely would admit it, then growing steadily, though still obscurely, outwards. "They tremble and are changed," flashed through her mind the horrid line that Sanderson had quoted. Yet the change was graceful for all the uncouthness attendant upon the size of so vast a movement. They had turned in her direction. That was it. *They saw her.*

In this way the change expressed itself in her groping, terrified thought. Till now it had been otherwise: she had looked at them from her own point of view; now they looked at her from theirs. They stared her in the face and eyes; they stared at her all over. In some unkind, resentful, hostile way, they watched her. Hitherto in life she had watched them variously, in superficial ways, reading into them what her own mind suggested. Now they read into her the things they actually *were*, and not merely another's interpretation of them.

They seemed in their motionless silence there instinct with life, a life, moreover, that breathed about her a species of terrible soft enchantment that bewitched. It branched all through her, climbing to the brain. The Forest held her with its huge and giant fascination. In this secluded breathing-spot that the centuries had left untouched, she had stepped close against the hidden pulse of the whole collective mass of them. They were aware of her and had turned to gaze with their myriad, vast sight upon the intruder. They shouted at her in the silence. For she wanted to look back at them, but it was like staring at a crowd, and her glance merely shifted from one tree to another, hurriedly, finding in none the one she sought. They saw her so easily, each and all. The rows that stood behind her also stared. But she could not return the gaze. Her husband, she realised, could. And their steady stare shocked her as though in some sense she knew that she was naked. They saw so much of her: she saw of them—so little.

Her efforts to return their gaze were pitiful. The constant shifting increased her bewilderment. Conscious of this awful and enormous sight all over her, she let her eyes first rest upon the ground; and then she closed them altogether. She kept the lids as tight together as ever they would go.

But the sight of the trees came even into that inner darkness behind the fastened lids, for there was no escaping it. Outside, in the light, she still knew that the leaves of the hollies glittered smoothly, that the dead foliage of the oaks hung crisp in the air above her, that the needles of the little junipers were pointing all one way. The spread perception of the Forest was focussed on herself, and no mere shutting of the eyes could hide its scattered yet concentrated stare—the all-inclusive vision of great woods.

There was no wind, yet here and there a single leaf hanging by its dried-up stalk shook all alone with great rapidity—rattling. It was the sentry drawing attention to her presence. And then, again, as once long weeks before, she felt their Being as a tide about her. The tide had turned. That memory of her childhood sands came back, when the nurse said, "The tide has turned now; we must go in," and she saw the mass of piled-up waters, green and heaped to the horizon, and realised that it was slowly coming in. The gigantic mass of it, too vast for hurry, loaded with massive purpose, she used to feel, was moving towards herself. The fluid body of the sea was creeping along beneath the sky to the very spot upon the yellow sands where she stood and played. The sight and thought of it had always overwhelmed her with a sense of awe—as though her puny self were the object of the whole sea's advance. "The tide has turned; we had better now go in."

This was happening now about her—the same thing was happening in the woods—slow, sure, and steady, and its motion as little discernible as the sea's. The tide had turned. The small human presence that had ventured among its green and mountainous depths, moreover, was its objective.

That all was clear within her while she sat and waited with tight-shut lids. But the next moment she opened her eyes with a sudden realisation of something more. The presence that it sought was after all not hers. It was the presence of some one other than herself. And then she understood. Her eyes had opened with a click, it seemed; but the sound, in reality, was outside herself. Across the clearing where the sunshine lay so calm and still, she saw the figure of her husband moving among the trees—a man, like a tree, walking.

With hands behind his back, and head uplifted, he moved quite slowly, as though absorbed in his own thoughts. Hardly fifty paces separated them, but he had no inkling of her presence there so near. With mind intent and senses all turned inwards, he marched past her like a figure in a dream, and like a figure in a dream she saw him go. Love, yearning, pity rose in a storm within her, but as in nightmare she found no words or movement possible. She sat and watched him go—go from her—go into the deeper reaches of the green enveloping woods. Desire to save, to bid him stop and turn, ran in a passion through her being, but there was nothing she could do. She saw him go away from her, go of his own accord and willingly beyond her; she saw the branches drop about his steps and hide him. His figure faded out among the speckled shade and sunlight. The trees covered him. The tide just took him, all unresisting and content to go. Upon the bosom of the green soft sea he floated away beyond her reach of vision. Her eyes could follow him no longer. He was gone.

And then for the first time she realised, even at that distance, that the look upon his face was one of peace and happiness—rapt, and caught away in joy, a look of youth. That expression now he never showed to her. But she *had* known it. Years ago, in the early days of their married life, she had seen it on his face. Now it no longer obeyed the summons of her presence and her love. The woods alone could call it forth; it answered to the trees; the Forest had taken every part of him—from her—his very heart and soul…

Her sight that had plunged inwards to the fields of faded memory now came back to outer things again. She looked about her, and her love, returning empty-handed and unsatisfied, left her open to the invading of the bleakest terror she had ever known. That such things could be real and happen found her helpless utterly. Terror invaded the quietest corners of her heart, that had never yet known quailing. She could not—for moments at any rate—reach either her Bible or her God. Desolate in an empty world of fear she sat with eyes too dry and hot for tears, yet with a coldness as of ice upon her very flesh. She stared, unseeing, about her. That horror which stalks in the stillness of the noonday, when the glare of an artificial sunshine lights up the motionless trees, moved all about her. In front and behind she was aware of it. Beyond this stealthy silence, just within the edge of it, the things of another world were passing. But she could not know them. Her husband knew them, knew their beauty and their awe, yes, but for her they were out of reach. She might not share with him the very least of them. It seemed that behind and through the glare of this wintry noonday in the heart of the woods there brooded another universe of life and passion, for her all unexpressed. The silence veiled it, the stillness hid it; but he moved with it all and understood. His love interpreted it.

She rose to her feet, tottered feebly, and collapsed again upon the moss. Yet for herself she felt no terror; no little personal fear could touch her whose anguish and deep longing streamed all out to him whom she so bravely loved. In this time of utter self-forgetfulness, when she realised that the battle was hopeless, thinking she had lost even her God, she found Him again quite close beside her like a little Presence in this terrible heart of the hostile Forest. But at first she did not recognise that He was there; she did not know Him in that strangely unacceptable guise. For He stood so very close, so very intimate, so very sweet and comforting, and yet so hard to understand—as Resignation.

Once more she struggled to her feet, and this time turned success-fully and slowly made her way along the mossy glade by which she came. And at first she marvelled, though only for a moment, at the ease with which she found the path. For a moment only, because almost at once she saw the truth. The trees were glad that she should go. They helped her on her way. The Forest did not want her.

The tide was coming in, indeed, yet not for her.

And so, in another of those flashes of clear-vision that of late had lifted life above the normal level, she saw and understood the whole terrible thing complete.

Till now, though unexpressed in thought or language, her fear had been that the woods her husband loved would somehow take him from her—to merge his life in theirs—even to kill him in some mysterious way. This time she saw her deep mistake, and so seeing, let in upon herself the fuller agony of horror. For their jealousy was not the petty jealousy of animals or humans. They wanted him because they loved him, but they did not want him dead. Full charged with his splendid life and enthusiasm they wanted him. They wanted him—alive.

It was she who stood in their way, and it was she whom they intended to remove.

This was what brought the sense of abject helplessness. She stood upon the sands against an entire ocean slowly rolling in against her. For, as all the forces of a human being combine unconsciously to eject a grain of sand that has crept beneath the skin to cause discomfort, so the entire mass of what Sanderson had called the Collective Consciousness of the Forest strove to eject this human atom that stood across the path of its desire. Loving her husband, she had crept beneath its skin. It was her they would eject and take away; it was her they would destroy, not him. Him, whom they loved and needed, they would keep alive. They meant to take him living.

She reached the house in safety, though she never remembered how she found her way. It was made all simple for her. The branches almost urged her out.

But behind her, as she left the shadowed precincts, she felt as though some towering Angel of the Woods let fall across the threshold the flaming sword of a countless multitude of leaves that formed behind her a barrier, green, shimmering, and impassable. Into the Forest she never walked again.

And she went about her daily duties with a calm and quietness that was a perpetual astonishment even to herself, for it hardly seemed of this world at all. She talked to her husband when he came in for tea—after dark. Resignation brings a curious large courage—when there is nothing more to lose. The soul takes risks, and dares. Is it a curious short-cut sometimes to the heights?

"David, I went into the Forest, too, this morning; soon after you I went. I saw you there."

"Wasn't it wonderful?" he answered simply, inclining his head a little. There was no surprise or annoyance in his look; a mild and gentle *ennui* rather. He asked no real question. She thought of some garden tree the wind attacks too suddenly, bending it over when it does not want to bend—the mild unwillingness with which it yields. She often saw him this way now, in the terms of trees.

"It was very wonderful indeed, dear, yes," she replied low, her voice not faltering though indistinct. "But for me it was too—too strange and big."

The passion of tears lay just below the quiet voice all unbetrayed. Somehow she kept them back.

There was a pause, and then he added:

"I find it more and more so every day." His voice passed through the lamp-lit room like a murmur of the wind in branches. The look of youth and happiness she had caught upon his face out there had wholly gone, and an expression of weariness was in its place, as of a man distressed vaguely at finding himself in uncongenial surroundings where he is slightly ill at ease. It was the house he hated—coming back to rooms and walls and furniture. The ceilings and closed windows confined him. Yet, in it, no suggestion that he found *her* irksome. Her presence seemed of no account at all; indeed, he hardly noticed her. For whole long periods he lost her, did not know that she was there. He had no need of her. He lived alone. Each lived alone.

The outward signs by which she recognised that the awful battle was against her and the terms of surrender accepted were pathetic. She put the medicine-chest away upon the shelf; she gave the orders for his pocket-luncheon before he asked; she went to bed alone and early, leaving the front door unlocked, with milk and bread and butter in the hall beside the lamp—all concessions that she felt impelled to make. For more and more, unless the weather was too violent, he went out after dinner even, staying for hours in the woods. But she never slept until she heard the front door close below, and knew soon afterwards his careful step come creeping up the stairs and into the room so softly. Until she heard his regular deep breathing close beside her, she lay awake. All strength or desire to resist had gone for good. The thing against her was too huge and powerful. Capitulation was complete, a fact accomplished. She dated it from the day she followed him to the Forest.

Moreover, the time for evacuation—her own evacuation— seemed approaching. It came stealthily ever nearer, surely and slowly as the rising tide she used to dread. At the high-water mark she stood waiting calmly—waiting to be swept away. Across the lawn all those terrible days of early winter the encircling Forest watched it come, guiding its silent swell and currents towards her feet. Only she never once gave up her Bible or her praying. This complete resignation, moreover, had somehow brought to her a strange great understanding, and if she could not share her husband's horrible abandonment to powers outside himself, she could, and did, in some half-groping way grasp at shadowy meanings that might make such abandonment—possible, yes, but more than merely possible—in some extraordinary sense not evil.

Hitherto she had divided the beyond-world into two sharp halves—spirits good or spirits evil. But thoughts came to her now, on soft and very tentative feet, like the footsteps of the gods which are on wool, that besides these definite classes, there might be other Powers as well, belonging definitely to neither one nor other. Her thought stopped dead at that. But the big idea found lodgment in her little mind, and, owing to the largeness of her heart, remained there unejected. It even brought a certain solace with it.

The failure—or unwillingness, as she preferred to state it—of her God to interfere and help, that also she came in a measure to understand. For here, she found it more and more possible to imagine, was perhaps no positive evil at work, but only something that usually stands away from humankind, something alien and not commonly recognised. There *was* a gulf fixed between the two, and Mr. Sanderson *had* bridged it, by his talk, his explanations, his attitude of mind. Through these her husband had found the way into it. His temperament and natural passion for the woods had prepared the soul in him, and the moment he saw the way to go he took it—the line of least resistance. Life was, of course, open to all, and her husband had the right to choose it where he would.

He had chosen it—away from her, away from other men, but not necessarily away from God. This was an enormous concession that she skirted, never really faced; it was too revolutionary to face. But its possibility peeped into her bewildered mind. It might delay his progress, or it might advance it. Who could know? And why should God, who ordered all things with such magnificent detail, from the pathway of a sun to the falling of a sparrow, object to his free choice, or interfere to hinder him and stop?

She came to realise resignation, that is, in another aspect. It gave her comfort, if not peace. She fought against all belittling of her God. It was, perhaps, enough that He—knew.

"You are not alone, dear, in the trees out there?" she ventured one night, as he crept on tiptoe into the room not far from midnight. "God is with you?"

"Magnificently," was the immediate answer, given with enthusiasm, "for He is everywhere. And I only wish that you—"

But she stuffed the clothes against her ears. That invitation on his lips was more than she could bear to hear. It seemed like asking her to hurry to her own execution. She buried her face among the sheets and blankets, shaking all over like a leaf.

IX

And so the thought that she was the one to go remained and grew. It was, perhaps, first sign of that weakening of the mind which indicated the singular manner of her going. For it was her mental opposition, the trees felt, that stood in their way. Once that was overcome, obliterated, her physical presence did not matter. She would be harmless.

Having accepted defeat, because she had come to feel that his obsession was not actually evil, she accepted at the same time the conditions of an atrocious loneliness. She stood now from her husband farther than from the moon. They had no visitors. Callers were few and far between, and less encouraged than before. The empty dark of winter was before them. Among the neighbours was none in whom, without disloyalty to her husband, she could confide. Mr. Mortimer, had he been single, might have helped her in this desert of solitude that preyed upon her mind, but his wife was there the obstacle; for Mrs. Mortimer wore sandals, believed that nuts were the complete food of man, and indulged in other idiosyncrasies that classed her inevitably among the "latter signs" which Mrs. Bittacy had been taught to dread as dangerous. She stood most desolately alone.

Solitude, therefore, in which the mind unhindered feeds upon its own delusions, was the assignable cause of her gradual mental disruption and collapse.

With the definite arrival of the colder weather her husband gave up his rambles after dark; evenings were spent together over the fire; he read *The Times*; they even talked about their postponed visit abroad in the coming spring. No restlessness was on him at the change; he seemed content and easy in his mind; spoke little of the trees and woods; enjoyed far better health than if there had been change of scene, and to herself was tender, kind, solicitous over trifles, as in the distant days of their first honeymoon.

But this deep calm could not deceive her; it meant, she fully understood, that he felt sure of himself, sure of her, and sure of the trees as well. It all lay buried in the depths of him, too secure and deep, too intimately established in his central being to permit of those surface fluctuations which betray disharmony within.

His life was hid with trees. Even the fever, so dreaded in the damp of winter, left him free. She now knew why. The fever was due to their efforts to obtain him, his efforts to respond and go—physical results of a fierce unrest he had never understood till Sanderson came with his wicked explanations. Now it was otherwise. The bridge was made. And—he had gone.

And she, brave, loyal, and consistent soul, found herself utterly alone, even trying to make his passage easy. It seemed that she stood at the bottom of some huge ravine that opened in her mind, the walls whereof instead of rock were trees that reached enormous to the sky, engulfing her. God alone knew that she was there. He watched, permitted, even perhaps approved. At any rate—He knew.

During those quiet evenings in the house, moreover, while they sat over the fire listening to the roaming winds about the house, her husband knew continual access to the world his alien love had furnished for him. Never for a single instant was he cut off from it. She gazed at the newspaper spread before his face and knees, saw the smoke of his cheroot curl up above the edge, noticed the little hole in his evening socks, and listened to the paragraphs he read aloud as of old. But this was all a veil he spread about himself of purpose. Behind it—he escaped. It was the conjurer's trick to divert the sight to unimportant details while the essential thing went forward unobserved. He managed wonderfully; she loved him for the pains he took to spare her distress; but all the while she knew that the body lolling in that armchair before her eyes contained the merest fragment of his actual self. It was little better than a corpse. It was an empty shell. The essential soul of him was out yonder with the Forest—farther out near that ever-roaring heart of it.

And, with the dark, the Forest came up boldly and pressed against the very walls and windows, peering in upon them, joining hands above the slates and chimneys. The winds were always walking on the lawn and gravel paths; steps came and went and came again; some one seemed always talking in the woods, some one was in the building too. She passed them on the stairs, or running soft and muffled, very large and gentle, down the passages and landings after dusk, as though loose fragments of the Day had broken off and stayed there caught among the shadows, trying to get out. They blundered silently all about the house. They waited till she passed, then made a run for it. And her husband always knew. She saw him more than once deliberately avoid them—because *she* was there. More than once, too, she saw him stand and listen when he thought she was not near, then heard herself the long bounding stride of their approach across the silent garden. Already *he* had heard them in the windy distance of the night, far, far away. They sped, she well knew, along that glade of mossy turf by which she last came out; it cushioned their tread exactly as it had cushioned her own.

It seemed to her the trees were always in the house with him, and in their very bedroom. He welcomed them, unaware that she also knew, and trembled.

One night in their bedroom it caught her unawares. She woke out of deep sleep and it came upon her before she could gather her forces for control.

The day had been wildly boisterous, but now the wind had dropped; only its rags went fluttering through the night. The rays of the full moon fell in a shower between the branches. Overhead still raced the scud and wrack, shaped like hurrying monsters; but below the earth was quiet. Still and dripping stood the hosts of trees. Their trunks gleamed wet and sparkling where the moon caught them. There was a strong smell of mould and fallen leaves. The air was sharp—heavy with odour.

And she knew all this the instant that she woke; for it seemed to her that she had been elsewhere—following her husband—as though she had been *out*! There was no dream at all, merely this definite, haunting certainty. It dived away, lost, buried in the night. She sat upright in bed. She had come back.

The room shone pale in the moonlight reflected through the windows, for the blinds were up, and she saw her husband's form beside her, motionless in deep sleep. But what caught her unawares was the horrid thing that by this fact of sudden, unexpected waking she had surprised these other things in the room, beside the very bed, gathered close about him while he slept. It was their dreadful boldness—herself of no account as it were—that terrified her into screaming before she could collect her powers to prevent. She screamed before she realised what she did—a long, high shriek of terror that filled the room, yet made so little actual sound. For wet and shimmering presences stood grouped all round that bed. She saw their outline underneath the ceiling, the green, spread bulk of them, their vague extension over walls and furniture. They shifted to and fro, massed yet translucent, mild yet thick, moving and turning within themselves to a hushed noise of multitudinous soft rustling. In their sound was something very sweet and winning that fell into her with a spell of horrible enchantment. They were so mild, each one alone, yet so terrific in their combination. Cold seized her. The sheets against her body turned to ice.

She screamed a second time, though the sound hardly issued from her throat. The spell sank deeper, reaching to the heart; for it softened all the currents of her blood and took life from her in a stream—towards themselves. Resistance in that moment seemed impossible.

Her husband then stirred in his sleep, and woke. And, instantly, the forms drew up, erect, and gathered themselves in some amazing way together. They lessened in extent—then scattered through the air like an effect of light when shadows seek to smother it. It was tremendous, yet most exquisite. A sheet of pale-green shadow that yet had form and substance filled the room. There was a rush of silent movement, as the Presences drew past her through the air,—and they were gone.

But, clearest of all, she saw the manner of their going; for she recognised in their tumult of escape by the window open at the top, the same wide "looping circles"—spirals it seemed—that she had seen upon the lawn those weeks ago when Sanderson had talked. The room once more was empty.

In the collapse that followed, she heard her husband's voice, as though coming from some great distance. Her own replies she heard as well. Both were so strange and unlike their normal speech, the very words unnatural:

"What is it, dear? Why do you wake me *now*?" And his voice whispered it with a sighing sound, like wind in pine boughs.

"A moment since something went past me through the air of the room. Back to the night outside it went." Her voice, too, held the same note as of wind entangled among too many leaves.

"My dear, it *was* the wind."

"But it called, David. It was calling *you*—by name!"

"The stir of the branches, dear, was what you heard. Now, sleep again, I beg you, sleep."

"It had a crowd of eyes all through and over it—before and behind—" Her voice grew louder. But his own in reply sank lower, far away, and oddly hushed.

"The moonlight, dear, upon the sea of twigs and boughs in the rain, was what you saw."

"But it frightened me. I've lost my God—and you—I'm cold as death!"

"My dear, it is the cold of the early morning hours. The whole world sleeps. Now sleep again yourself."

He whispered close to her ear. She felt his hand stroking her. His voice was soft and very soothing. But only a part of him was there; only a part of him was speaking; it was a half-emptied body that lay beside her and uttered these strange sentences, even forcing her own singular choice of words. The horrible, dim enchantment of the trees was close about them in the room—gnarled, ancient, lonely trees of winter, whispering round the human life they loved.

"And let me sleep again," she heard him murmur as he settled down among the clothes, "sleep back into that deep, delicious peace from which you called me…"

His dreamy, happy tone, and that look of youth and joy she discerned upon his features even in the filtered moonlight, touched her again as with the spell of those shining, mild green presences. It sank down into her. She felt sleep grope for her. On the threshold of slumber one of those strange vagrant voices that loss of consciousness lets loose cried faintly in her heart—

"There is joy in the Forest over one sinner that—"

Then sleep took her before she had time to realise even that she was vilely parodying one of her most precious texts, and that the irreverence was ghastly…

And though she quickly slept again, her sleep was not as usual, dreamless. It was not woods and trees she dreamed of, but a small and curious dream that kept coming again and again upon her: that she stood upon a wee, bare rock in the sea, and that the tide was rising. The water first came to her feet, then to her knees, then to her waist. Each time the dream returned, the tide seemed higher. Once it rose to her neck, once even to her mouth, covering her lips for a moment so that she could not breathe. She did not wake between the dreams; a period of drab and dreamless slumber intervened. But, finally, the water rose above her eyes and face, completely covering her head.

And then came explanation—the sort of explanation dreams bring. She understood. For, beneath the water, she had seen the world of seaweed rising from the bottom of the sea like a forest of dense green—long, sinuous stems, immense thick branches, millions of feelers spreading through the darkened watery depths the power of their ocean foliage. The Vegetable Kingdom was even in the sea. It was everywhere. Earth, air, and water helped it, way of escape there was none.

And even underneath the sea she heard that terrible sound of roaring—was it surf or wind or voices?—further out, yet coming steadily towards her.

And so, in the loneliness of that drab English winter, the mind of Mrs. Bittacy, preying upon itself, and fed by constant dread, went lost in disproportion. Dreariness filled the weeks with dismal, sunless skies and a clinging moisture that knew no wholesome tonic of keen frosts. Alone with her thoughts, both her husband and her God withdrawn into distance, she counted the days to Spring. She groped her way, stumbling down the long dark tunnel. Through the arch at the far end lay a brilliant picture of the violet sea sparkling on the coast of France. There lay safety and escape for both of them, could she but hold on. Behind her the trees blocked up the other entrance. She never once looked back.

She drooped. Vitality passed from her, drawn out and away as by some steady suction. Immense and incessant was this sensation of her powers draining off. The taps were all turned on. Her personality, as it were, streamed steadily away, coaxed outwards by this Power that never wearied and seemed inexhaustible. It won her as the full moon wins the tide. She waned; she faded; she obeyed.

At first she watched the process, and recognised exactly what was going on. Her physical life, and that balance of the mind which depends on physical well-being, were being slowly undermined. She saw that clearly. Only the soul, dwelling like a star apart from these and independent of them, lay safe somewhere—with her distant God. That she knew—tranquilly. The spiritual love that linked her to her husband was safe from all attack. Later, in His good time, they would merge together again because of it. But, meanwhile, all of her that had kinship with the earth was slowly going. This separation was being remorselessly accomplished. Every part of her the trees could touch was being steadily drained from her. She was being—removed.

After a time, however, even this power of realisation went, so that she no longer "watched the process" or knew exactly what was going on. The one satisfaction she had known—the feeling that it was sweet to suffer for his sake—went with it. She stood utterly alone with this terror of the trees... mid the ruins of her broken and disordered mind.

She slept badly; woke in the morning with hot and tired eyes; her head ached dully; she grew confused in thought and lost the clues of daily life in the most feeble fashion. At the same time she lost sight, too, of that brilliant picture at the exit of the tunnel; it faded away into a tiny semicircle of pale light, the violet sea and the sunshine the merest point of white, remote as a star and equally inaccessible. She knew now that she could never reach it. And through the darkness that stretched behind, the power of the trees came close and caught her, twining about her feet and arms, climbing to her very lips. She woke at night, finding it difficult to breathe. There seemed wet leaves pressed against her mouth, and soft green tendrils clinging to her neck. Her feet were heavy, half rooted, as it were, in deep, thick earth. Huge creepers stretched along the whole of that black tunnel, feeling about her person for points where they might fasten well, as ivy or the giant parasites of the Vegetable Kingdom settle down on the trees themselves to sap their life and kill them.

Slowly and surely the morbid growth possessed her life and held her. She feared those very winds that ran about the wintry forest. They were in league with it. They helped it everywhere.

"Why don't you sleep, dear?" It was her husband now who played the rôle of nurse, tending her little wants with an honest care that at least aped the services of love. He was so utterly unconscious of the raging battle he had caused. "What is it keeps you so wide awake and restless?"

"The winds," she whispered in the dark. For hours she had lain watching the tossing of the trees through the blindless windows. "They go walking and talking everywhere to-night, keeping me awake. And all the time they call so loudly to you."

And his strange whispered answer appalled her for a moment until the meaning of it faded and left her in a dark confusion of the mind that was now becoming almost permanent.

"The trees excite them in the night. The winds are the great swift carriers. Go with them, dear—and not against. You'll find sleep that way if you do."

"The storm is rising," she began, hardly knowing what she said.

"All the more then—go with them. Don't resist. They'll take you to the trees, that's all."

Resist! The word touched on the button of some text that once had helped her.

"Resist the devil and he will flee from you," she heard her whispered answer, and the same second had buried her face beneath the clothes in a flood of hysterical weeping.

But her husband did not seem disturbed. Perhaps he did not hear it, for the wind ran just then against the windows with a booming shout, and the roaring of the Forest farther out came behind the blow, surging into the room. Perhaps, too, he was already asleep again. She slowly regained a sort of dull composure. Her face emerged from the tangle of sheets and blankets. With a growing terror over her—she listened. The storm was rising. It came with a sudden and impetuous rush that made all further sleep for her impossible.

Alone in a shaking world, it seemed, she lay and listened. That storm interpreted for her mind the climax. The Forest bellowed out its victory to the winds; the winds in turn proclaimed it to the Night. The whole world knew of her complete defeat, her loss, her little human pain. This was the roar and shout of victory that she listened to.

For, unmistakably, the trees were shouting in the dark. There were sounds, too, like the flapping of great sails, a thousand at a time, and sometimes reports that resembled more than anything else the distant booming of enormous drums. The trees stood up—the whole beleaguering host of them stood up—and with the uproar of their million branches drummed the thundering message out across the night. It seemed as if they all had broken loose. Their roots swept trailing over field and hedge and roof. They tossed their bushy heads beneath the clouds with a wild, delighted shuffling of great boughs. With trunks upright they raced leaping through the sky. There was upheaval and adventure in the awful sound they made, and their cry was like the cry of a sea that has broken through its gates and poured loose upon the world...

Through it all her husband slept peacefully as though he heard it not. It was, as she well knew, the sleep of the semi-dead. For he was out with all that clamouring turmoil. The part of him that she had lost was there. The form that slept so calmly at her side was but the shell, half emptied...

And when the winter's morning stole upon the scene at length, with a pale, washed sunshine that followed the departing tempest, the first thing she saw, as she crept to the window and looked out, was the ruined cedar lying on the lawn. Only the gaunt and crippled trunk of it remained. The single giant bough that had been left to it lay dark upon the grass, sucked endways towards the Forest by a great wind eddy. It lay there like a mass of drift-wood from a wreck, left by the ebbing of a high springtide upon the sands—remnant of some friendly, splendid vessel that once had sheltered men.

And in the distance she heard the roaring of the Forest further out. Her husband's voice was in it.

STORY SOURCES

'The Willows', Algernon Blackwood, *The Listener and Other Stories*, London: Eveleigh Nash, 1907

'Ancient Sorceries', Algernon Blackwood, *John Silence: Physician Extraordinary*, London: Eveleigh Nash, 1908

'The Wendigo', Algernon Blackwood, *The Lost Valley, and Other Stories*, London: Eveleigh Nash, 1910

'The Man Whom the Trees Loved', Algernon Blackwood, *Pan's Garden: A Volume of Nature Stories*, London: Macmillan & Co., 1912

British Library Tales of the Weird collects a thrilling array of uncanny storytelling, from the realms of gothic, supernatural and horror fiction. With stories ranging from the nineteenth century to the present day, this series revives long-lost material from the Library's vaults to thrill again alongside beloved classics of the weird fiction genre.

We welcome any suggestions, corrections or feedback you may have, and will aim to respond to all items addressed to the following:

The Editor (Tales of the Weird),
British Library Publishing
The British Library
96 Euston Road
London, NW1 2DB

We also welcome enquiries through our Twitter account, @BL_Publishing.